ONE
LAST
SHOT

Also by John David Anderson

Sidekicked

Minion

The Dungeoneers

Ms. Bixby's Last Day

Posted

Granted

Finding Orion

Stowaway

JOHN DAVID ANDERSON

ONE LAST SHOT

WALDEN POND PRESS
An Imprint of HarperCollinsPublishers

Walden Pond Press is an imprint of HarperCollins Publishers.
Walden Pond Press and the skipping stone logo are trademarks and
registered trademarks of Walden Media, LLC.

One Last Shot
Copyright © 2020 by John David Anderson
www.harpercollinschildrens.com

ISBN 978-0-06-264393-3

21 22 23 24 25   PC/BRR   10 9 8 7 6 5 4 3 2 1
❖
First paperback edition, 2021

For Boo

The game has such a hold on golfers because they compete not only against an opponent, but also against the course, against par, and—most surely—against themselves.

—Arnold Palmer

Waka waka.

—Pac-Man

HOLE #1

<u>Par 2</u>

A gentle downhill slope leads to a solitary stone hazard blocking the cup, which is located just behind the rock and out of view. Your average golfer will settle for two, but with the proper angle and appropriate force, you can make it in one.

And everyone knows one is better.

It's a beautiful, sunny day here in Williams Bay, Wisconsin, where twenty-four talented young golfers are getting ready to tackle this monster of a course.

That's right, Bill. This one is a killer. Each hole more challenging than the last. Expect to see some serious bogeys on the cards today. We've got sand. We've got water. But this ain't no day at the beach.

You said it, Jim. And here we have the underdog: twelve-year-old Malcolm Greeley in the dark blue polo. What do you make of him?

Well, his ears are a little big, Bill. They're just not in proportion to his face. Sort of like a Mr. Potato Head. And those shorts his mother picked out for him are hideous. He looks like he just waded waist deep through Mustard Creek. A little yellow goes a long way out here on the green, Mrs. Greeley.

No, Jim. I mean what do you think of the kid's chances? Do you

think he has what it takes to bring home the Morris-Hirschfield Tro-
phy this afternoon?

"Malcolm."

Well, it's a challenging field, Bill. A lot of talented golfers out here
today. But the odds-on favorite has to be returning champion Jamie
Tran, who has dominated just about every mini golf competition he's
played in this year.

"Malcolm."

No question, Tran has the skills, Jim. I suspect he's going to
annihilate the likes of Malcolm Greeley. Really rub his face in the—

"Malcolm!"

Mom snaps her fingers. Her freckled face is only inches
from mine. I can smell her perfume, the stuff Dad puts in her
stocking at Christmas every year. It's flowery but also sort of
sweet smelling. Like rose petals and vanilla frosting.

"You okay?"

I lick chapped lips and give her two nods. Normally two's
enough to convince her, but not today. I could nod until
my head snapped off and she would still know better. Given
everything that's going on, how could either of us be okay?

"You're up," she says, touching me softly on the shoulder.
"Don't be nervous. Just relax. Visualize." My mother takes a
series of deep, cleansing breaths—in through the nose, out
through the mouth. She probably learned that in yoga class.
I don't understand the point of paying someone to teach you
how to stand like a tree, but she likes going. It relaxes her, she

says. I'm pretty sure I don't relax her. She places her hand over her heart as if she's about to recite the Pledge. "You're going to do great."

I know she thinks so. But not everybody's definition of *great* is the same.

I scan the crowd—the hundred or so people who have turned out for the tournament, most of them parents or grandparents. A few hold up poster-board signs with colorful bubble names and drawings of golf clubs. Many more hold Starbucks cups. Most of the siblings who have been dragged along already have their faces in their phones. I've seen some of them before. Heard these same parents telling their respective kids to take their time, to relax their elbows, to focus. They've probably never tried to relax their elbows. It's harder than it sounds.

Mom scans the crowd too. She looks disappointed. Or maybe I just *want* her to look disappointed. The announcer comes on over the PA system. His voice muffled and mechanical, nothing like the voices in my head.

"Up next on hole one, Malcolm Greeley, age twelve, from Falls Point, Illinois."

"That's you," Mom says. I know it's me, even if I'm not always crazy about the fact. Out of the corner of my eye, I spot Jamie Tran talking to his coach by the Coke machine that's really a Pepsi machine. Jamie's coach whispers something and both he and Jamie look my way. I look down at my feet and wonder what I've done to get their attention. Not that it matters. I can only assume today will end the same way as last time. There's no way I can win. And at this point I'm not even sure if it matters.

He's not coming.

That's what the voice inside my head says.

He's not coming.

Which sucks. Because this was maybe my last chance to fix things. To make him happy. To convince them both that this is all worth it, the three of us together. It's foolish, I know—it's just miniature golf—but I figured it was worth a shot.

Except the voice in my head is right. He's *not* coming.

And I still can't help but feel like it's somehow my fault.

I've heard voices ever since I can remember. But I didn't hear *that* voice until one night a little over three years ago.

The night I almost died.

Dad says it's an exaggeration. He says I would have had to sustain some sort of physical trauma. A car accident. A heart attack. A mauling by a mountain lion. You need to pass out, or at least be bleeding from your ears and eyeballs, as my salty old Granny Allison would say. *Then* you can say you've almost died. Dad says you can't almost die of freaking out, which was what *I* was doing.

I know he's right. I know I just panicked. But at the time, I felt like I'd lost everything.

It was buy-one-admission-get-one-free day at the fair. Also the day of the big horse race, although that part didn't interest me; those horses always look like they want to trample me, snorting and pawing the ground, just like some of the bigger kids at school. Going to the county fair was a Greeley family tradition. Every year for as long as I can remember. I mostly went for the ice cream, though that year I had another prize in mind.

I needed a goldfish.

At school, Susan Stottlemeyer was always bragging about the goldfish she'd won at the same fair two years ago, playing that game where you have to toss the Ping-Pong ball into the bowl with the colored rim. Her fish's name was Willy McGilly, and she'd managed to keep it alive for two years already. She said that proved she would make an excellent mother someday. Susan wasn't exactly a friend—I didn't have a lot of those—but she had awesome scented markers that she shared and orange hair that reminded me of a campfire.

"Fish are marvelous," she informed everyone at our table. "They listen to everything you have to say and never talk back, and they always give you something to watch when you've used up your screen time." I was always maxing out my screen time, so I figured I could use a fish. Besides, it might be nice to have someone else to talk to besides myself.

After two weeks, I'd almost convinced Mom and Dad through a delicate mixture of nagging and begging. I figured if I were to win one at the fair, they'd have no choice but to let me keep it. Dad weighed in, saying the last thing we needed in the house was another mouth to feed, until I informed him that a goldfish's mouth is about the size of a freckle and promised I'd buy the food with my allowance.

Dad frowned. Mom said, "We'll see." They left it at that.

For the ten days leading up to the fair, I practiced the carnival game in the kitchen, using a Ping-Pong ball and whatever containers I could find—mixing bowls, flower vases, empty orange juice cartons—the ball click-clacking across the linoleum. Mom watched silently, smiling whether I made it or not. I knew better than to practice when Dad was around; I didn't need that much advice.

By the time Saturday arrived, I could sink my shot from ten feet away more than half the time, which meant, with three balls per try, I was destined to make at least one shot in the bowl. I would be the Steph Curry of the Allen County Fair goldfish game. I overheard the kids on the bus talking about Steph Curry a lot, so I figured he must be good.

We gave the grumpy lady at the entrance our coupons, and she asked us if we were coming to see the pigs. "Not unless they are slow-roasted and smothered in barbecue sauce," Dad said. The lady smiled politely, but her eyebrow twitched. I notice these kinds of things. We grabbed a program with a picture of a dancing cow on the front and entered the fairgrounds, and I was instantly reminded of what I *didn't* like about the fair. It had nothing to do with the pigs—roasted or otherwise.

It was the people.

There were always way too many of them. You couldn't help but bump shoulders as you walked, and there were places where everyone was pushed together, noses to necks, sweaty and musky, jostling to get a look at something—the fattest sow, or the longest cucumber, or the most accurate butter sculpture of Abraham Lincoln. Bodies against bodies. And because I was too busy navigating around those bodies, I always ended up stepping in something brown and gooey that caused my shoes to stick to the pavement so that every step made a little ticky-tack sound. Disgusting.

But it was still worth it to see my parents having a good time.

We worked our way slowly along the road, dodging the golf carts and the little kids dueling with balloon swords. We bunched up against the fence to see the baby goats. Mom grew up in the country, three doors down from a farm, and she used to spend her afternoons helping her neighbors. She missed those days, so she insisted on petting every four-legged creature she saw. "Aren't they just adorable, Malcolm?"

"Their eyes are creepy," I said. The goats had hyphens for pupils, like cyborgs. They looked like they were planning to take over the world.

"He's right. They do look kind of demonic," Dad seconded, making little horns on top of his head.

"Well, *I* think they're cute." Mom stuck her hand between the slats of the fencing to pet the closest baby goat; it nipped at her fingers and she jerked back.

"Adorable," Dad said.

We moved through the rest of the animal pens quickly after that. My mother kept her hands at her sides. I kept mine in my pockets. I almost always keep my hands in my pockets. Not because I'm afraid to touch stuff—though that's true too—but because there's always something in them to fiddle with. A gum wrapper. A paper clip. A chewed-on eraser. Usually, though, it was a lucky nickel given to me by my grandfather, Grandpa Ellis, before he passed away. A Denver-minted 1929 buffalo head worth about fifty bucks. It was supposed to be good luck; I brought it to help with the goldfish getting. Mr. Curry probably had a special pair of lucky socks or something that he wore for big games too.

"Smell that?" Dad inhaled deeply, which seemed like a dangerous thing to do considering we'd just exited the cow barn. I took a tentative whiff as we stepped beneath the flashing sign for the midway. Sure enough, the smell of manure was quickly overpowered by a bouquet of buttered popcorn and caramel apples. It was like sniffing all of Susan Stottlemeyer's scented markers at once. "Smells like destiny."

The midway was even more crowded than the rest of the fair. People were roped into lines, waiting to ride the Himalayan and the Whirligig. The dancing lights pushed back against the dusk, and rock oldies blared out of unseen speakers. I watched every step I took like a minesweeper, wary of the brown glop that was waiting to swallow my shoes, and kept my distance from the cardboard-box trash cans that were swamped with bees.

"Let's ride until we puke," Mom said.

Dad bought a strip of twenty tickets without even

complaining about the price, and the three of us tackled a few of the tamer rides. Dad couldn't do anything that went up and down or spun around real fast—they gave him a headache—so I picked rides all three of us liked. I didn't bother to ask about the goldfish game yet, even though I could see it in the center of the midway next to the Bottle Toss. My parents always insisted on doing the games last on the off chance we'd actually win something; no sense lugging around a giant Pikachu all night.

A half hour later we stepped out of the Fun House, which was neither fun nor a house, and Dad rubbed his belly. "Think I'm going to go get a funnel cake. You could help me tackle a funnel cake, couldn't you?" I nodded, hoping that splitting a funnel cake didn't exclude me from getting ice cream later.

Mom frowned. "Do you know how much grease is in those things?"

I held my breath. Grease was one of the things my parents didn't agree on. It ranked somewhere in the middle of a very long list, alongside which brand of toilet paper to buy and whether opera was beautiful or boring. The list was so long, I sometimes lost track of who stood where on what, but this one was obvious. Dad was pro grease.

"That's what makes them taste so good," he countered.

I watched my parents' faces carefully, waiting to see if this would turn into something bigger. I knew all of their cues. The sudden crease of my mother's mouth. The pinch of my father's eyebrows. The way she cleared her throat before she said something that would make him mad, as if priming her vocal cords for battle. I'd catalogued all my father's sighs. The exasperated sigh—huffy and pronounced. The dismissive sigh—which was really more of a snort, a nasal sound that meant "you're wrong, but it's just not worth telling you why you're wrong because it's just *so* obvious." The defeated sigh—long and drawn out, usually punctuated by a head sag.

This time he delivered a combination, a little huff and a little snort. "Malcolm wants one, don't you, bub?"

Bub was one of the things my dad sometimes called me. *Bub* and *buddy* and *little man*. It wasn't just me. He called everybody by some nickname or another, neighbors, coworkers, friends. Except my mother. He called her Nicole. Not Nickie, or Nic, like everybody else. Not honey or sweetie or babe. And she called him Matt. Matt and Nicole.

Mom and Dad.

And me.

Mom rolled her eyes, conceding the point, but she wanted the eye roll down for the record, to let him know that he only won because she *let* him win. I knew all of this about my parents. I'd been watching them for years. Triumphant, Dad took off, following the scent of funnel cake, my mother watching after him. Then, as if she'd just realized I was standing right next to her, she looked at me and smiled. "Come on," she said. "Let's go try *that* thing."

She pointed to the Wild Mouse, a kind of multitiered coaster that reminded me of a human-size Rube Goldberg machine.

It was the biggest ride at the fair next to the Ferris wheel. Definitely not the sort of thing we could do with Dad. Mom took my hand as we stepped in line. The woman in front of us had a tattoo of a bleeding heart with a knife sticking out of it covering her shoulder. I wondered what it was supposed to mean. Love hurts? Judging by the size of the knife, it must hurt a lot. The guy with her had a tattoo of Mickey Mouse on his neck. I liked his better.

Beside me, Mom hissed a bad word then immediately apologized. "Sorry. Pretend you didn't hear that." She didn't realize that I already knew at least thirty curse words, including three in Russian that I learned from the school custodian, Mr. Popov. I gave her a what's-wrong? look and she held up five tickets. The Wild Mouse ride cost three each. "Do you think you could ride it without me?"

I shook my head emphatically. If I rode by myself, there was a chance they would stick me with a stranger. Better to not ride it at all. Of course, Mom knew the answer before she even asked. She spun in place. "Do you notice how your father is always gone when you need him?" The line inched forward. We were still a ways from the loading platform. She pointed to a booth with a bright yellow sign. "See there? I'm just going to run over and get us a few more tickets. You hold our place, 'kay?"

I glanced around, hoping to spot Dad in the crowd. I didn't like this idea. We could always just jump out of line and jump back in. But the ticket booth was close. Less than fifty feet away. I almost said no. Almost.

"I won't be gone but a second," Mom said. "Keep me in your sights."

She made a pair of pretend binoculars with her hands and put them up to her hazel eyes. I imitated the gesture. It was one of our things, just hers and mine, something we'd done since I was little and she would take me to the playground. *Go play with the other kids,* she'd say. *They won't bite, I promise. Besides, I've got you in my sights.* Then she'd put her fingers in circles. Circles to eyes. Always on the lookout.

I watched her hurry over and get in line behind one other couple, fishing her credit card out of her wallet and turning and waving it at me. I still had my binocular hands pressed to my face.

"Hey, kid. . . ."

My hands darted back into my pockets, and I looked at the two teenage boys standing behind me, clearly older, the top of my head barely coming up to their necks. The one who had called out to me had a White Sox ball cap on and an annoyed look on his face. I wondered what I'd done. Maybe I was wearing the wrong brand of shoes. Or maybe it was just because I was suddenly by myself, unprotected. He pointed, and I could see his frustration growing, jabbing his finger at me like he was about to stab me with it. "The line, idiot," he said.

I spun to see the gap I'd made. The line had moved up while I'd been staring after Mom. "Sorry," I said, and stumbled forward, glancing back over my shoulder, trying to look past the two boys laughing and shaking their heads at me. The mouse-shaped cars ahead filled quickly, taking on passengers and zipping along the track. I could hear the *cachick, cachick, cachick* of the chain hefting them up the lift hill, the screams of the riders sliding into each other on the hairpin turns. There were only eight or so people in line ahead of me now. I could feel the two boys start to press closer, and I twisted back around, expecting to see my mother walking toward me, tickets in hand.

My eyes darted to the bright yellow sign, to the window where she'd been standing only seconds ago.

Gone.

There was a man standing at the booth instead. I quickly scanned the crowd, looking for the navy blue coat, the chestnut hair that was already turning gray at forty—*Partially your fault,* she joked, *but mostly your father's*—expecting to see her pushing her way through, apologizing for cutting back in.

Nothing. I froze, staring at a dozen strange faces in line behind me. Two dozen more filling the street between me and the ticket booth. All of them older than me. Bigger than me. Crowding around me. Unbreathably close.

"Next."

My hands jerked out of my pockets, making circles, binoculars up to my eyes, but I couldn't spot her anywhere.

"Next," the voice said again, less patient this time, though I could barely hear it over the rush of blood in my ears. I felt dizzy. I reached out with one hand and grabbed the railing that led into the ride, eyes leapfrogging, face to face to face.

"C'mon, kid, are you riding or not?"

I looked at the teenage boy with the ball cap, pointing again, not at me, but at the empty car. I turned to see the man at the ticket booth, heavy mustache barely hiding a scowl. I shook my head dumbly. The two boys brushed past me, tickets in hand, and I stumbled out of line, spinning with each step, looking everywhere now for the blue coat, for my father's white shirt and broad smile, listening for my name being called, but there was too much buzzing and clanking and screaming. I clutched my hands to my stomach, suddenly feeling ill.

I reached the ticket booth with the yellow sign and spun around again. She was right here a minute ago, standing right in this spot. Where could she be?

That's when I heard it. The voice. Coming from somewhere deep inside.

They're gone, it said.

My throat closed. I struggled for a breath.

They left you.

This voice sounded like me, like my own voice, except with an edge, the words cutting and cruel.

You're alone.

I started to walk, eyes darting, hands over my ears to block out the noise of the crowd, but I could still hear that voice muttering the same thing over and over.

Alone, it said. *Alone. Alone.*

Something touched me on the shoulder. A hand, dark skinned, grown-up. Lots of rings. Coat, not blue. Shirt, not white. Face, unknown.

"Hey, sweetie, you all right? You look a little sick."

Her hand still on my shoulder. Holding me. Trapping me. It was too much.

I bolted. Back into the crowd. Away from the hand. Away from the Wild Mouse ride. Toward the center of the midway with all the games. I called out for Mom and Dad, but my mouth was dry, and it came out as a squeak, impossible to hear over the music. I turned with every other step, trying to look in every direction at once, afraid I would miss them, certain I'd missed them already, that every time I looked left, they'd already passed by on the right.

They're gone, the voice said again. *They left you.*

An explosive sound from behind. Bells screeching, like the fire alarm at school. The man who'd just won the Test Your Strength game held the sledgehammer high above his head like Hercules. Everywhere I looked, lights blinked and blazed. I felt dizzy again, the whole world spinning like a teacup car. I took another step and backed into a girl holding a drink, knocking it out of her hands. It splashed across the front of her jeans, down onto her shoes, onto my shoes.

"Jesus! Watch where you're going!"

The girl glared at me with murder in her eyes. She had rainbow-colored braces crisscrossing her bared teeth. I didn't stop to apologize, I just ran, pushing back into the crowd, the sticky soda soaking through the tops of my sneakers into my socks. I tried to talk over the voice in my head. "They're here. They have to be here."

They left you.

"They would never do that."

You don't know that.

"Stop it!" I shouted. "Stop it! Stop it!" I stumbled from the busy center street and pressed my back against the side of the nearest booth. I closed my eyes and wished it all away. The crowds. The music. The rides. The voice. Wished I was back home, back in my living room, curled onto our couch with my parents sitting on either side. Warm and secure. I dropped into a crouch and wrapped my arms over my head, burying my face between my knees, squeezing out hot, stinging tears.

I wanted to go home.

Alone.

Stop.

Alone.

Don't say that.

Alone. Alone. Alo—

"Malcolm!"

I blinked through the blur. Navy blue coat. Frizzy hair. Purse tucked under her arm. She broke through the crowd and knelt down in front of me, pulling me tight against her. I leaked snot all over her collar. She grabbed my shoulders and held me at arm's length.

"Malcolm. Malcolm, I'm so sorry. The man at the booth—their credit card machine was down. But he said there was another ticket booth right around the corner. I wasn't thinking."

I wiped tears on the back of my sleeve. I didn't say anything. I didn't know what to say.

"I came back to the ride and couldn't find you. Why didn't you wait there for me?"

See? It was your fault.

It was all my fault. My cheeks continued to burn. Before I could answer, I saw Dad appear over Mom's shoulder, a partially eaten funnel cake in one hand, his phone in the other. "You found him. Where was he?" He turned his eyes on me. "Where were you?"

They were both looking at me, waiting for an answer.

"I'm sorry. I didn't mean to . . ."

Dad shook his head. "You've got nothing to be sorry for," he said, giving my mother a sideways glance, the kind that said, *I left him with you*, but Mom didn't even look at him. Instead she helped me stand up and fished in her purse for a tissue.

"It's all right," she whispered. "You're all right now. Calm down."

I pulled my jacket tight around me. The top of my sock was soaked through with soda. Warm snot smeared across my lip.

"C'mon," Mom said. "Deep breath."

I did my best, my breaths long and shuddering. I nodded twice to let her know I was okay. I was safe. They were here. I wasn't alone. Dad held out the paper plate with oil spots soaking through the bottom.

"I saved you the half with the most sugar," he said; then he pointed to the booth we were all standing next to. "And look where we are."

I hadn't even realized where I'd ended up, where I'd gone to hide. I could see now the picture of the goldfish painted on the side.

"You okay?" Mom asked, but before I could respond, Dad chipped in.

"Of course he's okay. Aren't you, sport?"

I nodded. Sniffed. Nodded again.

I wasn't, though. I could still hear him. Way down, little more than a whisper. That new voice inside of me. The one I hadn't invented, that didn't have a name. The one I couldn't control or ignore like all the others. That sharp, insistent voice, telling me that I was the one responsible. That I was the one to blame.

Dad put his arm around me, strong and heavy. He and Mom exchanged a glance, and I realized the look that I thought was anger before could just be worry. "Let's go play some games, huh?" he said.

I nodded again. Dad kept his arm around my shoulders, Mom took my hand, and I let them lead me back into the crowd, the whisper in my head now drowned out by the sounds of the fair. I was okay. I wasn't bleeding. I hadn't died. I'd just freaked out.

I kept the voice to myself.

That night I came home with two goldfish. My father won the first for me on his first bounce. "See, Malcolm. Now *that's* how it's done." I won the second, though it took me four tries. I named the first fish Nemo and the second one Jaws. Dad said two fish were good because now they would each have a friend, and friends were important. He was always saying things like that.

Nemo died the next day. I found him floating belly up, Jaws circling underneath him like he was waiting for his mouth to get big enough to swallow his dear friend whole. Mom fished him out with a slotted spoon and flushed him down the toilet.

That was three years ago.

Jaws is still happily swimming in his bowl on my dresser, all by himself, which maybe means I will grow up to be a good father someday. I still feel bad whenever I have to leave my room, though, knowing I'm leaving him all alone, so I always promise him that I'm coming back.

I don't want him to freak out.

I stand at the tee and eyeball my shot, visually verifying the angle. Miniature golf is all about angles. Angles and slopes and curves. Trajectory and velocity and muscle memory, but not luck. There's none of that in mini golf, despite the nickel in my pocket. Just physics and geometry and practice. Maybe you could point to bad weather or the conditions of the course, but for the most part it's just you and the hole. When you miss, you have only yourself to blame. That's part of what I love about it. And what I don't like about it, too.

It's definitely possible to love something and not like it all the time.

My putter already feels hot and sticky in my hands. I can sense a hundred pairs of eyes on me, watching me, waiting for me to go, as if there wasn't enough pressure already. As if I didn't have enough on my mind. I stand at the tee and think about everything that's gone wrong. I can't help it. I think about Dad's last words to me before he drove away two nights ago and how I didn't say anything back. I think about Frank lying there in his ugly green gown, chewing on a Starburst, the box beside him tracing the pattern of his heart.

I think about Michael and how hard it must have been.

I wish they were here. I wish they were all here.

The official, a college-age kid with a T-shirt that says VOL-UNTEER on it, says, "Whenever you're ready."

I'm so not ready. I don't know if I'll ever be ready.

Then I hear another voice inside my head. It's not one of the regulars—not Jim and Bill or Aleck or Granny Allison. And it's not that other one, either, the one I first heard at the fair three years ago.

It's Lex. Somehow, she's wiggled her way in, broken through the noise.

You've got this, she says.

"I've got this," I whisper, but it doesn't sound as confident when I say it.

Still, I square up and hit the ball the way I've practiced a thousand times, knees slightly bent, arms in tight. Elbows as relaxed as I can make them. It feels right. I trace the ball's path to the wall, where it glances off with a hollow metal *thunk*, changing course, losing a little momentum, but not too much, until it disappears behind the stone in the middle of the green and I lose sight of it, only for a second.

A second can seem like forever. In a second you can turn around and find the people who love you are gone. You can feel like the world's about to swallow you whole.

But then I hear it, the hollow thud of the ball hitting the bottom of the cup. I hear my mother's voice, her hissed *"Yes"* coming from the line of parents off to the side, most of them standing in pairs. Two by two.

It's an ace. A hole in one.

One is the best number you can hope for in miniature golf.

But not in everything.

HOLE #2

<u>Par 2</u>

Three hills provide constant shifts in momentum, with the cup situated in the dip between hills two and three. Golfers must provide just the right amount of force. Too little and they won't breach the second hill. Too much and they may skip over the hole altogether, cresting the third slope and ending up against the back wall. You want to find a happy medium, but that middle ground can be hard to judge.

Jaws was the first thing I'd won in a while. And even that took four tries.

You hear about prodigies who started golfing or dancing or running at age four. Who came sprinting out of the womb with a football cradled in their elbow or a tennis racket in hand, destined to be one of the greats.

That's not me.

Instead, you hear about these other kids who aren't so talented, but who work hard every day, giving it 110 percent. And because of their passion and determination, they are also destined for greatness.

That's not me either.

I'm the kid with the participation trophy. The one who is informed at dinner one night that he's going to do Little League over the summer because it's good to be part of a team and to go out and get exercise and to learn how to catch a pop fly. Because knowing how to catch stuff is important. For all those times when people decide to throw things at you.

There's no catching in miniature golf, unless you bounce your ball on the cement, which you shouldn't, because sometimes it gets away from you and skitters like a frightened rabbit, rolling under the fence and getting lost in the parking lot underneath some stranger's pickup truck, and then you have to go ask for another one, which is embarrassing.

Miniature golf is also technically not a sport. That's what Dad says. He says for it to count as a sport you have to sweat when you're playing. He should know. He was a star athlete growing up: lacrosse, football, baseball. He was even a wrestler for a year in middle school but quit because, as he puts it, there's such a thing as too much sweat, especially when it's coming from other people's armpits.

I've seen pictures of my father when he was my age. Tall and lean, with muscles stretching his shirt. Broad smile. Close-cropped blondish hair. Olive eyes; we have those in common. He doesn't have a lot of that wheat-colored hair left, but he still sweats a lot. He runs two miles every day before work. I come downstairs most mornings to the *thwop-thwop-thwop* of his feet pounding the treadmill. He likes to run. My mother and I used to go with him, just out through the neighborhood, along the path that circles the pond, Dad pushing me in one of those three-wheeled strollers, sometimes stopping to feed the geese from a stash of stale bread until they waddled too close and made me cry. But then five years ago, Dad turned the office into an exercise room and got a treadmill and we stopped running together as a family.

Running is obviously a sport, but it's not Dad's favorite. Not by a long shot. For him, nothing beats baseball.

There's a desk in the exercise room that used to be an office, and on the desk sits a ball signed by Ryne Sandberg, encased in glass, right next to a picture of me in my Little League uniform. Ryne Sandberg played second base for the Chicago Cubs ages ago and he was good. Really good. I know this because Dad's told me a million times. Something about golden gloves and silver slugs and being in the Hall of Fame. Supposedly my father wanted to name me Ryne, but Mom wouldn't have it. That's at least one argument I'm glad she won.

Ryne Sandberg is one of Dad's heroes. He has a lot of heroes, and all of them are sports figures. He says it's important to have role models. People you look up to and aspire to be like.

I always thought that's what parents were for.

I remember the first time I ever watched a football game with my dad, from start to finish, with all the beer and truck commercials in between.

Most Saturday and Sunday afternoons I could find him planted on the couch, shouting at the TV, bag of chips by his feet. I'd sit in the corner of the family room and build with Legos or play on the iPad or read the funnies from the newspaper that Mom insisted on buying even though Dad complained that she was murdering trees. Sometimes she would sit with me and help me find the right pieces or make domino runs on the hardwood while Dad asked players who couldn't hear him what-the-heck-they-were-getting-paid-for. Whenever he shouted, I'd look up to see a bunch of grown men jumping around or hanging their heads; then I'd go back to what I was doing.

Until one Sunday, I didn't look away in time. Dad caught me and suggested we should watch a game together. We could make an afternoon of it. Break out some root beer. Open a jar of queso. Slouch on the couch side by side with our bellies sticking out.

I nodded. I knew almost nothing about football despite sitting in a room where it was being played every autumn weekend for most of my life. But if it came with root beer and a never-ending bowl of corn chips, I would try it.

The following Sunday, Dad microwaved a bowl of cheese and twisted the caps off of two glass bottles of Virgil's with his bare hands and the two of us settled next to each other on the living room sofa—a big brown monster that took up half the room. Mom was outside raking up a thick carpet of leaves from our unmurdered trees. Normally she'd ask me to help her, but today I had an out. Father-son time.

I scooted closer to him, putting myself right next to the chips. "Who's playing?"

"Steelers and Titans," he said.

I puzzled over the names. I knew what a Titan was. I'd

started reading the Rick Riordan books and seen *Hercules* twice. "Stealers? You mean like bank robbers?"

"No. Like steel, dude. Metal. Tough. Like *hurrggh*." Dad made a weird gesture, flexing his biceps. My father had big arm muscles for a regional marketing manager, though I hadn't met enough regional marketing managers to know for sure.

"Pff," I said. "Steelers are going to lose."

Dad seemed offended. "And why is that?"

"Titans are giant monsters with superpowers. Steelers are men who work with metal. The Titans can just melt them with their lava breath." It seemed like sound logic. I was ten.

"Yeah. Pretty sure lava breath is illegal in the NFL," Dad said.

"Titans are still going to win," I insisted.

"Wait and see."

So I waited. And sure enough, the Steelers seemed to be the better team. They scored the first touchdown and then, a minute later, also got something called a safety, which seemed like a terrible name considering some guy got clobbered by three bigger guys and lay on the ground for a while. When it happened, Dad said, "Wow. You don't see *that* every day."

I sure hope not, I thought. If you *did* see people getting slammed to the ground every day, you'd probably never leave your house. But I didn't say that. I ate chips and dripped cheese on my shirt, sucking it out of the fabric. Dad explained the rules as the game went on, but no matter how much he explained, I still had questions.

"What's the throwy guy's name again?"

"Rothlisburger," Dad said.

It sounded like a brand of dog food. "Not his name, name. I mean, like, his job."

"Oh. Quarterback, remember?"

"And the runny guy?"

"Halfback."

I nodded. I did the math. "So the runny guy's twice as good as the throwy guy?"

Dad looked at me, confused. "What? No. That's just what they call them. Everybody has a position, see?" He got up and started pointing at the little men on the TV. "Quarterback. Halfback. Tight end. Guards. Tackles. Linebackers. Safeties."

"Safety. Like when the throwy guy got smooshed in the goal by the tackly guys?"

"No. That's a different kind of safety."

I shook my head. My father was speaking a different language. But the chips were good and salty. I took a sip of root beer and summoned the best burp I could, though it was weak compared to all of his. On the TV one of the Titans started freaking out. "Why's that guy so angry?"

"He's not angry. He's pumped."

"He looks angry."

"He's just excited. He got a sack."

I didn't even bother to ask what a sack was.

"You know what?" Dad said. "Maybe we should just sit here and enjoy the game for a little bit." Which was his way of

29

telling me to stop asking so many questions.

I took another sip and kept the bottle pressed to my lips. I told myself I would quietly watch until the end of the quarter, which was only three minutes away. Except three minutes took twenty. "You know what they should call this game?"

"What should they call it?" Dad asked with a sigh.

"Zoneball. Think about it. The goal of baseball is to go around the bases and the goal of basketball is to get the ball in the basket. The goal of football is to get the ball in the in-zone."

"End zone."

"What?"

"You said in-zone. It's *end* zone. Like, the end of a race."

"It could be in-zone," I said.

"But it's not," Dad insisted.

"But you go *in* it. If they want it to be a real end zone, then getting there should be the end of the game. You know. Like catching the Snitch."

Dad looked at me blankly, the way my neighbor's dog does when you tell it to sit.

"Quidditch?" I prompted, staring hard at my father. "Harry Potter?"

"Oh," Dad said. "Right."

I couldn't blame him—he'd never read any of the books, and he'd slept through the movies—but still. It's *Quidditch*.

"You know what would make this game better?"

"I'm pretty sure you're going to tell me," Dad said.

"Trampolines."

"Trampolines?"

"Yeah. Just replace some patches of grass with trampolines. Then the catchy guys—"

"Receivers."

"Right, the receivers would run to the trampolines because they could jump higher to get the ball from the throwy guy."

"Quarterback," Dad corrected.

I hadn't forgotten; I just liked "throwy guy" better. "And they should put one right in front of the in-zone, too. Then you could call it trampball. How cool would that be?"

The look on Dad's face told me he thought trampball was a terrible idea. "How about you go rustle us up a couple more root beers?"

I shuffled off to the kitchen, and when I came back I really tried to get into the game, but around halftime I got bored and started playing with my empty root beer bottle, blowing in it, jamming my thumb in it, seeing if I could balance it on my head. Dad noticed—I saw his sideways glances—but he didn't tell me to stop. Occasionally he would hiss a "yes" or a "c'mon, ref" and I'd look up to check the score. And every now and then, Dad would look over at me and smile and I'd smile back.

I wanted him to think I was having a good time.

And I was. Sort of. Because of the chips. And the soda. And the company.

When the Steelers scored the game-winning touchdown with seven seconds left, Dad stood up and cheered. I don't think I'd ever seen him so excited about anything. I cheered too, imitating him, even though I'd secretly been rooting for the Titans.

Five minutes later I grabbed my jacket and went out back to jump in the pile of leaves Mom had gathered. We made leaf angels and then I helped her rerake the mess and get it into bags.

"How was the game?" she asked as we hauled the leaves to the curb.

I shrugged. "Okay, I guess. Confusing. And it takes for*ever*. Quidditch is better."

"Yup. Nothing beats Quidditch," she said.

I knew she would understand.

I square up, squinting at the hole. With my ace on hole one, I'm tied for the lead with eleven other junior golfers out of a field of twenty-four. But the first hole is a cakewalk. Or as Granny Allison would say, *Easy as falling off a log that's rolling down a mountain,* which sounds like it would be more easy *and* painful.

Hole two, on the other hand, requires a little more finesse.

The cup doesn't get any smaller, I remind myself. It's the

same size, every hole. Wherever you want to go, there's always a path that will get you there. But there's a difference between knowing something and believing it.

Which is why I hear that voice creeping back inside my head. That's what it's like. Creeping. The other voices aren't like that. I don't give them too much thought, but I always know they're coming. But *this* voice sneaks up on me.

You won't make it, it says.

"I've made shots like this before," I whisper to myself.

Not this time. It's too hard.

I shake my head, trying to regain my focus. I glance to the right and spot Mom with her thumbs up, surrounded by a bunch of strangers.

Maybe it's better this way. He won't be disappointed.

Everything tenses: shoulders, calves, neck, I can even feel it in my elbows. I grit my teeth and whack the ball without even taking a practice swing. I know the moment I make contact that I hit it too hard. My only hope is that it's straight enough that it finds the hole somehow, drops right in.

But the voice was right. I don't make it. The ball skirts the left edge of the cup, climbs the last hill, and rolls down the other side, banging against the back wall. It takes me another shot to get back over the hill and a third to find the cup. My first bogey of the day and we are only two holes in.

I look at Mom, who shrugs as if to say, *Don't sweat it—you'll do better next time.* Except you don't always know if there's going to be a next time. Sometimes the end sneaks up and surprises you and only when you look back afterward do you realize that there were warning signs all along.

After two holes, I'm sitting at par, no longer sharing the lead. After two holes, I'm barely breaking even.

And I get this sinking feeling to go with the voice inside my head, telling me it's all downhill from here.

HOLE #3

Par 2

Two irregularly spaced stone hazards split the green, providing three possible approaches—left, right, or center—none of which offers a straight shot to the hole in the back corner. Shooting the narrow gaps between the rocks or the walls is so difficult that some golfers choose to just close their eyes and whack it, hoping for the best.

This approach seldom works.

I am not left-handed.

That's a line from one of my favorite movies. It also happens to be true. Not that it's unusual; most people aren't left-handed. My mom's not either, so I guess I get my right-handedness from her. I also got her nose, her short stature, and, hopefully, some of her musical talent; she's played the piano since she was six, when she sat down and started plunking out tunes she heard on the radio. She never seems to miss a note. She's kind of a musical genius.

I can play "Chopsticks" and "Hot Cross Buns." I miss notes all the time.

Our piano, a mahogany Baldwin upright and the same one that Mom grew up with, sits in our living room next to a corduroy papasan. I sometimes curl up in that chair like it's a bird's nest and listen to her play. She says it's nice to play when there's an audience. Dad used to sit in there and listen too sometimes, but doesn't as much anymore.

Mom also plays for the Methodist church three blocks down the road, weddings mainly, and she fills in for the organist when he's out of town. For a while, when I was little, she gave lessons to the neighborhood kids, but it didn't pay enough. Now she's an administrative assistant at a doctor's office. It pays better and comes with free trial bottles of hand sanitizer. We keep them in a basket by the door for anyone to take. I'm sure the neighbors think we're germophobes.

Granny Allison—my mom's mom and my favorite grand-parent—used to say that my mother could have become a professional musician if she'd stuck with it, maybe traveled with a band or landed a spot in a city orchestra, but she married my father instead.

Granny Allison always said this with a frown, and only when Dad wasn't in the room.

Mom insists she was never good enough to play profession-ally, but I don't believe her. The way her fingers gallop up and down the keys, hands like dancing spiders, the notes making whirlwinds in my ears, makes me dizzy.

I'm scared that my musical genes came from Dad instead. He says he can't even play the radio properly. But he could play baseball. And unlike Mom and me, he *is* left-handed.

That's important because if Dad hadn't been a lefty, he might not have been good enough to get a college scholarship as a pitcher. And then he might not have even *gone* to college, because his grades were only so-so and his parents couldn't afford to send him otherwise. Which means he might not have met my mother, his college sweetheart. Which means they might not have gotten married. Which means I might not even have been born.

Which means I basically owe baseball my life.

And because I owe baseball my life, I had no choice but to try it. As soon as I was tall enough to swing a real aluminum bat without falling over. And then again, every summer, for the next three years.

At least, I watched baseball being played in front of me. I had an excellent vantage point from far left field. Occasionally a fly ball would be hit so close that I couldn't really expect the center fielder to come running after it, so I would have no choice but to try and catch it. Most of the time, I missed. I'd chase it down and throw it to the closest person I could find, whether that was the right person or not, because I had what they call a spaghetti arm. "They" being my teammates. When they thought I wasn't listening.

Still, it wasn't so bad being out in left field. I spied on the birds perched along the fence. I scanned the clover for bumblebees. I pretended my glove was a leathery, face-hugging alien, and I'd fight with it, holding my left hand back with my right to prevent the glove-monster from sucking my eyeballs out. I looked at the snack shack and thought about what kind of candy I would get when the game was finally over. Fun Dip, if they had it. Runts if not.

It was harder to just sit back and watch when I was up to bat. I was always placed last in the lineup. Even after Joshua "Mouse" Wilder, who at least had a "good eye." That meant Mouse got a lot of walks. He was even shorter than me and had a strike zone the size of a button. He was also the only kid on the team I really talked to.

So for three years I spent my summers staring at my cleats wondering if they would allow me to climb up the sides of buildings like Spider-Man, sharing the Goldfish crackers Mom packed me with Mouse, and watching the bigger kids practice their spitting. Jace Miller could launch a saliva missile twenty feet. He played first base and was also the only one of us who could hit a home run. The team called him "The Mace" because he could clobber the ball. And it rhymed.

They called me *you*. As in, *you coulda had that.*

At least Dad wasn't the coach; that would have been worse. He would have made me the lead-off man or made me play first base (Jace's position—Jace the Mace who plays first base). He would have done these things because he knew I could be good if I wanted it bad enough. That's how he felt about everything.

Instead I was coached by a gum-chomping police officer named Coach Parker. Coach Parker had no preconceptions about how good I could be. Hence, bottom of the lineup, far left field. Coach and I had an understanding: we both knew why I showed up every summer. He said the same thing to me, every game, every practice, every at bat. "Just do your best."

So I camped out in my grassy corner of the outfield, wondering why baseball pants had to be so tight, my head itchy from the hat, holding my breath every time the batter swung, occasionally glancing over to the bleachers were my mother sat with her coffee between her knees, my father leaning forward telling me to "look alive," probably wishing he could grab his glove and come show us all how it's done.

It's hard not to at least *try* when you owe your life to baseball. It's hard not to try with your dad in the stands telling you to keep your head in the game.

But it's also hard to look alive when you're dreaming of being anywhere else.

There's that moment in sports movies when the hero has his back to the wall, and he's got a broken leg and a black eye and two teeth knocked out, and his team is down by just-enough-to-lose, and the crowd is speechless, holding its breath, and the music is building to a big finale. And you get the close-up of the hero's face, and you can see the determination in his eyes. And he looks to his coach or his fiancée or his former-nemesis-who-recently-became-his-best-friend and gets *the nod*.

And then the hero does that move, the one that shouldn't work because it's never been done before. And in that moment, the music stops as you watch the move in slow motion, and you hold your breath too, even though you know exactly what's going to happen. The crowd explodes. The music swells. And the hero hoists the trophy as he's surrounded by his cheering teammates.

Believe it or not, that kind of stuff does happen. I should know.

It was the fifth game of the season—my fourth summer in Little League and only a couple of months until I'd start the sixth grade—and it was looking like the Cardinals would be taking their fifth loss. Coach Parker, for all his smiling and after-game pep talks, was itching for a win just so parents would stop giving him advice. I knew my dad was one of the advice givers; I overheard the two of them talking strategy more than once.

Top of the sixth. Last inning in Little League. Two outs. Down by one. Mouse Wilder at the plate. First pitch: ball.

"Good eye. Good eye," Coach Parker said.

Four games. Four losses. None of them close. We'd even had one game end on the mercy rule after giving up ten runs in one inning. This time, though, the Cardinals had a chance.

Second pitch. Ball two.

Mouse Wilder. Strike zone the size of a dime.

"Wait for your pitch, honey!" Mrs. Wilder called out. From my spot on deck, I could see the pitcher kick the dirt in frustration. He wanted Mouse to swing already. *I* wanted Mouse to swing. Swing and miss. Three times. Just as long as I didn't have to go up to the plate again. I'd been up three times already that game. Two strikeouts and one weak little grounder to first base. "Way to make contact," Coach Parker had said after that one. Because at least it was *something*.

I leaned over my bat, the one Dad had bought me at the start of the season. I got a new bat and mitt every year. It was a tradition. I remembered standing in the sporting goods aisle of the Target with my brand-new mitt tucked under my armpit, eyeing the new Lego sets three aisles down while he droned on again about sweet spots. I tried to look excited. I stood in the aisle and pointed to a black bat that looked like all the others.

"That one's junk," Dad said, picking out one that cost three times as much. Then he made me practice swinging it in the aisle until I almost took out an entire shelf of tennis rackets.

Now my sixty-dollar bat was getting sweaty in my hands as I waited on deck. Pitch three was way above Mouse's head. He would have had to whack it like a piñata. He was going to walk. And then it would all be on me.

"Good eye," Coach repeated. Coach Parker curved his fingers when he clapped, making *C*s with his hands. The other coach called for time and jogged out to talk to the pitcher, probably to assure him that it was no big deal if Mouse walked. I could almost hear the conversation: *Don't sweat it. You'll definitely get the next guy.* The pitcher nodded and twisted the ball in his glove.

Three balls and no strikes. You never swing at the fourth pitch if you've got three balls and no strikes. Even I knew that. The pitcher delivered.

Mouse, inexplicably, incomprehensibly, swung.

I heard the plink of the aluminum bat, saw the ball arc heavenward, briefly, before curving toward right field. Watched as two kids ran toward it. Mouse streaked around first. Behind me, everyone on our bench stood up. I know what they were thinking: Drop. Just drop.

Catch it, I thought. *Please catch it.*

It dropped. Mouse slid into second before the throw came in. The Cardinals bench went crazy, whooping and stomping. In the bleachers I saw Mrs. Wilder with her arms up. Mouse dusted off his pants and pumped his fist. Still two outs, but now the tying run was on.

I looked at home plate, at the kid staring back at me from behind his catcher's mask, looking like a gladiator sent from the future. Coach Parker called my name. "Greeley. You're up."

He always called me Greeley. Probably because that was what was printed on the back of my shirt. I started slowly toward the plate, dragging my bat behind me, but halfway there I took a detour until I was standing face-to-chest with him.

"I don't feel so good, Coach," I mumbled.

Coach Parker looked at the home-plate umpire and put up his finger, then turned back to me. "What's up?" Coach Parker was a big guy. Bulky. Bulging. I wouldn't want to be the crook cornered by him in a dark alley.

"My stomach hurts." It wasn't a lie. I could feel a sharp pain in my middle, as if my intestines were being wrung out like a wet rag.

Coach rubbed his jaw, looked over at the other players on the bench. "I mean, we could pinch hit for you," he said. "You know, if you're feeling bad."

He was offering me an out. To get around the *easy* out we both knew was coming. I started to nod, but as I did, Coach Parker looked over at the stands. I made the mistake of looking with him and saw my father, standing on the top row of the bleachers, hands cupped to his mouth; he was shouting my name. "Go, Malcolm! You can do it!"

Coach frowned, then turned back to me.

"You know, it's all right to be nervous," he said. "I get it. But whatever happens up there, it's not on you. We're a team. We win or lose as a team. You just go up there and do your best. Give it *your* best shot. That's all you gotta do, right?"

That's all I had to do. But it felt like I needed to do a whole lot more. I could still hear Dad shouting. Coach Parker gave me a pat that turned into more of a push toward home plate. None of the kids in the dugout were clapping or cheering. They just watched me with stone-hard stares, except for our third baseman, Tyler Tines, who had his eyes closed. I think maybe he was praying.

I stepped up to home plate.

"Go, Malcolm! Smack that sucker out of the park!"

Dad continued to clap above his head. Mom sat beside him, elbows on her knees. From his spot on second, Mouse pointed at me, which only made things worse. I choked up a little on the bat like Dad taught me. If I could just get on base somehow, the *next* guy up could come hit the game-winning home run. Or not. I just didn't want to be the last out. Not again.

I watched the first pitch go by.

"Strike!"

"That's all right. That's all right," Coach Parker said. "Be patient. Wait for your pitch."

Wait for my pitch. I'd heard that before. But how would I know it was mine? Would it be screaming, *Hit me, you fool,* as it spun toward me? The pitcher, who looked at least two years older than me, wound up and released. The ball didn't say a word, except maybe *fwish.*

"Strike two!"

From our bench, Jacc the Mace called out: "C'mon, Greeley. Swing, man. That pitch was perfect!"

Maybe that was my problem. I didn't know what perfect looked like.

That's when I heard the voice. The same one from the night at the fair.

You can't do this.

You don't know that, I thought. It's possible. Anything's possible if you want it bad enough.

Not this, the voice insisted. *Not you.*

I could still hear Dad cheering from the stands. In that moment, I wanted it more than anything. Because I knew how happy it would make everyone else. Dad. Coach Parker. The kids on the team. The *parents* of all the other kids on the team. They wanted it enough to make me want it.

The pitcher wound up and threw. I saw the ball hurtling toward me. Then silence. That quiet, still space between heartbeats. I closed my eyes and swung as hard as I could.

I imagined the crack of the bat, the ball launching like a bottle rocket, up into the clouds. *It's going. It's going. It's . . . it's . . . it's out of here! A two-run shot by Malcolm Greeley to win the game, and the crowd goes—*

"Strike three!"

I opened my eyes and looked down to see the ball peeking out of the catcher's mitt. The opposing outfielders were already running in to celebrate. I stood there, unmoving, my expensive bat drooping in my hands. "Good game, kid," the ump said, patting me on the back.

On the mound, the pitcher was being surrounded by his teammates. I was pretty sure he could hear the triumphant fanfare in his head. The sweeping violins. The blaring trumpets. The cheering fans. Striking out the last batter to get the win. Just like in the movies.

As he walked past me, Mouse said, "You tried." Over on the Cardinals bench my teammates were looking anywhere but at me.

"Heckuva swing," Coach Parker said. "We'll get 'em next time." Then he called out to the rest of the team to line up for congratulations. I stood in the very back of the line and slapped hands with everyone on the opposing team, then watched as my own team scattered. None of them said a word to me. They didn't need to; I knew what they were thinking. I knew what everyone was thinking.

"That one was close," Dad said as he helped me pack up my gear. Mom offered to buy me anything I wanted from the concession stand, even the king-sized Reese's. I shook my head. The sharp pain in my stomach was gone, but it had been replaced with something else, a heaviness, like cement just starting to harden. I said I just wanted to go home.

The first three minutes in the car were silent, except for Dad's fingers on the wheel, a steady tap like a dripping faucet. I was about to ask Mom if she'd turn on the radio when he finally spoke.

"It was way out of the zone, you know." He tilted the rearview mirror so that he could see me in it. I looked up to see only his eyes, like my eyes, the bridge of his nose not at all like my nose. Depending on what feature you looked at, we were either eerily similar or completely different. "That last pitch. You had a solid swing, but the ball wasn't even close. There was no way you were going to get a piece of it. The pitcher gave you a couple of good looks, but that third one . . . you should have laid off."

"Okay," I said. I didn't tell him that I'd had my eyes closed when I swung. I wasn't sure it would have made any difference.

"You have to make the pitcher work for it," Dad continued. "Don't give 'em an easy out. Don't go chasing balls out of the zone."

47

I pressed my forehead to the window and tried to see shapes in the clouds, but they all looked pretty much the same: wads of cotton stretched too thin. It felt like you could blow them apart with a good, strong breath, scattering them like dandelion seeds. I spotted a girl riding her bike along the sidewalk. She looked like she was enjoying her summer immensely.

Dad continued. "Because with two strikes, you had to know he was going to try and get you to chase one. That's what I'd do. Low and away. Make you dig in the dirt. That's when you just lay off. Wait for something better."

Wait for something better. That was good advice.

Mom twisted in her seat and caught my eye, but I quickly looked back out the window at the girl. "It's just a game," she said softly before turning back. She was speaking to me, but Dad heard. She'd meant for him to hear.

I chewed on the inside of my cheeks. I knew what was coming. Like when you're watching someone try to carry too many groceries at once, their arms full, and then it all starts to slip, the carton of eggs spilling out of the top. I counted to five in my head, *One, two, three—*

Dad sighed. His exasperated sigh. The one with the exclamation point on the end.

"What?" my mother said.

"I didn't say anything."

"You went *hmph*."

"Well . . . I don't think that's helpful, is all," Dad replied.

"What's not helpful?"

For a moment it seemed like he might drop it. I wanted him to drop it. In my head I *begged* him to drop it. *Drop it. Drop it.* But I'd seen this happen before. It happened more and more lately.

"Saying it's *just* a game. I mean, yes, it *is* a game. But the way you said it, I think maybe you're giving our son the wrong impression."

I was *our son* now. Like I wasn't in the car anymore. I fiddled with the leather ties on my glove. It was a nice glove. Forty bucks. The insides were lined with some kind of fur. Hopefully fake. I'd hate to think something had died just so I could stand in left field and fantasize about eating candy.

Mom's volume clicked up a few notches. "The wrong impression? It's Little League, Matt. It's not the World Series."

"I didn't say it was the World Series. But you say *just* a game like it's not important."

"Because it's *not* that important."

Dad's forehead creased. "Well obviously it's important to Malcolm, or he wouldn't be upset. And it's important to his teammates. And I can guarantee you that, even with his *let's go out there and have fun* attitude, it's important to Stan Parker. And it's important to the parents in the stands."

"One of them, at least," Mom snipped.

Dad turned and fixed his eyes on her. I kept mine on the road, afraid he might hit something, ready to warn him. "What? You think I'm the only one sitting there who wants the team to win a game?"

"I didn't say that."

"Then what? You're saying *you* don't want him to win?"

"I didn't say that either. I'm just saying maybe don't make such a big deal out of it."

"Oh, come off it, Nicole. Really? Did you see the look on those kids' faces when Malcolm struck out? They were crushed."

I hadn't seen their faces. I was watching the winning team celebrate on the pitcher's mound instead. I'd barely glanced at the other kids on my bench and all the parents on the bleachers sitting behind them. But now I knew, because Dad said so: they were crushed.

"I don't think that's fair," Mom said.

"What's not fair?"

"One, that you blame Malcolm for them losing—"

"I didn't say it was his fault—"

"And two," Mom continued, "that you assume everyone cares as much as you do."

"Fine." Dad angled to face me in the mirror again. "Tell me honestly, bub. Did you want to win that game today or not?"

I couldn't escape. Couldn't slink up to my room. Couldn't sneak into my special hiding spot. I was trapped in the back seat of the car, with Dad's reflection staring at me, waiting for my answer.

Did I want to win?

Of course I wanted to win. Because if we'd won, we wouldn't be having this conversation. *They* wouldn't be doing *this*, again. And Dad would be watching the road in front of him instead of looking at me.

I nodded.

Dad nodded back and finally turned his eyes forward.

"What did you expect him to say?" Mom said. She turned and looked out her window at the same thin stretch of clouds, giving Dad the back of her head.

After another two minutes of silence, he reached back between the two front seats and found my knee, giving it a squeeze. "Don't sweat it, dude," he said. "There's always next game. Maybe we can get in a little extra batting practice this weekend—how does that sound?" His eyes in the mirror again, watching me.

I thought of the girl riding her bike. Just riding her bike in the sun.

What was I supposed to say?

After the first two holes I am sitting at par along with eight other players. Still sixteen holes to go. A lot can happen in sixteen holes. A lot can change.

Except Jamie Tran is already in the lead with two birdies, making the shots that I didn't. Sometimes it feels like everything is easier for other people. There are kids like that at school. Kids who just seem to glide along, everything going according to some prewritten script. Straight As. Lots of friends. Varsity sports. Lead in the school play. I imagine the parents of those kids brag about them constantly. I imagine their shelves at home are cluttered with ribbons and awards.

Sitting on the corner of the registration desk, the Morris-Hirschfield Trophy sparkles in the sun, its dimpled silver top glinting like a disco ball. I can't quite picture it sitting on my dresser, surrounded by my Lego MOCs. For that to even happen I would need everything to go according to script, and so far nothing has.

I don't even try to split the rocks on three. There's too good a chance I'm going to swing and miss, so instead I skirt the edge and settle for two.

The crowd claps politely.

HOLE #4

Par 2

Three sand traps situated near the cup necessitate a measured approach on this curvy par two. In addition, a slight downhill slope can add unwanted momentum that can carry you past the hole and into the waiting pits. Proceed with caution lest you fall into a trap.

The gears in my head are always turning. They just aren't always turning the right way.

That's what Mrs. Rumford told me in the third grade. I looked up one afternoon to see her standing right behind me. She'd caught me daydreaming when I was supposed to be circling all the nouns in a sentence. Instead of getting mad, though, like some other teachers, she asked me what I was thinking about.

Vampires, I said. And vitamin D.

"What about vampires?"

She kept looking at me, so I went on to explain that vitamin D is produced naturally by the human body in response to exposure to sunlight, but that's a problem for vampires, for obvious reasons. So where do they get their vitamin D? Do they just have brittle bones from a vitamin deficiency?

Or does it even matter because they're immortal? Or maybe their digestive system is capable of extracting the necessary vitamins and nutrients from the blood of their victims, which would make sense, but what if their victims were indoorsy types and had a deficiency as well?

When I was done explaining, Mrs. Rumford pointed to my head.

"You have an awful lot going on up there, I can tell. The gears are always turning, which is awesome. But right now you need to switch those gears and find the nouns in this sentence. Then it can go back to contemplating the dietary needs of vampires."

I nodded. Then I circled the nouns and underlined the verbs and drew a picture of a bottle of chewable multivitamins shaped like drops of blood. I don't remember what any of the sentences were, but I never forgot what Mrs. Rumford said.

Always turning.

Honestly I'm not sure about gears, but there's almost always a conversation happening up there. It's not like that spooky whispering you see in a scary movie. The voices in my head aren't evil demons. They're *my* voices—it's just that nobody else can hear them.

But it's okay, because everybody talks to themselves. At least that's what Mom said the one time I asked her about it.

It was a Friday afternoon, which was the best kind. Mom always took off early on Fridays so that she could pick me up from school and we could spend a couple of hours together, just the two of us—"to decompress." We'd spend them browsing at the library or walking around the park or just lying on the couch watching baking contests on TV while Dad worked late. It had become a tradition. Decompressing was one of my favorite things to do. I was good at it. We both were.

That particular afternoon we'd stopped at the grocery store to pick up a few things. With Mom "a few things" usually ended up being a cartful: whatever she needed plus whatever I could sneak in. That Friday I was standing in the cereal aisle admiring a box of Lucky Charms when a voice inside my head with a bad Irish accent said, *Go on. Get them. They're magically delicious.* I casually dropped the box into the cart and then looked at Mom.

"Do you ever hear voices?"

I could tell by the long breath that my question took her by surprise. And not a breakfast-in-bed-on-your-birthday kind of surprise. "What *kind* of voices?"

"You know. Just like regular voices. In your head." I didn't want to go into details. I just wanted to know if *she* thought it was normal. I just wanted her to tell me I was okay.

"You mean like talking to yourself?"

I nodded, because that was mostly what it was. Except the voices I heard didn't always *sound* like me. Sometimes it was Granny Allison, who used to call me "Twizzler" because of my skinny legs and always tried to fatten me up with Girl Scout cookies bought by the case. Granny Allison lived in town near us right up until she passed a little over four years ago. She was full of odd sayings and had a scratchy, bullfrog voice from smoking two packs a day. The voice in my head sounded just like that: like a frog with emphysema and a Southern accent left over from a childhood in Tennessee.

Then there were the announcers, Bill and Jim—sounding like all those Sunday afternoons in the family room with football on, popping in to provide commentary on whatever I was doing at the time—even the most mundane, everyday things.

Greeley's in position. Looks like he's not putting the seat up this time. That could cost him.

Yes it could, Bill, but the rookie's aim has been spot on as of late. He's got a good stance. He lines up. . . . He shoots. . . . He scores! And the crowd goes wild!

In my head the crowd always goes wild.

Then there's Aleck. Aleck is ornery. That's a Granny Allison word. Aleck doesn't pop in often, but when he does, he says things that I would never dare say out loud. "Why's your hair sticking up?" *Because I forgot to brush it, duh.* "Is there a reason you're not working on your math assignment?" *Probably because I finished it five minutes ago, duh.* "Do you want fries with that?" *It's a cheeseburger, duh.* Aleck's favorite word is "duh." But Aleck is mostly harmless, because I knew better than to repeat after him.

Those were the main voices. The regulars. But sometimes there were others.

"So you don't think it's weird?" I asked.

"Weird? Of course not. I talk to myself all the time," Mom

said. "Just this morning I was like, 'Seriously, Nicole, don't you *dare* hit that snooze button again, you lazy bum.'" I knew she didn't listen to her voice because she was late for work that morning. "It's natural. We all do it. There's even a name for it . . . internal something-or-other."

"Monologue." I'd already googled it, which I guess meant that Mom was technically my second opinion.

"See? So you already know it's no big deal." Mom bent over the cart and removed the Lucky Charms, putting them back on the shelf and grabbing a box of bland, flavorless bran flakes instead. "These voices . . . you hear them *all* the time?"

"Not *all* the time," I said, which was true. "Just sometimes. If I'm bored. Or nervous. Or spacing out."

So, a lot of the time.

"And do you, like, talk *back* to them? Like . . . out loud?"

She looked worried again. She probably pictured me sitting alone at the lunch table at school, hands gripping the sides of my tray, mumbling whole conversations to myself, the other kids taking their food to go sit somewhere else. I did eat alone sometimes, but not because kids got up and left, just because they never sat down in the first place. "It's not like that," I told her. "I'm not schizofrantic."

"Schizophrenic," Mom corrected. "And people with schizophrenia don't necessarily hear voices. You're thinking of multiple personality disorder. But I don't think you have that either. You just have a big imagination. Remember Rocky the Robot Rocket?"

I frowned. Rocky the Robot Rocket was an imaginary talking spaceship and also my best friend when I was five. He started as a cardboard refrigerator box the three of us decorated with markers and glitter and duct tape, but when the box collapsed and got recycled, Rocky's spirit somehow lived on in my head. Rocky and I would fly to the moon together and have adventures where we battled an army of evil unicorns lead by Dr. Hornnoggin. We could both transform and shoot missiles out of our fingers. Then, right about the same time Granny Allison had her stroke, Dad suggested that I was too old to be playing with imaginary friends and Rocky disappeared.

The voices in my head weren't like that, though. I could summon Rocky whenever I wanted, but I had to stop and think about it. These other voices just sort of happened. They popped up like little cartoon thought balloons. I wasn't sure I could explain the difference to Mom, so I nodded and tucked a box of Froot Loops into the cart.

"Nice try," she said, reaching in and putting the box back. "Do *you* think it's a problem? These voices?"

I stood in the aisle, taking a moment to consider what would happen if I said yes. Would she go home and tell Dad? Would he make a bigger deal out of it than she was? Could it lead to a fight somehow, one of them blaming the other? Suddenly I regretted even bringing it up, afraid I'd already ruined our Friday afternoon.

"Nope," I said. "Just curious."

She nodded, but she didn't look convinced. The little folds at the corners of her mouth deepened. "You know you can talk to me about this kind of stuff whenever you want. That's what I'm here for." She touched my shoulder and then glanced down into our cart, somehow finding the box of Cocoa Pebbles I'd stealthily buried beneath the paper towels. She held it up with her eyebrows raised.

"They contain eleven essential vitamins and minerals," I explained, pointing to the back.

Mom sighed and put the Cocoa Pebbles back in the cart. Victory at last.

I felt better after that. At least she knew. But I hadn't told her everything. I didn't tell her about the one voice, the one I didn't really have any control over, the one that didn't have a name. I didn't tell her how it came to me that night at the fair. Or how I suspected it had been there all along. Or how it made me feel. Like everything was going wrong.

And like it was all my fault.

The day after I asked my mom about the voices, I had to lace up my cleats again.

A full week had passed since the blind swing that caused the Cardinals to lose their fifth game in a row. I got to miss Tuesday's practice because of a dentist appointment. I'd been saved from Wednesday's game and Thursday night's practice because of rain. Which meant I hadn't been back on the field since that game-ending strikeout. A full week baseball free, though Saturday's doubleheader loomed over it like a dark shadow. To make matters worse, Mom informed me that she was going to have to miss the first game. She'd promised to volunteer at the library book sale; it had been on the calendar for months.

"Sorry, kiddo." She lifted my cap and kissed the top of my head before wiggling the hat back down.

"Don't worry," Dad said, adjusting the cap so it was sitting straight again. "I'm going to take him to breakfast and stuff him full of pancakes. Then we're going to grab a couple of *W*s for the team. Isn't that right, bub?"

Grab a couple of *W*s. Dad had a way of making everything sound easier than it was.

All the way to the IHOP, he recounted highlights of some of his best games pitching for Ohio State University. How he'd struck out eight in a game against Wisconsin. How he'd gotten Purdue's best hitter to ground into a double play to win the Big Ten Championship. How his buddies bedazzled his jockstrap with fake rhinestones and then superglued it to his locker. I sat in the back with my head against my glove, glove against the window, feeling ornery. Aleck's voice piped up. *Who wants to hear about your sparkly old jockstrap?*

"Sounds fun," I said aloud.

We found a table by the window because Dad knew I liked to look outside. He filled the silence with more baseball stories while I made a tower out of coffee creamers. It was ten high when the waitress brought our food.

"You want syrup, hon?"

I looked up at her. *They're pancakes. Duh.*

I nodded politely and poured until the pancakes were two spongy lily pads floating on a pond of sweet brown liquid, but I still couldn't bring myself to take a bite. In less than an hour I would be sitting in the dugout again, dreading my first at bat. This was how it would be for the rest of the summer.

"Not hungry?" Dad asked, noticing my still-full plate.

I shrugged.

"Nervous?"

I nodded.

"That's all right," he said. "I used to get worked up before a big game too. It's normal."

Big game, Aleck said. *The Jackson County Little League thriller between the Cardinals sponsored by Mitch's Meat Market and the Nationals sponsored by Dr. Patel's Family Eye Care. Get your tickets today.*

I used my fork to make little dimples in my pancake. "I guess."

Dad eyed me for a moment behind his glasses, then leaned back in the booth, his long arms still reaching halfway across the table. He had long fingers too. Piano player's fingers, Mom called them. Also good for putting spin on the ball. I wondered if Dad would still be pitching if he hadn't injured his shoulder back in college, before he got the comma-shaped scar that I sometimes stared at whenever we went to the pool. Maybe he could have made it to the majors. He was that good.

Dad sighed. I knew all of his sighs. I could tell what was coming: the motivational, go-get-'em pep talk that he gave me every game day. I had most of it memorized.

Then he threw me a curve.

"I'm getting the impression you don't like baseball much anymore."

That wasn't how the speech normally started.

In my head, Aleck snorted. *Anymore?*

"It's all right," I said, looking at my plate to avoid looking across the table.

"Just all right?" Dad repeated. He paused, and I looked up to see him giving this some thought. "You know I don't care if you're the best player on the field," he continued. "I just want you to go out there, work hard, and do your best."

Every year. Whether you want to or not.

"You know, be part of a team. . . ."

Far left field. Bottom of the lineup. Last seat on the bench.

"And have some fun. . . ."

Striking out. Losing the game. Having your teammates glare at you.

"But you're not having very much fun, are you?" Dad prodded.

Duh-duh-duh-duhh! Aleck said, channeling Beethoven's Fifth, a song Mom sometimes played on the piano.

I shrugged, afraid to say yes, afraid to say no. But a shrug always leans toward no. At least this one did.

Dad sensed it. "Well, if it's not any fun . . . ," he started to

63

say but stopped, as if he couldn't imagine the possibility. He'd played baseball for nearly half of his life. It *was* his life. At least for a while. He crossed his arms and squinted at me, silently studying me for a moment. I studied him back. I had his ears, too. The too-big ears. His ears and eyes, but my mother's nose and mouth—a mouth that I kept shut. Which was good, because I might have missed what came next, he said it so quietly.

"You know you can quit if you want to."

Freeze. I couldn't possibly have heard that right. Quit? I had never heard my father say that word. Not about baseball, at least. Aleck was struck speechless, so I jumped in. "Wait, what?"

"You heard me," he said.

"You mean just stop playing? Like, today? Right now?" I tried not to sound too excited. It felt like a trap. And it was. Sort of. Dad continued to frown.

"Of course it *is* the middle of the season," he said, weaving those long fingers together. "And this isn't just about you. You have your team to think about. And your coach."

My team? The kids who never talked to me? Jace the Mace, who laughed in my face because I thought Mike Trout was a cartoon character. Sure, Mouse might be a little disappointed, but he could find somebody else to share candy with. Coach Parker would probably try to talk me out of it, but only because he felt like he had to. But the rest of the team would probably launch a volley of farewell loogies to show me the way out of the dugout.

"It's a lot to consider," Dad continued. "You made a commitment. You'd be letting them down."

I knew what he was trying to do—my parents used this strategy on each other all the time. But Mouse, Mace, Coach Parker—they weren't the reason I started playing. They weren't why I said yes every time Dad asked, "We're doing baseball again this summer, right?"

We.

There was only one person I was afraid of disappointing.

Do it. Just ask him, Aleck prodded.

"Would you . . . you know . . . would you be mad?"

Dad seemed to think for a moment. "No. Not mad." His voice trailed off, leaving a big blank space for me to fill in.

Sometimes conversations are full of blank spaces. Like Mad Libs. Somebody will say something and then pause, waiting for you to think what they were too frightened or embarrassed or polite to say. My parents ended a lot of their sentences this way when they talked to each other. They had whole conversations that seemed to be filled with unspoken words, little pits of quicksand for the other person to walk into.

This blank was easy to fill. He wouldn't be mad, but he might not look at me the same way for a while.

"Listen, Malcolm, I know baseball's not your favorite thing in the world. . . ."

And the understatement of the year goes to . . .

"But I don't want to see you unhappy either."

I wasn't even sure what my favorite thing in the world was, but I knew it wasn't baseball.

"So just tell me, straight up, do you want to quit or not?"

There it was. The slow, easy pitch. Right in the zone. I just needed the guts to swing.

I thought about the last three summers. The gleam in Dad's eye during our trips to the store to buy new gear. The look he got when we parked by the field and he heard the ping of balls rocketing off aluminum bats. The pumped fists and the sound of my name shouted from the bleachers on those rare occasions when I managed to catch a pop fly or somehow get on base. I knew what he wanted me to say, but for once I didn't say it.

"Yes."

"Yes what?" He needed to hear the word. I swallowed hard.

"I want to quit."

I startled, nearly jumping out of the booth as Dad suddenly slapped his hands on the table hard enough that his silverware rattled. "It's settled then." His voice had changed. He was talking quickly now, but he wasn't looking at me anymore. "I'll call Coach Parker as soon as we leave and let him know we won't be there today. You can call him again later and tell him why you quit." He picked up his fork and dug back into his food without even looking up.

He said not mad, but he sure seemed mad.

I let him get his bite in. Then I said, "Sorry."

"What are you apologizing to me for?" Dad asked. "I'm not on your team."

On the way home after breakfast, Dad informed me we were stopping by the hardware store. He suddenly had the afternoon free; he might as well fix the sagging gutter over the front porch.

"Have you ever fixed a gutter before?"

"No."

"Can't you just pay someone to do it?" I suggested.

"I could. And I could probably pay somebody to fold my laundry too. But I won't, because it's something I'm perfectly capable of doing myself. That's called fulfilling your responsibilities."

I didn't say anything more about it, just followed quietly behind him through the store. When we checked out, the cashier noticed my uniform. "Big game today?"

I was about to nod, figuring it was the easiest way to avoid a conversation, but before I could, Dad said, "Not anymore." I stared at the ground, wondering if it was possible to fold myself in half, and then quarters, and then eighths, again and again until I was so small that nobody noticed me anymore. The cashier nodded and rang up the rest of our stuff without another word.

I followed Dad out to the car, hoping we could just ride home in silence. Part of me wanted to change my mind, to tell him to just drive to the baseball diamond, that I was wrong. We could still make it in time for the first game. But he would know I didn't mean it. You can't take back something like that. You can't lie *after* you've already told the truth.

We had almost made it out of the parking lot when our Honda came to a sudden stop. Dad sat at the wheel, looking thoughtful. I braced myself for whatever came next.

"Huh," he said.

I looked where he was looking. Directly behind the Home Depot was an auto body shop, but behind that was something unfamiliar: Fritz's Family Fun Zone. Fritz was an alligator who wore yellow suspenders and a red baseball cap, at least according to the chipped, faded statue sitting out front.

Behind the alligator stood a one-story building with neon signs advertising pizza and games. On one side of the building stood a row of batting cages, and just behind it was a miniature golf course. You could see a windmill and a waterfall from the parking lot, the former moving almost as slowly as the second hand of a clock, the latter churning up sickly, greenish water.

"What?" I asked from the back seat.

"You remember this place? We brought you once when you were little. Like, *really* little. You could barely hold the club, so you'd just pick the ball up and plop it right in the hole. It closed down not long after that, so we never came back."

It wasn't closed anymore. There were at least a dozen people on the golf course and a couple more in the batting cages. You could hear the clink of bats over the tinny music playing through speakers somewhere. The sound made my stomach churn. Dad started driving again, but instead of turning onto the road and taking us home, he cut through the parking lot and pulled into an empty space in front of the alligator. "We've got time to shoot a round, don'tcha think?"

This was unexpected. Another curve. "Don't you have to fix the gutter?" I asked.

"No rain in the forecast," he replied, glancing up at the clear blue summer sky before getting out of the car.

Fritz's might have just reopened, but it probably looked like it did back when I was a toddler. There were a bunch of ancient-looking pinball games. The Skee-Ball machine had some lightbulbs missing. There was even an old-fashioned Pac-Man machine that still took quarters, tucked away in a corner. The walls were decorated with 1980s movie posters. *Ghostbusters*, *Gremlins*, and *Goonies*, just to name the Gs.

The little concessions area was baking up pizzas even though it wasn't yet noon. A slushy maker churned in the background. The teenager at the counter looked up from her phone long enough to swipe Dad's credit card and ask what color ball we wanted. Dad went with red, his favorite. I went with orange just because it was the only orange one left, which meant either it was the best color and everybody else was using it, or that it was one of a kind. Either way was fine with me. We headed through the back door to Fritz's two courses.

"Look. They still have the dinosaur."

Dad pointed to a ten-foot-tall brontosaurus that straddled

one of the holes, its front feet acting as an obstacle. It seemed strange having a dinosaur sitting alongside windmills and lighthouses. Then again, the whole layout was a hodgepodge. One hole looked like a safari, complete with miniature plastic lions and zebras. Another had an igloo with a penguin sitting on the roof. Another had a loop meant to simulate a roller coaster. Another hole was guarded by ceramic lawn gnomes. It was as if Fritz—or whoever actually owned the place— decorated the course with whatever he could find at the local flea market. And wherever giant plastic dinosaurs are sold.

"It's busy," Dad remarked, taking in the other golfers. He stood near the entrance to the course, deciding whether to play the Blue Course or the Red one. The sign for Red claimed it was harder, so that's where we headed.

I watched as the people around us took their shots, squinting one eye, sticking out their tongue, hissing when the ball bounced off a rock. One little girl, a few years younger than me, just kicked her ball with her feet.

"I've been here a couple of times, actually. Before we brought you here, your mom and I used to play," Dad said as we made our way to the first hole—a vaguely star-shaped green with a straight shot—no hills or hazards. "You know. For date night."

Date night. I tried to remember the last time my parents had one of those, going out just the two of them. There were lots of nights when one of them was gone. Lately half of my time was spent with only one parent.

"You're up," Dad said.

I placed my ball on the tee and stood next to it, holding my club like a toilet plunger.

"No. Not like that. Like this." Dad took my hands, twisting them in his, closing my fingers back around the sticky rubber handle, making me wonder what the kid who'd used it before me had been eating.

"Like a sword?" I said, holding the club out.

"Sure. If that's how you want to think of it."

I stood next to the ball again and looked at the hole, less than twenty feet away. That's when it struck me. The simple truth of it.

I couldn't miss.

I mean technically I *could*. It was possible I could swing too hard and totally whiff, but the odds of that were slim. The ball was just sitting there, waiting for me to whack it. I didn't have to wait for "my pitch." There was no chance of striking out. The game wouldn't end just because I screwed up. No teammates would mope and groan. No coaches would give me sympathetic looks. If I didn't sink the ball on the first try, I would get another shot at it. And another. And another. Until it went in the hole.

I hadn't even taken a shot yet, and I already liked this game ten times better than baseball.

Dad stood behind me, looking over my shoulder, but it didn't bother me. Not like it usually does. I gave the ball a tap. It rolled halfway across the green and stopped.

"Not quite hard enough," Dad said, as if I hadn't figured that one out. "It's all about applying the proper velocity."

Dad set up and then gave his ball a whack that sent it shooting past the hole like a bright red comet, rebounding off the back metal wall. It came to rest only an inch from the cup.

"That was close," I said.

"It's all about the angles," Dad replied.

Apparently, miniature golf was all about a lot of things.

Dad tapped in his second putt and marked his score. I made mine in three, which meant he was ahead already, but that was okay. He'd played this game before. He'd played all the games before. That's when Dad started talking about birds. On a golf course named after an alligator. Decorated with a dinosaur.

"Par is sort of the average—what you're expected to get. One under par is a birdie. Two under par is an eagle, though I think all of these are a par two, so that's impossible. One *over* par is called a bogey."

"What kind of a bird is a bogey?" I asked.

"I don't think bogey is a bird. It just means you didn't do so hot."

I got a bogey on my first hole. Not so hot. Still, something about the word "bogey" amused me. It was nothing like "strikeout," which sounded violent and final and depressing. I whispered the word over and over to myself—"bogey-bogey-bogey-bogey"—until Dad gave me a funny look.

We came up to hole two, which looked a lot like hole one

except for the giant fake rock stationed right in the middle of the green. A tunnel had been carved through its center. I crouched down to get a better look. If you hit it perfectly straight, the ball could pass right underneath the rock and get in the hole in one shot. But that was a big if. The tunnel was narrow, barely two ball widths wide. There was plenty of room to go around the rock. In fact, if you hit it just right, banked it off the wall, you could probably sink it in one that way, too.

"Let the old pro show you how it's done," Dad said, teeing up. "Shortest distance between two points is a straight line." He squared his shoulders and swung.

Thunk. Right off the front of the rock.

Dad turned to me and shrugged. "That's why they put them there, I guess."

By "them" he meant the rocks, but I wondered who "they" were. The mysterious designers of mini golf courses? I pictured little elves coming out from behind the trees after midnight, busily cobbling together tunnels and traps. Like the word "bogey" and the plastic penguin and the dinosaur with the paint peeling off its hide, there was something fun and goofy and harmless about this place. But there was something else. A kind of logic to all those angles and hills and tunnels that made sense to me.

Dad managed to bang his ball through the rock on his second swing, though it missed the hole and rolled into a corner. He ended up with a four. On a par two. He didn't tell me what that was called. A mega bogey? A bogus? A booger?

"Be careful," he said. "You have to hit this one just right."

There were three dimples on the rubber mat at the start. I placed my ball on the dimple to the left.

"You'll want to use the middle one," Dad said. "Trust me."

But I didn't want to use the middle one. I kept the ball where it was and eyed the left wall. It seemed to me you could hit it just about anywhere near the center of the wall and clear the rock, but if you wanted to get a hole in one, you needed to find just the right spot. I'd learned some basic geometry in fifth grade. I'd also played a lot of Angry Birds when I was little.

I glanced up to see the look on Dad's face, his lips pressed tight. I could tell he wanted to say something, to tell me I was standing the wrong way or my ball was in the wrong place or that my toes were pointed incorrectly. But it was my shot. He'd already had his. So he just watched.

And I heard other voices inside my head. Not Aleck this time.

And here we have Malcolm Greeley, age twelve, on the second hole. He bogeyed the first one. But here he's taking a different approach.

That's right, Jim. I think Greeley is going to try and avoid the center rock entirely and go for the bank shot. An unorthodox strategy that his dad clearly doesn't approve of, but today seems to be the day for disappointing your father, so what the hey.

I lined up the groove in the middle of my putter's head with the center of the ball. The angle seemed right, but there was still the question of speed. I had no idea how hard to hit it off the metal siding. I decided to give it a little extra.

And here's the shot.

Click. The ball left my putter. Rolling and then . . .

Clonk. Off the side of the wall. Still rolling and then . . .

Dink. Right in the hole.

And it's a birdie for Malcolm Greeley. And the crowd goes wild!

Except there was no crowd. Just Dad. And he wasn't going wild. He was staring at the cup, looking at my bright orange ball sitting on top of his faded red one.

"Beginner's luck," he said.

I shrugged. A shrug means maybe, but it usually leans toward no.

In the sixteen holes that followed, I only had one more hole in one, but I had mostly twos and threes. There was just one hole where I had to take the maximum score of six. That was hole number sixteen, a crazy uphill climb that led to a flat section barely big enough to stand on. If you didn't hit the ball just right, it rolled back down the other side, forcing you to hit it up the hill again. And again. And again. That was the only other hole that Dad beat me on. He finished with a score of fifty-eight.

I finished with a forty-six. It was the first time I'd ever beaten my father at anything.

And yet it didn't even feel like we were playing against each other so much as working against the course. Each hole was a puzzle to be solved. Half the time I didn't even know what

Dad got—I was too busy sizing up my own shot.

Still, I knew that a forty-six was better than a fifty-eight.

And I knew he knew I knew.

Mom was surprised when she pulled into the driveway that afternoon to find our other car parked there. She was popping in to change clothes before heading out to the field for the second game. Instead, she found me on the porch reading *Squirrel Girl* and Dad on the ladder attending to the sagging gutter.

"What are you two doing home? Did the game get canceled?"

I looked up at Dad, wiping his hands as he stepped off the ladder. The whole ride home, he hadn't mentioned baseball, me quitting, the phone call to Coach Parker, none of it. Instead we talked about other things, like Skee-Ball, and whether it was worth it to try for the hundred-point holes in the corners or just aim for the fifty in the middle. Dad went for the corners. I always played it safe and rolled it right down the middle.

Now, with Mom home, I could sense it coming. *Your son decided to quit baseball.* That's how it would start, and then each of them would blame the other for the poor decision I made. It would be another tense night at the dinner table, with the two of them circling like combatants in the Colloseum.

Instead, Dad smiled and said, "We played Putt-Putt, actually."

Mom looked confused, then glanced at me for confirmation. I nodded, feeling no need to volunteer additional information.

"So no baseball?" she ventured.

There was a pause. "I think we might be done with baseball for the time being," Dad said.

Mom's eyebrows nearly lifted clear off her head, like some anime character's. "Ookaaay . . . ," she said, drawing the word out as long as her breath would allow. I tried giving her a look that I hoped meant *Please don't ask.* She must have gotten the hint. "So where did you go to play Putt-Putt?"

"That old place off of County Line Road? Next to Home Depot. You remember. We used to have date nights there?"

Judging by the look on her face, Mom couldn't quite remember the last time they'd had a date night either. "You mean Fritz's? I thought that place closed down."

"New management," Dad said. "Fresh coat of paint, but still all the same holes and stuff."

"There was a dinosaur," I added.

Mom smiled. She remembered the dinosaur.

"I have to admit, your son's pretty good." *Your son.* That's how he put it. But it didn't come out sounding how it usually does.

"Yeah? How good?"

"I got two birds."

"Birdies," Dad corrected.

Then, because I couldn't help myself, I blurted out, "*And* I beat Dad."

Eyebrows up again. My mother, clearly impressed.

"It's true," Dad confirmed. "By, like, ten strokes."

Mom gave me a high five and told me I was her hero. Then we sat on the porch, the three of us, eating cheap plastic-tube Popsicles I fetched from the fridge. Red for Dad, green for Mom, orange for me. We sat and watched our neighbors walking their dogs and listened to the geese squawking at the pond across the street. It was one of the best summer Saturdays I'd had in a while.

It felt so good, I didn't even bother to correct Dad on his math, because it didn't really matter.

Though for the record, I'd beaten him by twelve.

Hole four is tough. If you get stuck in one of the sand traps, you have no choice but to take a one-stroke penalty. Miniature golfers don't get to use sand wedges. Most miniature golf courses don't even use real sand, they just use beige-colored turf to give the *suggestion* of sand, but this course is swanky—not at all like Fritz's—which means the hazards here are real.

Still, I manage to make par. My first shot is way too strong, shooting past the hole and banging off the back wall. I sink a tricky second putt past the sand, though, ignoring Admiral Ackbar's voice in my head—*It's a trap!*—and sighing with relief when the ball drops.

Frank Sanderson would call that a good recovery. He'd say that there are very few shots in golf—miniature or otherwise—that you can't recover from if you know what you're doing.

I want to believe that. I want to believe that no matter how deep you get, you can always dig yourself out of the hole you're in. I want to believe that things can always be salvaged, even if it means only breaking even.

I think about where Frank is right at this moment and I whisper a prayer under my breath as I retrieve my ball. A birdie on this hole would have been nice, but sometimes you take what you can get.

Sometimes just making par is good enough.

HOLE #5

<u>Par 2</u>

Hole five begins with a steep uphill climb leading to a pipe that funnels your ball to the level below, providing your most direct line to a hole in one. Alternatively, you can bypass the pipe and simply plummet over the top ledge. It should be noted that even if you manage to hit the mouth of the pipe on your first shot, an ace is not guaranteed.

Sometimes a blind leap over the edge is your best option.

My dad has something hidden in his closet. It's not a gun, or a box of letters from some girl he met before Mom, or a super-hero outfit from his secret life as a crime-fighting vigilante. It's not even something that should have surprised me. But it did.

I discovered it by accident. It had been two weeks since that Saturday at Fritz's. Two baseball-less weeks filled with trips to the park and the pool. We were headed to a fancy dinner to celebrate a promotion Dad had gotten at work, which meant scratchy pants and a tie. Except I didn't own any ties. Dad told me to run up to his closet and pick out a thin one; he'd show me how to tie it and tuck the extra into my shirt.

As I stood in front of Dad's sliding closet door, I realized I hadn't looked in it in years. During games of hide-and-seek I'd always picked Mom's walk-in, because there was plenty of stuff to huddle behind: long dresses and winter coats and piles of unfolded laundry you could burrow under. She kept hers messy, like I did. I slid the door to my father's closet open, and the first thing I saw was the rack of ties at the far end. There were dozens.

I picked the first skinny one I saw—dark blue with silver stripes—and started to slide the door shut when a glimmer caught my eye. I took two steps away and looked to the top of the closet and found them, shoved toward the back but lined up in a neat row: Dad's trophies. From his ball-playing days.

They easily outnumbered his ties.

I'd just assumed they were in a box somewhere—the back half of the attic, maybe. But here they were, on parade in the dark closet, easy to miss if you weren't looking up. I took in the small army of gold and silver athletes. The bigger ones held baseball bats or were winding up for a pitch. The smaller ones showed someone cradling a football or holding a lacrosse stick. One just had a star on top; that one was for wrestling, proba-bly. I grabbed one of the big plastic tubs from Mom's closet and dragged it over, taking a glance in the hallway to make sure it was empty. Standing a couple feet taller, I reached for the clos-est one: a gold figurine perched atop an emerald pedestal. The engraved plate along the base had my father's name: *Matthew Greeley.* And underneath, the words *First Team All-State, 1995.*

It was twenty times more impressive than my baseball par-ticipation trophies, yet here it was, stashed away in the top of the closet for nobody to see.

It was heavier than I expected. But not dusty at all. That surprised me too.

I took down another, a trophy for winning the county championship—almost no dust on that one either. Even the Lego models I had sitting on the shelves in my bedroom had gathered a powdery coat. Sitting up here in the dark there should have been cobwebs hanging from these athletes' elbows.

Unless someone regularly took care of them.

I pictured my dad, cloth in one hand, pulling each trophy down and holding it for a moment, maybe thinking about the good old days before wiping it off and putting it back. Did he sneak up here and dust them while Mom was at the store? Was it something he was ashamed of for some reason? Or was it something he just didn't want to share with anyone else? How had I never noticed them before?

How come he never showed me?

"Hey, bub, did you find a good one?"

It was Dad's voice, calling me from the stairs. I quickly replaced the trophies and shut the closet door, scooting the storage bin back where I'd found it. I'd been told to get in his closet, but it still felt like I'd crossed a line. Like I'd seen something I shouldn't have.

"Come on. It's almost time to go."

As I shut off the light, I glanced back at Dad's closet and imagined all those little men suddenly coming to life, starting a pickup game in the dark, a strange combination of baseball, football, and lacrosse. The Top Shelf Championship. And Matt Greeley as the obvious MVP.

There was no kids' menu at L'Oie d'Or, but there were grilled pork chops with mushroom sauce that could be mostly scraped off. Mom made me eat the asparagus that came with it, which was saggy and soggy but could be washed down with plenty of Sprite. There was also seven-layer chocolate cake at the end that almost made up for it.

And there were stories. Mom and Dad spent most of dinner remembering life way back when. Before me. Back even before they were Mrs. and Mr. Greeley, when they were just Nicole and Matt, two college students falling for each other. Dad teased Mom about their first date at the bowling alley—a story I'd heard a half-dozen times. ("Seriously, Malcolm. First ball . . . not a single pin. And the bumpers were up! I mean, how is that possible?") Mom called Dad out on his choice of gift for their first Valentine's Day together. ("Chocolates would have been fine. Flowers. A nice dinner. But hockey tickets? For Valentine's Day?") I just chewed my mushroomy pork chop and listened. Mom would say something about Dad and then they would both laugh. He'd tease her right back and they'd laugh again. I held my breath every now and then, anxiously waiting for one of them to say something that would sour the mood, cause everything to shift, but it never happened. It was as if everything around us—the chandeliers, the fancy napkins, the stiff waiter who refilled my cup after

84

every sip, the piece of chocolate cake as big as my head—all of it created a kind of force field around us. A bubble where snippy remarks or uncomfortable silences weren't allowed.

They were happy. I was happy. The asparagus was tolerable. The cake was delicious. As we walked back to the car after dinner, Dad suggested we head over to Fritz's and play a round. "I want to get your mom on the green," he said, "see if *she* can beat you."

Summer was drawing to a close and Fritz's was packed. It was mostly teenagers eating pizza and playing video games. Dad paid and chose the red ball again. Mom picked yellow. The orange one was still there. This time I thought I was being clever. "You know, 'cause yellow and red make—

"Yeah, I get it," Mom said.

Dad insisted on doing the harder course again. He told me to go first. I looked down the green and remembered not hitting it hard enough the first time, so I made an adjustment.

Tap. Roll. Drop.

Down goes the birdie. A little surge of satisfaction bubbled up inside of me.

"Wow. You *are* good at this," Mom said.

"Well, it *is* just a straight shot," Dad interjected. He then proceeded to get a three on the hole, his second shot circling around the cup but not falling. "Come on! You both saw it. I was robbed!"

"Whatever helps you fall asleep at night," Mom teased. She squared up, closed one eye, pressed her lips tight. Her swing sent the ball skipping over the artificial turf, right past the hole, rebounding hard off the center of the rusted back wall, and then bouncing backward . . . straight into the cup. "Would you look at that?" she said. "I got a hole in one *too*." Mom gave me a high five and we both turned to Dad. "You got that, right?" she said, pointing at the scorecard in his hand. "That's a one for me, and a one for Malcolm, and then whatever you got."

Dad muttered something to himself as he wrote on the card with the tiny pencil and went to the next hole. Mom rolled her eyes. "I don't know if you've realized this about your father yet," she whispered to me, "but he hates to lose."

"I can hear you," Dad said over his shoulder. "And you saw it yourself: that ball should have gone in."

We followed him to hole two and I noticed that Dad placed his ball on the far left of the tee this time. He didn't get a hole in one, but he avoided the rock and did better than last time. Mom managed to hit her ball straight through the tunnel on the first try, though not quite hard enough to sink it. We all settled for par and no one complained.

When we were finished with all eighteen, Dad tallied up the scores, announcing them loud enough for the people standing next to us to hear. Then he bought me an ice-cream bar from the concession stand, even though I'd already had seven-layer chocolate cake. "To the victor go the spoils."

"I think we all did good," I said. Mom and Dad had both gotten scores under fifty.

"A win is a win," Dad said.

I didn't argue. After all, I was the one holding the ice cream.

That night I did three things that I would pay for later.

I ate the asparagus and it made my pee stink. Like dead skunk and rotten eggs and burned garlic. It was gross. And fascinating.

I scored a thirty-nine at Fritz's, which was even better than last time and only three shots over par. Mom stuck the score-card to the fridge.

The last thing happened as soon as we got back in the car. Dad turned around before turning the key. "You really like mini golf, don't you?" he asked.

I didn't think about it. If I had, I might have seen where the question was leading. "Yeah. It's fun," I said. Because it was. There was something about it. Lots of things, really. I liked how colorful it all was. I liked the video-gamey nature of the obstacles and the strange, mismatched décor. I liked the word "putter"—even better than the word "bogey." I liked stand-ing at the tee, tracing the potential path of the ball with my eyes. I liked the sound it made when it dropped into the plas-tic cup, sometimes bouncing once at the bottom—*clu-clunk*. "A lot of fun."

Dad nodded as he turned back around. The headlights came on and I could see Fritz the Alligator staring back at me, a vacant look in his big black eyes.

"Things are always more fun when you're good at them," Dad said.

It was still several days before what I'd said in the car came back to bite me in the bum, as Granny Allison would say. By then school had started up again. It seemed like it started earlier and earlier every year.

Life at Longview Intermediate School ranged from tedious to tolerable. A typical day looked something like this:

- Forty-four minutes listening to other kids gossip and make inappropriate jokes. Usually about body parts. Or teachers. Or some combination of the two.
- Sixteen minutes trying not to get trampled in the hallway by kids who are bigger than me, i.e., horses at the fair.
- Thirty-three seconds wondering if Melissa Danforth's hair felt as smooth and silky as it looked, but always way too scared to touch it and find out.
- Thirty-three minutes actually learning something interesting, usually in science.
- Twenty-seven minutes doodling in my writing notebook. Usually pictures of robots. Or dinosaurs. Or robot dinosaurs.
- Fifteen seconds at the drinking fountain hoping that none of those same bigger kids pushes my head down into the spray.
- Fifty-six minutes daydreaming plans for the afternoon (if

it wasn't Friday), or thinking about what I would do
if everyone in my class suddenly turned into a pack of
zombies and tried to eat me, or guessing how many Oreos
I could consume in one sitting, or reflecting on the sad fact
that I will probably only set foot on .000001 percent of the
Earth's surface in my entire life.

- Two hundred and forty-seven minutes of fidgeting in class,
  praying I won't get called on. Not because I don't know
  the answers, but because I don't want kids looking at me.

Then at 2:55 the bell rings and I make my escape, sitting in
the front of the bus, close to the door, hugging my backpack.
When I get home, I use the garage code to get in, find something to eat (Cocoa Pebbles if I'm lucky), and then head up to
my room.

That's where I was on the Thursday of the first week of
school, sitting on my bed, Spider-Man comic in hand, listening to the sounds of Dad coming home from work: the
purr of the car in the driveway, the jingle of his keys on the
kitchen counter, the footsteps coming up the stairs, turning
left instead of right, which meant he was heading my way.

Why was he heading my way?

He gave three quick knocks before opening the door himself. Mom always waited for me to come let her in. Dad . . .
not so much.

"Hey, bub, how was school?" His tie hung limp around his
neck like a sleeping snake.

"Okay," I said, hoping he didn't want the minute-by-minute breakdown, but that was usually Mom's thing. He sat down next to me on the bed, a folded piece of paper in hand.

Warning. Parental lecture incoming, Aleck said.

I wondered what I'd done wrong. I'd only been in school for three days. I hadn't been kicked out of any classes or sent to the principal's office. But the paper had nothing to do with school.

"So I did some research into this whole miniature golf thing," Dad began, flipping the paper over and over in his hands, "and did you know that there's, like, an actual *league* for this stuff. Like an *association* of mini golfers?"

I didn't say anything. I didn't even blink. I could see where this was going already.

"It looks pretty legit. There are membership dues. And a monthly newsletter. And here's the best part: they help sponsor tournaments and competitions all across the country."

Dad stared at me, waiting for a response.

Here we go.

"Wow," I said.

"I know, right? And get this," Dad continued. "Believe it or not, there's actually one coming up at Fritz's at the end of next month."

He unfolded the paper to show me. It was a printout of an email announcing a junior mini golf tournament sponsored by Leroy McClucker's Chicken Shack. There was a picture of a chicken laying a golf ball at the top. It was kind of wrong.

"It's just for kids, ages eight to fourteen. One round. Only ten bucks to enter, and there are prizes for the top three places. So what do you think? Pretty cool, right?"

Dad licked his lips. I looked at the golf-ball-laying chicken. *Good luck eating* that *egg,* Aleck snarked.

I shrugged. "Could be fun, I guess."

Dad nodded eagerly. "That's what I was thinking. Could be fun. I mean . . . you're pretty good," he ventured. "Better than me. And it's something you enjoy. I mean . . . it's nothing like baseball, right?"

Even just hearing the word made me tense. I sat cross-legged on my bed and stared at my hands; my fingernails still had the little smiley faces I'd drawn on them in social studies. Dad held the paper out to me, but the excitement he'd burst through the door with seemed to be fizzling. When he spoke again his tone had changed.

"It's no biggie. I just thought I'd mention it." He offered a quick smile, set the printed email announcement on the bed between us, and stood up to go. I watched him shuffle out, noticing how one hand cupped the back of his neck, rubbing it slowly. I could tell what he was thinking, how he was feeling. I knew how it felt to strike out.

I let him get as far as the door.

"Sure."

Dad stopped. Turned. "Yeah?"

"Yeah. Let's do it," I said.

And Greeley comes through at the last second with the save.

I could tell by the big grin that I'd said the right thing. "Cool. I'll look into getting us signed up." He started to leave and then stopped again. "And don't worry: it's still over a month away. We've got plenty of time."

Plenty of time for what?

But before I could ask, Dad had gone, shutting the door behind him. I listened for his footsteps on the stairs and then scooted to the edge of my bed and looked at Jaws. "Don't worry. It's just miniature golf. We *like* miniature golf."

Jaws made little fish kisses with his mouth, then went and hid behind his plastic castle, as if he knew something I didn't.

But there was no way either of us could have known what would happen next.

Hole five is sneaky. The pipe at the top of the ramp is tempting for more than just the potential ace. Everyone likes to hit their ball into the cool tunnel or through the windmill. It's not as much fun if you don't make use of the gimmicks and contraptions. But the truth is that top hole is a trap. It requires just the right amount of force, and there's a good chance you will go too soft for fear of skipping over it and your first shot will come rolling right back down to your feet, costing you a stroke. And even if you do manage to hit that top hole and travel down the pipe to the lower level, it's just as likely that your ball will have too much momentum and will shoot past the cup or will come out of the mouth of the pipe at an off angle; then you're stuck with a two-putt anyway.

Better to skip the top hole entirely. Smack the ball hard enough to crest the hill and drop over the cliff on the other side. You probably won't get a hole in one, but you won't have to worry about a rollback, and why fight against the inevitable?

I play it safe, go off the cliff, and make par.

Jamie Tran manages to drop it in the top hole and gets a one.

HOLE #6

Par 2

Hole six—often called "The Mound"—begins with a narrow approach that opens onto a gentle slope up to a wide plateau with the cup at its center. The biggest mistake you can make is hitting the ball too softly, which can lead to wishes for a mulligan on what may be your best chance for a hole-in-one on the entire course. The key is to commit to cresting that hill and making the most of the opportunity once you're at the top.

Most of the time, the voices in my head are easy to shut off.

The voices outside of my head are harder. Especially when those voices belong to my parents.

Even more when they are talking about me.

Most of my parents' arguments *aren't* about me—they are about money, or work, or something somebody said three weeks ago that the other person remembers verbatim. They are pointed and sharp. Back and forth. One jab and then another until somebody says, *Have it your way.* That's the difference between a conversation and an argument: conversations don't have winners and losers.

When the voices get too loud, when it stops being a conversation and turns into a fight, that's when I retreat into the Cove.

That's my name for it. Dad calls it my hidey-hole. It's really just part of the attic that I can access through my bedroom. There's a thin wood door, three feet high, painted to blend in with the wall. It's meant to give access to vents and cables. I have to duck to enter; Mom and Dad have to get down on their hands and knees. There is another entrance to the attic, a set of fold-out stairs in the garage that lead to the back half where Mom and Dad keep the sleds and the Halloween decorations, where I once imagined Dad's trophies were stowed.

My door leads to a hideaway. There are Christmas lights strung through the rafters. There's a small shelf for books and sudoku magazines. Two beanbag chairs purchased at a garage sale provide the only places to sit. I'm not allowed to keep any food in there—Dad's afraid it might attract mice or bats—or jump up and down—Mom's afraid I'll come through the ceiling and drop into her lap on the couch—but otherwise I can do whatever I please.

Mom gave it its name. I didn't even know the word until she explained it. "A cove is a little sheltered stretch of water in the ocean, like a little pool. Sort of peaceful and tucked away. The waves usually don't crash as big there."

So the Cove is where I go when the yelling starts.

Unless I hear my name. Then I keep listening no matter what. Because if I know what I've done wrong, maybe I can figure out a way to undo it.

My parents weren't yelling the morning of the day I met Frank Sanderson, but I could tell they were on edge. It started with my dad saying my name followed by something I didn't quite catch. I sat near the top of the stairs, concealed by the half wall, the best place to eavesdrop. You could hear most everything coming from the kitchen or dining room, which were the usual sparring grounds.

"Who?" Mom asked, suddenly sounding irritable.

"Frank Sanderson. He was formerly a ranked player in the PGA. Like, *worldwide* ranked. I mean, he was only nine hundred and something. But still, that's a big deal."

I'd never heard the name Frank Sanderson. I wasn't sure what the PGA was either. My only guess was Parental Guidance Association—the people who gave all the interesting-looking movies R ratings so I couldn't watch them. Mom must have known what it was, though I could tell by her tone that she wasn't impressed. "You don't play golf. Why is he coming here?"

"Because I asked him to be Malcolm's coach," Dad said.

From out of nowhere, a lump in my throat. Another in my stomach. Did he just say *coach*?

Mom wasn't sure she'd heard right either. "His coach? Wait. You mean for *Putt-Putt*?" She said it like a dirty word. Like, *Do you know what these two were doing in the backyard? I caught them playing Putt-Putt.* "Are you serious?"

Dad's voice was calmer, quieter, and I held my breath so I wouldn't miss a word. "It's just a few lessons, once a week for an hour or two, and he's not charging much. I'm not sure what you're getting so worked up about."

"I'm not worked up," Mom said, louder than before. "But come on. A Putt-Putt coach? Where did you find this guy? Google?"

"Facebook," Dad admitted. "But it's not like that. We're old friends. We went to high school together, one year apart. He lives here in town."

There was a pause. At least I thought it was a pause. Or maybe they were whispering. I scooted down a few more stairs so I could see into the hallway. My father stood with his back to me, his hands on his hips, talking into the kitchen. I couldn't see my mother, but when she spoke again, I could hear her just fine.

"Malcolm doesn't need a coach."

"Why not? He's good. And he *likes* it. This isn't like Little League, all right? Or any of the other things we've made him try."

"*You've* made him try," Mom corrected.

"Excuse me? What about gymnastics?"

"He was four!" Mom snapped. "And you can't call that gymnastics. They rolled around the floor to music."

She was right. That was Little Stars Gymnastics. One hour of rolling around, playing Simon says, and jumping into foam pits. All good until we started the balance beam and the other kids started showing off, seeing who could stay on longer. That's about when I quit.

Dad sighed. His frustrated sigh. "I can't win with you. You complain that I don't take an interest in the kinds of things he likes. Then when I do, you don't like that either."

"There's a difference between taking an interest in something and making a huge deal out of it."

"Who's making a huge deal out of it?"

"You hired a *coach*, Matt."

"Yeah. So he can get better before the tournament."

"*What?*"

"Oh, come on. I told you about that," Dad snapped. "I showed you the paper. Malcolm said he wanted to do it."

"You mean the chicken thing?"

"It's not a chicken thing. It's just a local competition. But I think if Malcolm practices, gets a little better, he could actually win."

"Maybe he doesn't *want* to get better. Maybe he's good enough as he is."

There was a clunk as Mom dropped something in our metal sink. I watched Dad run a hand across his thinning hair. He muttered what came next. It was impossible to catch all of it, but I could make out the words "settle" and "average."

Mom obviously heard the whole thing, though. And whatever she'd heard, it was enough.

I ducked out of view right as she turned the corner out of the kitchen, catching a glimpse of the red splotches on her face. Her cheeks always seemed to catch fire when she was mad.

"Where are you going?" Dad called after her.

"For a walk," she snapped. "To think about the things I've had to settle for."

"Nicole, I didn't mean—"

But anything else Dad might have said got cut short by the door slamming. I heard him coming down the hallway, so I scrambled back up the stairs and into my bedroom, shutting my own door softly, listening for the click, then ducking into the Cove, where the waves didn't crash as big. Where I could think about what I'd just heard. About Frank Sanderson. The former high school friend and big deal. Ranked nine hundred and something on the PGA.

The man who would be my coach.

That evening brought a knock on my bedroom door.

The knocker waited for me to open it, just like Mom always did, but it definitely wasn't Mom. It was a man in baggy gray track pants, a black Nike polo, and camouflage flip-flops. He had a dark blond goatee, pink cheeks, and foggy blue eyes set deep. He filled the doorway.

"What's up?" he said, the way an uncle who comes over every Sunday for dinner would.

"Um . . . nothing?" I said, the way a kid with a complete stranger standing in their doorway would.

Dad's face appeared over the bigger man's shoulder. "Hey, Malcolm. This is Frank Sanderson. He's an old friend of mine. *And* a professional golfer."

"Former professional golfer," Frank corrected. The man's voice was gravelly and breathless. Sort of like Granny Allison if Granny Allison had been a baritone. Except Granny Allison had been shaped like a ferret, long and slinky. This man was shaped more like a bulldozer. He was intimidating. Even with flip-flops on.

"Fine," Dad said. "He *used* to golf professionally. Now he . . . what, you sell phones, right, Frank?"

"Not the actual phones," Frank said. "Just the accessories."

Who is this guy? Aleck smirked.

My father clearly knew almost nothing about him either. When I overheard the conversation from this morning, I was pretty sure this was a bad idea. Now I was positive.

"Frank is here because he knows a thing or two about sinking putts." Dad looked at Frank for confirmation; the man smiled thinly. "And since I signed us up for that thing next month, I thought, what the hey, couldn't hurt to get a little expert advice."

A moment of awkward silence. Dad looked at me. I looked at the floor. Frank scratched at his goatee. Jaws darted back and forth in his bowl, bumping into the glass as if looking to bust free.

"How about you just give us a couple a minutes to talk?" Frank said finally. "You know, golfer to golfer."

My eyes darted to my father, hoping to get his attention and blink out an emergency message, something along the lines of *Don't you dare leave me alone with this strange man,* but Dad smiled and nodded. "Sure. Sounds good. I'll be right downstairs if you need me."

I already needed him, but he left anyways. He kept the door

open at least. I shoved my hands in my pockets, finding my grandfather's nickel in one and a rubber band in the other. I took out the rubber band and started twisting it around my finger. Frank waited for my father to hit the stairs. Then he pointed to my desk chair.

"Mind if I sit?"

I shook my head. So far I'd only said two words. And that's if you counted "um."

Frank settled awkwardly into the black swivel chair that had come with the desk. It was a good size for me, but I was small for my age. I sat on the edge of the bed directly across from him. Now that I could get an even better look at his feet, I noticed his toes were unusually hairy. Like a hobbit's.

Frank noticed me looking at his feet and clicked his flip-flops together. "You like 'em? I got 'em at the dollar store. Bet you can't guess how much they cost."

Bah-dum, tshh. Aleck's rimshot rang out in my head.

I gave a polite snort. Sort of a cross between a cough and a laugh. Except more cough.

"Your dad and I were on the baseball team together for one year back in high school," Frank continued. "Did you know that?"

I shook my head.

"You like baseball?"

His eyes settled on me, searching. Was this a trick question? Had Dad told him about me quitting? How much did Frank

Sanderson know about me already? "It's okay," I said. And it was. Just so long as I wasn't forced to play it. Or watch it. Or talk about it.

"Yeah, that's kinda how I felt about it, too. Turned out I was better at swinging a golf club than a baseball bat. That I was actually *good* at. But you know what being good gets you?"

I shook my head.

Frank spread his hands as if to say, *You're looking at it.*

I took it all in. The camo flip-flops. The furry toes. The hair, thinning, just like Dad's. The chubby squirrel cheeks. Frank Sanderson smelled like a curious mixture of spicy cologne and nacho cheese. It reminded me a little of school.

"Lots of people are just *good*," Frank continued. "You have to be *better* than good if you really want to be successful. You know what I mean?"

I wasn't sure. It seemed to me like being good at something should be enough. I was good at school. As and Bs. I could ride my bike with no hands, even through the turns. I could solve a Rubik's cube in under thirty seconds, which a very small number of kids at school thought was impressive. There were competitions for that too—solving cubes—but thankfully Dad didn't know about them.

"I guess," I said. Up to six words now.

"Your dad tells me you really like golf. At least the putting part."

Miniature golf wasn't real golf. I knew that. Frank Sanderson

103

played real golf. At least he used to, but he didn't look like any of the golfers I'd seen on TV. They were all skinny and wore nice slacks and white shoes. Most of them had bronzy tans. Frank had coffee stains on his teeth, but he was pale as a vampire. I wondered about his vitamin D intake. "Yeah. It's pretty fun," I said, breaking the two-word response barrier.

"Pretty fun," Frank repeated, eyes suddenly big with shock. "It's way better than fun, kid. Golf is . . . man . . . it's freakin' poetry in motion." He leaned forward in the chair. "There's nothing like standing out there in the early morning for tee-off, sun coming up over the green, little drops of dew on the grass tips, the feel of the club in your hands. The whistle of wind as the ball soars like a comet over the treetops. It's beautiful."

Frank's eyes seemed to glaze over for a moment. They were aimed at the Avengers poster behind me, but I got the impression he was somewhere else. He shook his head and focused back on me. "You know in my prime, I had one of the sweetest short games around. I could sink a twenty-foot putt on a downhill break in the middle of a tornado." He made a swooping motion with one hand—the ball sweeping into the hole maybe. Or maybe his hand was the tornado.

You are so full of it, Aleck said.

"Impossible," I translated. Frank stared at me. I cleared my throat, tried not to look right at him. "It's just that tornados have wind gusts up to three hundred miles per hour. That's enough to lift a semi truck off the ground." I'd read a few books about natural disasters last year as part of the class reading challenge.

Frank smiled. "You're pretty smart, kid. Fine. No tornado. But I was kind of a stud back in my prime. I even got a chance to play against Ernie Els."

I didn't know who that was. It sounded like a Sesame Street character. Tiger Woods was the only real golfer I could name. "Did you beat him?" I asked.

Frank glared at me. "Are you kidding me? It was Ernie freakin' Els."

I took that as a no.

"Doesn't matter," Frank continued. "All I'm saying is, at one time I was good enough to play with the best, and it sharpened my game. And that's what I can do for you. Because right now, you're like . . . you're like . . ." He looked around the room, presumably to see what I might be like. His eyes passed over comic books and a laundry hamper and a darting fish. "You're like a butter knife," he decided, though there were no butter knives lying around. "There's potential there, but not much of an edge, see. But by the time I'm done with you, you'll be a freakin' samurai sword."

I wasn't sure we were still talking about Putt-Putt.

"Katana," I said.

"What?"

"The swords that samurai used. They're called katanas. Or

wakizashi—those were the short ones, but you're probably thinking of the long ones." I'd read a couple of books about feudal Japan, too.

"Katana. Wakasushi. Whatever. Still better than a butter knife, right?"

Unless you're trying to make a sandwich, Aleck quipped.

I just nodded.

"Your dad says you're pretty good. How long you been playing?"

I held up two fingers.

"Two years?"

"Two times," I corrected. "And once when I was three, but that time I just dropped the ball in with my hands."

Frank frowned. Wrong answer, I guess. "Know what?" he said. "That's okay. Just means you haven't developed any bad habits that I gotta deal with. Now we can just develop the right ones."

"The right ones?"

"You bet your sweet butt cheeks. I'm going to teach you how to stand properly. And swing properly. I'm going to teach you how to adjust for the weather and the conditions of the course. I'm going to teach you how to gauge slope and pitch and speed. I'm going to teach you the difference between a heel shaft and a center shaft. I'm going to show you how to work the dance floor with your chicken stick and give you the confidence you need so you never get the yips, you know what I'm saying?"

I had no idea what he was saying. He'd lost me at sweet butt cheeks.

"I'm saying that I am going to turn you into a putt-making machine, kid." Frank Sanderson leaned over, extending his thick arm with its big knob of a fist in my direction, like he was trying to punch me in slow motion. "So what do you say? Ready to learn from the master?"

The fist hung there, right in front of me. I didn't get a whole lot of fist bumps at school. The occasional shoulder bump, but those were mostly accidental. Mostly.

What was I supposed to say? I thought about Dad, probably standing at the bottom of the stairs, eavesdropping on me the same way I eavesdropped on him. I wasn't sure I wanted to learn how to dance with my chicken stick. Not with anyone. And definitely not with the man sitting across from me.

Then again, this might be a way to make up for quitting baseball.

"C'mon, kid, don't leave me hanging."

Frank's fist hovered between us, his eyebrows pinched together. In that moment, I got the impression that Frank Sanderson wanted this just as much as Dad did, and if I said no, I'd be letting both of them down.

Butter knife or katana?

I thought about the trophies in the top of Dad's closet. Thought about the email printout folded up on my desk— prizes to the top three finishers. I thought about the buzz I got every time my little orange ball dropped into the cup. Having a coach would at least give me an excuse to play more often. And no one would be counting on me to get on base or make the inning-ending catch. I'd be the only one on my team.

Besides, it would obviously make Dad happy. Give us something to talk about. And maybe him being happier would make Mom happier. We could all be happier.

It was worth a shot.

I reached out and tentatively touched my knuckles to Frank's. He made an exploding sound, complete with a spray of spit. Then he pulled himself out of my chair with a grunt and pushed it back under the desk. "It's settled then. I'll talk to your dad about setting up the first lesson. Probably this Saturday. Also gotta talk to the owner of the course and work out a deal so we can get some cheap playing time. Till then, just think about how awesome you're going to be."

Awesome? Me? Seemed unlikely. But maybe that was worth a shot too.

Frank smiled and started to leave, but there was one question I was curious about. "How much?"

Frank stopped in the doorway and turned his head. "How much what?"

"How much is my dad paying you?"

The question seemed to take him by surprise, but he quickly recovered. "It's not about the money, kid," Frank said. "It's about helping you reach your full potential."

I glanced at his shoes. In my head, Aleck started to gag.

Frank Sanderson sighed. "Fine. Twenty bucks an hour."

Twenty dollars? Dad only gave me five bucks for mowing the lawn. Front and back.

"Can't put a price on greatness, kid," Frank said. Then he shut the door, leaving me and Jaws with our mouths hanging open.

Hole six is a straight shot, a welcome change from the tricky ones that came before it. No banking. No angles. No obstacles. Just one giant hill at the end of the green, like the hump of a whale surfacing in the ocean, blowhole at its center. I know what Frank would say: *Looks can be deceiving, kid. Some things seem easy until you really dig into them. Other things seem impossible, but it's all smoke and mirrors. Once you clear your head, you see the path laid out in front of you. Then you just follow through.*

That's what he'd say if he were here, but he's not. I can't blame him . . . at least he has a good excuse.

Some paths are easier to see than others. I hit the ball just right, dead center, straight up the hill to the hole. *Cu-clunk.*

Poetry in motion.

I glance over at the leaderboard, which is really just a big dry-erase board on a stand, our names and current standings written in marker, the scores wiped clean and rewritten after every hole so that you have to glance down the numbers to see who is where. Jamie Tran is still in the lead, followed by Baez and someone named Miller. I'm two strokes down now after this birdie. Not terrible. If Jamie Tran ever missed a shot, the rest of us might have one.

But he never does. Miss, that is. It's sort of mesmerizing to watch. That kid knows how to dance with his chicken stick.

I look over at the crowd again and see Mom chatting with another set of parents. She notices me looking her way and cups her hands to her eyes, making binoculars. I lean my putter against my leg and circle my fingers around my eyes too.

A sharp voice comes from behind, and I turn to spy Jamie's coach standing beside him, arms gesticulating. I wonder what Jamie did wrong—nothing that I've seen, anyways, but I'm no expert.

Must be rough to have your dad as your coach. Not something I have to worry about.

Today I don't have either.

HOLE #7

<u>Par 2</u>

Like Scylla and Charybdis from Greek mythology, hole seven offers two paths, both risky. Going right will see your ball traversing a long, high-banked curve that is difficult to properly gauge, but the left is guarded by a large stone obstacle that offers only a narrow isthmus of green to travel along. The choice is yours, but whichever one you pick, you will probably regret it.

I learned a lot during my first lesson with Frank Sanderson, but not about putting. Mostly about Frank.

Like that he sticks his finger in his ear a lot, as if his skull is a leaking ship and he's trying to plug the hole. And then sometimes, when he thinks you're not looking, he examines the tip of the pinkie that went digging, sniffing it before wiping it on his pants. I kind of want to ask him if he found anything, but I don't.

I learned that someone once ran him over with a golf cart. Broke three ribs and sent him to the hospital. Frank said he couldn't tell me the rest of the story "because it's rated R for bad language and adult situations."

On what he called "a related note," I learned that Frank Sanderson was married for 167 days once. According to Frank, four of those days were the best of his life. "The advantages," he says, "of honeymooning in the Bahamas."

I also learned that he had an ingrown hair in his left armpit. He suspected it was infected because there was a little bit of oozing. He told me I really didn't want to see it, but I already knew that.

Mostly, though, I learned that Frank Sanderson likes to talk. About himself and his problems mostly, the biggest of which is that he's a forty-year-old bachelor who drives a fifteen-year-old Chevy and still eats bologna sandwiches for dinner. With mustard packets stolen from McDonald's.

I told him that if McDonald's didn't want you to take those little packets, they shouldn't just leave them sitting out like that.

He smiled at that and said we were going to get along just fine.

I wasn't so sure.

The first stop, I learned on the day of our first lesson, was and would always be the snack bar.

Frank was waiting for us right outside of Fritz's, dressed this time in black shorts and a cream-colored shirt that might have been white once. An old pair of Nikes covered his hobbit toes. Dad pulled up to the curb and unlocked the door. "See you in an hour or so." He waved to Frank, who waved back. Then I watched as our car drove off, leaving me alone with this man I'd only met once before.

I stood with my hands in my pockets, fiddling with a paper

clip and my lucky nickel. As nervous as I was about my first lesson with Frank, I was thinking it still might be better than being in the house with Mom and Dad. It had been a rough Saturday morning: Dad had run the dishwasher the night before but had forgotten to add the rinse aid.

"Nobody wants to drink out of these," Mom told him, holding up a spotted glass. "Now I have to wash them all over again by hand."

"I don't think a couple of spots are going to hurt anyone."

"No. But it would be nice not to have to come around and redo *everything* all the time."

I sat on the family room sofa, finishing my toaster waffle in front of the TV, wondering what it was they were really arguing about; it couldn't just be spots on the dishes. It was never just one thing. I was thinking that if some conversations are like Mad Libs with lots of empty blanks, others are more like a giant web with a big black spider waiting at the center: it doesn't matter what part of the web you touch—it could be the strand at the very edge, the tiniest little thing—the spider will still sense it and come after you. Mom and Dad took turns playing the spider.

"Seriously, how hard is it to remember the rinse aid? It's sitting right there on the counter."

"Fine. Leave them. I'll wash them again when I get back."

"Forget it. I'm already doing it."

I heard the faucet. Then Dad called from the kitchen and told me to finish getting ready.

Thirty minutes later I was standing at the concession counter next to Frank, wondering if other parents argued about spots on dishes. Or laundry that sat in the washer overnight. Or lids not being screwed back on all the way. Did they fight about it or did they just quietly go around fixing each other's mistakes?

Because that's what I would do. If I ever got married. Which wasn't likely.

"You want something to eat?" I looked at Frank and shook my head. He tapped on the counter to get the attention of the teenager behind it. "I know you technically aren't open yet, but any chance I could get a red slushy? And maybe some Fritos?" He turned back to me. "What color slushy you want?"

"It's ten thirty in the morning," I said.

"I'm not asking if you want a Bloody Mary, kid. It's a freakin' slushy. You pick or I pick."

My mouth *was* dry, but a cup of water would have been fine. Then again, Dad was paying him twenty dollars an hour. I went with blue.

Frank paid, grabbed both drinks, then led the way out to the courses.

The place was empty, which was by design. Frank had worked out a deal with the owner, whose name was not Fritz but Connor, and who happened to be a friend of a friend. According to the deal, we could show up a half an hour before the place opened on Saturdays and putt all we wanted, slushies not included.

Frank nodded toward the rack of putters up against the wall by the door. "Grab one that feels comfortable to you," he said. "We'll talk about getting a better one later."

I picked out a club with a blue head to match my slushy, then caught up to Frank at one of the tables on the cement clearing that separated the two courses. The tables were all the round metal kind with lots of small holes so the rain wouldn't puddle up on top. Pretty much everything at Fritz's was low maintenance, save for the windmill that just limped along getting no maintenance anyway. Frank set my cup in the middle of the table. "Go ahead. Have a drink before we get started."

I leaned my putter against the bench and reached for the slushy. Frank slapped my hand away.

"Ouch!" I said. It hadn't hurt—it was barely even a tap—but I certainly wasn't expecting it.

"Not like that," Frank said. "You want a drink, you're going to have to earn it."

I shook my unhurt hand for effect and looked over at my cup sitting in the center of the table. This was a test. And that was the reward. I probably wouldn't get to drink it until I sank a hole in one or something, and by then it could just be Kool-Aid.

It could be worse, I thought to myself. *It's Saturday. You could be standing out in far left field.*

Frank took a sip of his own slushy, then pointed to the club I'd picked. "What is this?" he asked.

I stared at the club. "Did I get the wrong one?" I'd grabbed

116

the first putter that looked about the right size.

Obviously, Frank knew more about it than I did. He shook his head and pointed again. "What . . . is . . . this?" he pressed.

"A putter?" I said, suddenly not 100 percent sure. Maybe it had a different name? Maybe this was the chicken stick.

"What is this?" Frank asked, grabbing my right arm and holding it up by my wrist.

"My arm?" In my head, Aleck desperately wanted me to add a "duh," but Aleck was imaginary and could get away with it. I was the one sitting here with a grown man slapping my hand away and asking me questions that shouldn't have been this hard to answer.

"Wrong," Frank said, shaking his head slowly. He pointed to the arm. Then to the club. "This and this . . . same thing." His finger—not the one he kept putting in his ear—jumped from one to the other. My eyes darted back and forth, following it. Arm. Club. Arm. Club.

This fella's nuttier than a port-a-potty at a peanut festival.

Granny Allison might be onto something. "I don't get it," I said.

Frank grabbed my putter and put it into my hands. "Your putter is a natural extension of your body. Like an infantryman and his rifle. Like an artist and his brush. Like a carpenter and his hammer. Same thing."

That's when he reached into his shorts pocket and pulled out a roll of duct tape.

I glanced around anxiously: one high school kid in a Fritz's

Family Fun Zone shirt inspecting the course, picking up trash. Other than that, there were no witnesses. I looked back at the roll of tape. "What's that for?" I squeaked out.

"Just hold on to the club with both hands, left hand on top. Hold it comfortably. And don't worry."

Someone saying don't worry has never stopped me before, but worrying is different than refusing. I curled my fingers tight, keeping one eye on the tape and the other eye on Frank's face, now pinched with frustration as he tried to find the loose end of the roll, freeing it with a fingernail. Then, before I knew it, he was wrapping the tape around my left wrist. "Hold still," Frank commanded as he circled the tape around and around, wrapping my left hand, then my right, working quickly, using up what seemed like half the roll, making a duct-taped *V* that started at my wrists and came to a bulbous point just below where my right hand gripped the club, completely encircling both hands in a cocoon of gray tape. He tore the end off with his teeth and smiled. "Perfect," he said.

I looked to see if the one teenager was even watching this, but he had apparently taken his trash out to the dumpster. I was alone with this man. I started to sweat. Frank smiled, eyeing the club now taped to me. "See. Same thing."

He was right. Instead of a club and an arm I had a clarm. I was a mutant. "Okay. But isn't it going to hurt when you take the tape off?" He *was* planning on taking the tape off, wasn't he? Surely I wasn't going to have to spend the whole hour like this.

118

"At least they're not as hairy as mine." He pointed at the slushy posted up in the center of the picnic table. "And now you can have your drink."

I just looked at Frank. So *this* was the challenge? To get a drink while permanently attached to the putter? I thought about telling him I wasn't thirsty, but that wasn't true. If anything, I wanted a drink even more. Plus there was a part of me that wanted to show him I could do it, that I could pass his test. It couldn't be that hard. There was a straw in the cup; I only needed to get up on the table and bend down and take a sip. I'd look silly, but there was nobody around to see.

As soon as I got one foot on the bench, though, Frank knocked it off with his hand. "Nope. Both feet on the ground at all times. Those are the rules."

"Whose rules?"

"My rules. Your rules. Same rules. The cup comes to you. Now use your one good arm and get a drink."

I looked down at the putter affixed to me. I looked back up at the cup on the table. I guess it was just like having a really long hook for a hand. If pirates could steer ships and buckle swashes with hooks for hands, I could probably manage to snag my slushy. I reached across the table with my one long arm, surprised at how heavy the putter was when you held it straight out. I hooked the head of the club around the bottom of the plastic cup. The holes in the iron tabletop made its surface bumpy and uneven, but still, all I had to do was slide it gently to the edge and—

Thunk. Splosh.

The cup tipped, the plastic lid popped off, and nearly half of my blue slushy spilled across the table and through the holes onto the concrete. I fumbled around, trying to turn the cup upright so that it would stop hemorrhaging slush, but my hands were now thirty-four inches long and equipped with one giant metal finger that I couldn't even bend, so I only managed to scoot the cup farther around the table, losing even more of its contents.

"Here. Let me help you with that," Frank said, righting the cup and sticking it back in the center of the table again. He didn't bother to put the lid back on, though at least the straw was still there.

I frowned at the cup, so far away, it seemed. A bright blue splotch had formed on the cement underneath the table.

Frank shook his head. "Precision. Control. When you're out there on the green, every tiny movement matters. You twist your wrists just a little, you lose your angle. You forget to square your shoulders, you miss the shot. This putter is a part of you."

"It is *now*," I mumbled, not quite loud enough for him to hear. Or if he did, he ignored it.

"Try again."

I planted my feet and took a deep breath. As I carefully snaked the head of the club around the cup, Frank took an extra-long, purposefully loud slurp of his own red slushy.

Shlllluuurrruuurrrppp. It made me shiver. "Careful now," he said. "Learn from your mistakes."

I gritted my teeth. What would Dad say if he saw what I was doing right now? This couldn't be what he had in mind when he hired Frank to be my coach. I eased the cup toward me again, watching it quiver, bumping over the small ridges in the table. I made it past the first wet smear of slush, being extra careful, keeping the head of the club low on the cup. Slowly. Slowly. Only about a foot from the edge.

Thunk. Splosh.

"You're not very good at this," Frank said.

I spun around to face him, forgetting, momentarily, that my hands were taped to my putter. It came around with me, swinging right toward Frank's head. He ducked out of the way, the end of the putter passing right by his nose.

"Watch where you're aiming that thing!"

"Sorry. I didn't mean to." I felt like Edward Scissorhands. Malcolm Putterhands. This was ridiculous. "How am I supposed to get the cup without knocking it over?"

"Carefully," Frank answered. "If golf is a game of inches, then miniature golf is a game of millimeters." He reset the cup. "Again."

I closed my eyes, took a breath, and turned back to the table, reaching with my metal appendage. Scoot. *Thunk. Splosh.* I groaned and let my clarm drop.

"Frustrated?" Frank asked.

I glared at the leaking cup lying on the table. I could feel Frank's eyes on me, but I was afraid to look at him, afraid I might say something I'd regret. Aleck already had a whole list of possibilities going in my head.

"Now imagine how frustrating it's going to be during a match after you've bogeyed three holes in a row. You can't give up just because things aren't going your way. You have more control than you think you do."

"The slushy's almost gone anyway," I said.

"This ain't about the slushy, kid."

"Easy for you to say. You already drank yours."

I stole a quick glance at Frank. I never snipped at grown-ups like that. Ever. Always better to keep your mouth shut. Be quiet. Be good. Stay out of the way. Don't do anything to rock the boat. That was the plan. That was always the plan. But this was too much.

Frank just smiled. "Good one, kid. Get it out. Stay loose. You let that frustration build and it'll get inside your head, throw you off your game."

Frank Sanderson had no idea what all was inside my head, but he was very much throwing me off my game. If I had any game to start with.

"Let's try something else," he said, grabbing the bag of Fritos. "Hold out your club." I held the club up straight while Frank balanced the snack-sized bag of chips on the end. "Now just keep it balanced on the head of the club. Don't let the bag drop."

The bag was light, but the club was heavy. "For how long?"

"No drooping," Frank replied, ignoring my question. "Whatever it takes to keep it steady." Frank sat back down on the bench and took out his phone. "Steady as she goes."

I wondered if I would at least get the Fritos if I did this right. Though I had hardly anything left to wash them down with. I held the club aloft. After a minute my arms started to burn. Then they started to shake. The bag of chips dipped a little. Then a little more. Drops of sweat dangled from my brow, threatening to slide into my eyes. I sensed the Fritos were about to tip and twisted my hands a little to keep them on, but it was too late. The bag dropped to the cement.

Frank hit a button on his phone. "Two minutes, fourteen seconds."

That was it? It felt like so much longer. Maybe they were football minutes. "That's still good, right?"

Frank shrugged. "Meh. An *hour's* good. Two minutes . . ."

An hour? What was he talking about? "No way," I muttered.

Frank didn't say a word. He put away his phone and went to the rack and got a club of his own. With one smooth motion he shoveled under the bag of Fritos with the head of his putter and tossed it into the air. Then, just as swiftly, he caught the bag, right on the edge, keeping it perfectly balanced. It was a smooth maneuver; I couldn't help but be a little impressed.

Frank held his chip-saddled putter with only one hand for a moment, then he stepped over and gently laid the club on the table, careful not to let the bag slip off. "Voilà," he said.

I looked at Frank. At the bag of chips still sitting on the head of his club now lying across the table. Back at him. I could feel my cheeks heating. "But you said I had to keep the bag balanced on the end of the putter. You didn't say I could prop the club up on the table." Not that I could have let go of my putter like he did, not with my hands taped to it, but at least it would have taken the weight off.

Frank shrugged. "I said not to let them drop. You just assumed you had to hold them up in the air."

"Because that's what I thought you were supposed to do."

"And do you always do what you're supposed to do?" he asked.

Yes, I thought. *At least I try.*

Frank motioned to the courses beside us, still empty save for the brontosaurus staring dumbly back at us. "You come across a hole in a big rock, right smack-dab in the middle of the green. The rock's got a tunnel, leads straight to the cup." He made a motion with his hands, like shooting an arrow. "But the tunnel's narrow. And you'd have to hit it just right if you wanted to make it through without banging against the inside walls."

He was talking about hole two on the Red Course, the one that I'd birdied on my first time here with Dad. The one that was supposedly "beginner's luck."

"Most people try to hit it straight up the middle because

that's what you're *supposed* to do. But that doesn't mean there's not an alternative. You have to look past the obvious. Study the angles. Consider the possibilities. You have to *see* it." Frank squinted at me, as if I'd suddenly blurred around the edges. "Do you see?"

Did I see?

Angles. Possibilities. Alternatives.

Slushies. Tunnels. Straight shot.

"I have to pee," I said.

Frank and I both looked down at my hands, completely encased in duct tape.

"I'll go find some scissors," he said.

When I came out of the bathroom, Frank was sitting at the table with a half-empty bag of Fritos and a full blue slushy. He handed the cup to me. "I told the guy that you accidentally spilled it; he gave me a free refill."

Frank seemed like the kind of guy who tried to talk his way into, and out of, a lot of things. "Thanks," I said.

"You earned it," he said.

As I slurped away, Frank sat across from me and told me about the rest of the deal he'd worked out: how we could play as many holes as we wanted before noon, provided we didn't get in anybody's way and always let the other paying customers play through.

I looked around. The clock hanging beside the door said it

was already after eleven. Fritz's was officially open, and customers were starting to file in. A family with two kids started the Blue Course, the kids screaming, trying to snatch each other's clubs.

"Benefits of being an only child, I guess," Frank remarked. "Though growing up I always wished I had a younger brother or sister to pick on. You?"

"Me what?"

"You ever wish you had a sibling? Someone to pester? To boss around?"

I picked at the duct tape residue still stuck to my fingers. "Not really," I said. Although if there had been someone else to play with all the time, there might not have been a need for Rocky the transforming robot rocket ship. Would have meant more work for Mom and Dad, though. There were probably days they felt like one kid was too many. They never said it, of course. Just the impression I got.

Frank scratched at his armpit, then squinted up at the sun. "Sorry if I went a little Yoda on you back there. This is my first time coaching miniature golf, believe it or not, so I'm kind of making it up as I go."

I ignored all the things Aleck was screaming in my head.

"It's okay. Yoda's cool," I said instead.

"Cool he is." Frank handed me my putter, also still a little sticky from the tape. "So how about it? You ready to actually go play some golf?" As he stood, he pulled on the drawstrings of his shorts to tighten them. That's when I noticed Frank Sanderson was actually wearing bathing trunks, not shorts. He noticed my noticing. "Built-in support," he said. "Eliminates the need for underwear and cuts down on your laundry."

This guy is a half dozen apples short of a bushel.

Or maybe not.

Study the angles. Consider the possibilities. Skip the underwear. I added this to the list of things I'd learned from Frank already.

And I still had yet to hit a ball.

Number seven is brutal; the curve to the right warps your speed and trajectory, but the stone hazard on the left is too close to the wall. Your best chance for a birdie is to hit that curve just so. You could stay left, but that would require shooting the gap and getting a perfect rebound off the back wall. The force required means you also run the risk of just slamming off the rock and sending your ball caroming right back to you.

Which is exactly what Grace Xin does. Maybe she misjudges her shot. Or perhaps her wrists turn just a little—it's a game of millimeters, after all. Or maybe she gets the yips. Whatever it is, her ball thunks right off the stone hazard and rolls all the way back, past the tee, off the green, forcing her to take a penalty stroke. She ends up with a four on the hole, dropping her all the way down to twelfth.

I pass her after I finish the same hole in two strokes, which is enough to move me up a little. "It's all right," I tell her. "Still plenty of holes left."

Grace gives me a sort-of smile that quickly turns back into a frown and then sulks off. That's when I notice that she's wearing black dress shoes that perfectly match her gray and black plaid jumper. The shoes are shiny with bright silver buckles that gather the sunshine and wink it right back.

They make me think of Lex.

There are a few things around here that remind me of her. The shiny shoes. The Pepsi machine. The little girl—somebody's younger sister, no doubt—twirling like a ballerina in the grass.

And of course the button attached to my waistband, pierced through one of my belt loops. My shirt is long enough to cover it, so nobody else can see it, but I know it's there, and it makes me feel better, just having it close. But like everything else I brought with me—the hand-me-down putter, the orange golf balls, the lucky nickel—it reminds me of what I'm missing.

And what I have to lose.

HOLE #8

Par 3

The first of the par threes on the course and also the first with a water hazard, though this one is easy to avoid by hugging the left wall. Golfers should be cautious of the three stone frogs forming a triangle to guard the cup. Rumor has it the statues were taken from the owner's flower garden without his wife's permission. Regulars who play the course insist that if your ball bounces off one of the amphibian sentries, it is due to the curse of the wife getting revenge for her stolen statuary. Probably, though, you just missed your shot.

There is a difference between being alone and being lonely. You can be the first without ever feeling the second.

Growing up I always had someone to talk to, even when I was by myself: a salty grandmother, a unicorn-fighting robot, a pair of bantering sports announcers, a sarcastic know-it-all. Mrs. Rumford was right: I had a head full.

Real-life friends were harder to come by.

I had them, but usually they were assigned to me. Cubby buddies and line partners and group project participants. Play dates set up by my mother at the bouncy gym. Siblings of students she gave piano lessons to who I was asked to keep entertained for thirty minutes at a time.

Kids at the playground would sometimes ask if I wanted to play freeze tag with them. Mom or Dad usually said yes for me and pushed me along. *He's a little shy,* they'd say, making excuses for my reluctance. I usually didn't get tagged anyway. Not because I was fast, but because nobody wants to chase after the kid they don't know.

I have friends at school, at least. The kids I sit with at lunch sometimes. Samantha Diggs, whose family collects stray animals as if they were stamps or rare coins: only two dogs, but seven cats. Seth Riker, who always puts his French fries inside his hamburger before he eats it. And Raul Wiśniewski, who has a dad from Poland and a mom from Cuba, so he knows curse words in a few different languages. I don't really talk to them much outside the cafeteria, and even when we're at lunch, I usually try to keep my mouth full of food. It gives me an excuse to just sit and listen. I make it a point to pack my own lunch. Granola bars. Peanut butter crackers. Swedish fish. Stuff that takes some jaw work.

There are other kids in my class who I talk to sometimes, about assignments or test scores or Marvel movies—but I never see them outside of school. None of them have ever been to my house. When I go to birthday parties, it's usually because everyone in the class got an invitation. Even then I sit on the sidelines, quietly watching other kids take turns being the center of attention.

Mom and Dad would talk about it sometimes, when they didn't know I was on the stairs, listening. Dad was a firm believer in having lots of friends. He'd had a ton in high school and then again in college. Even now he had a group of guys he played poker with every couple of weeks; Mom called them his cronies. She was a little different. She kept her circle small, just a few close friends. But that was a problem, too, because I didn't have any of those either.

I had them instead: Mom and Dad. And that was enough; I didn't feel like I was missing anything. But sometimes it takes having something before you realize you needed it in the first place.

My second ever lesson with Frank Sanderson started with a discussion of equipment. And how to handle it. Beginning with balls.

"Now, balls come in different sizes," Frank explained. "They can differ in bounce and hardness and texture, so it's important to use the right balls in the right situation. They can also get knocked around a lot, so you want to keep them safe and in good condition. And you want to make sure they're warm, too. Temperature can do funny things to balls, so on cold days, you can just rub them, like this. Or just keep them cupped in your hands, like so."

Frank held a golf ball in one hand, fingers wrapped tight around it. He looked deadly serious, even in cutoff sweatpants and a Game of Thrones T-shirt. His expression was straight as a pencil. I, on the other hand, had to bite down hard on the inside of my cheek to keep from laughing.

"Of course, some professionals will carry around a special bag for their balls, you know, to protect them, but those aren't really necess— What's the problem? You're turning red."

"Sorry," I said, still stiffling giggles.

It took Frank a second—then he started nodding. "Okay. You're twelve. I get it. But we're professionals, and this is an important conversation."

"I know. Sorry." I sat up straight, put on a serious face.

"Thank you," Frank huffed. "Now let's talk about putters. When it comes to shaft length—"

That was as far as he got. My lips were pressed tight, trying to hold it in, but they started to quiver. Frank shook his head and smiled, giving me permission to laugh.

So I did. Just a little. And he did too.

"Okay. Maybe we stop talking about equipment and get down to business." Frank went and picked a putter of moderate shaft length from the rack and pointed toward the Red Course. "Today we're going to focus on the back nine because they're harder. Fourteen's especially tricky." Fourteen was the one with the water hazard, a puddle that took up half of the green. I wondered what Frank would say about getting your balls wet. I wasn't about to ask.

He led me to hole ten—a challenge because of the three metal bars blocking half the green and the upward slope at the end. There was no straight line to the hole. I set my orange ball on the tee. Frank bent over and picked it right back up.

"Lie down," he said.

"Like, on the ground?"

Frank pointed to the artificial turf on hole number ten. "On your belly. Chin up. Toes on the tee."

It wasn't eleven yet according to the clock; the doors hadn't opened to the public, but there was still one Fritz's employee outside. I was pretty sure she was watching us out of the corner of her eye. "You want me to just lie down. Right here."

One look at Frank's face told me he was back in Yoda mode. I thought about my blue slushy dripping to the cement as I dropped to my knees, stretching out, fitting myself between the long metal rails. The artificial grass felt rough on my elbows. It was already warm from the sun.

"Look straight ahead," Frank said. "Tell me what you see."

I rested my chin on the back of my hand and looked. I was a lot closer to the obstacles now. Right ahead of me was the first of the three metal hazards, a foot-long block that reminded me a little of an old train car, painted a rusty red. Just past that I could make out parts of the other two blocks, and then the hill that followed, sloping up six inches or so, enough that I couldn't see the hole at the top, not from where I was lying. I was close enough that I could see the individual plots of artificial grass, though, all hooked and meshed together. Close enough that I could follow an ant crawling up the metal sidewall. "I see green," I said. "And a big hunk of metal in my way." I could make out the hundreds of tiny dings and dents where golfers hadn't quite managed to go around the first obstacle safely.

"Good. What else?"

"I don't know. An ant. Some chips in the paint. The hill

looks a lot bigger from down here. I can't even see the hole."

"Good. Hop up." I stood back on the tee, wondering when I was going to get my ball back. "Now what do you see?"

"Same stuff," I said. Obstacles. Walls. The hill. Fake grass.

Frank shook his head. "Try again."

I looked again. And this time I realized I could see *everything*. The start. The finish. The spot in the back right corner where I banked my shot the last time I played this hole. The distances between the obstacles. All the different routes you could take to get around them.

"I see which way to go," I ventured.

"Beautiful, isn't it? Down there you were looking at the trees," Frank said, "but up here you see the whole freakin' forest, you know what I mean?"

I nodded. This time I actually *did* know. At least I thought I did. Down there, chin to the ground, pressed up close, everything was bigger, blurrier, out of proportion. Up here it was clear. Like those Magic Eye posters. You can't just stare at one part. You have to step back and take the whole thing in for the secret image to appear.

"That's one good thing about miniature golf," Frank continued. "There are no surprises. You know exactly how many feet it is from one obstacle to the next. You know exactly how big the rock is that's standing in your way. You can see where the turf is worn, where it dips and rises. You are omniscient."

"Still doesn't mean you won't screw up," I said.

"True. But at least you'll know what you did wrong and you can get it right the next time. Not like life, where sometimes things go south and you have no idea why."

Frank and I stood next to each other for a moment, just staring down at hole ten, me wondering if that was true, if there were screwups that just happened and you didn't know why, or if there was always some way you could go back and find out what you'd done wrong, even if it was too late to fix it. I wondered if there were things in Frank's life like that, where he was still trying to figure where he made the wrong turn. Ending up here. At Fritz's. With me.

Frank crossed his arms. "This is probably a little like how God feels," he said wistfully.

I doubted God wore sweatpants. But maybe.

I picked my club off the ground and asked if it was okay to start putting.

If you have all of the information, if there are no surprises, then it's simply a matter of execution. And by execution, Frank meant practice. And by practice he meant endless repetition.

Which is why I spent the next half hour doing the same holes over and over. I would line up my shot and then Frank would come behind me, making adjustments, telling me to bend over or straighten out, turning my shoulders, rotating my club. When I missed, he'd help me to see what I could have done better, and when I made a good putt, he'd pretend to shoot the ball into the hole with his finger and then blow the imaginary smoke from the imaginary barrel of his imaginary gun.

Even if I got it in, though, I still had to do it over again. And again. And again.

"Muscle memory, kid. By the time we're done, I'll be able to blindfold you and tell you what hole you're at, and you'll ace it without even looking. You'll be a putt—"

"Making machine," I finished.

I felt like a machine, going through the same motions over and over. I followed orders, though, because Frank knew a lot more about golf than I did.

He also knew a lot about Transformers, beer, and divorce. He managed to tie all three together while I was practicing on hole eleven.

"'The entire collection's probably worth a couple of grand," he said, describing the shelves full of plastic robots he had sitting in his one-bedroom apartment. "I mean, I own most of the originals . . . out of the box, of course, but near-mint condition. Bumblebee. Prime. Megatron. But no Starscream. Not anymore."

Judging by the length of the sigh that followed, I knew that there was more to the story. "What happened to Starscream?"

"Danielle. My ex. We were having an argument, and I guess I'd had a few beers and said something I shouldn't have, and she just lost it. Picked up my nine iron and smashed him to pieces." Frank looked grief-stricken. I guessed he really missed that robot. "It was a first generation. Still had the missile launchers and everything. And she demolished it. Can you believe that?"

I tried to picture Mom grabbing a rolling pin or a hammer or even my now-neglected baseball bat and taking it upstairs to Dad's closet, smashing the rows of trophies lined up on top, but it was hard to imagine. That wasn't their style. My parents believed in using your words to solve conflicts. And start them. And keep them going. Besides, Frank didn't tell me what he said. Maybe he deserved it. Maybe he was lucky it was just one of his toys she swung at.

I fished the orange ball out of the hole and went back to the start. Frank dug in his ear and wiped his finger on his shirt. "Think I might get me some coffee. You want some coffee?"

"I'm twelve," I reminded him.

"So? My niece is already addicted to frappuccinos and she's eight. Maybe I'll just bring you back a scone or something."

I was almost positive the concession stand at Fritz's didn't serve scones. I wasn't even sure they served coffee, but Frank was already walking away.

"Wait, where are you going?" I called after him.

He pointed beyond Fritz's rusting metal fence. "There's a Starbucks right around the corner. I'll only be gone a minute."

Only a minute.

Immediately I thought about the Wild Mouse ride at the fair. The ticket booth. The girl with the dagger tattoo. The crowd closing in. The flashing lights. That one voice inside my head. *Alone. Alone. Alone.* "Hold on. How are you supposed to coach me if you aren't here to tell me what I'm doing wrong?"

"If you don't make it on the first try, you did it wrong."

With that, Frank left me standing at the tee.

"Fine. Just go then," I muttered to myself. At least he couldn't tape my hands together again this way.

I took my shot on eleven, missing the cup by inches, not millimeters. I started over and did it wrong five more times and got fed up. There were a few people on the course now, but no sign of Frank, so I moved on to the next one. Hole twelve was more fun anyway. It had a fence of iron-bar letters that spelled out FRITZS—you had to sneak your ball in between the slats. Your best bet was between the *F* and the *R*. So much of miniature golf was making the right choices before you even took your first shot, which was okay because, as Frank pointed out in his own unique way, you could see everything. There were no surprises. At least there weren't supposed to be.

I teed up.

"Five!"

I glanced in the direction of the shout just in time to see a bright red ball bouncing across the concrete walkway, hopping over the side railing of hole twelve, skidding across my own green, rebounding, and coming to a rest only a few feet from the cup that I was about to shoot for. I traced the path of the ball back to the person who'd hit it.

A girl. And she was headed my way.

She looked older than me, but most girls my age looked older than me. Her thick-rimmed glasses made her eyes look large compared to the rest of her face, which was kind of pointed around the nose. She had a mole on her right cheek that looked like a Cocoa Pebble. Her black-haired ponytail made little swishes when she walked toward me with a sense of purpose. She was frowning. I braced myself.

"Sorry," she said, sort of breathless, pointing to her ball intruding on my green. "Unfortunate miscalculation of required force."

As the girl bent over to pick up her ball, I noticed her backpack. It was covered in buttons, most of them round but lots of different sizes. Buttons for bands and cartoons and restaurants. Smiley face buttons and narwhal buttons and one button that looked like a giant M&M. I'd never seen anyone bring a backpack to miniature golf before, button covered or otherwise. When she stood back up, her glasses had slipped a little; she pushed them back into place with her thumb. "Hope I didn't mess up your shot." She was less than five feet away. I somehow stood my ground.

"I hadn't taken it yet," I said, nodding at my own ball still waiting on the tee.

"No harm, no foul." The girl smiled, and I saw she had

slightly crooked teeth, the bottom row kind of crashing together like they were all trying to get to the front of the line. Mine were crooked too, but mostly in the back where you couldn't see. I looked at the ball in the girl's hand, wondering why she wasn't taking it back to the hole she came from. "You here by yourself?" she asked.

I looked to the fence line. I couldn't even see the sign for whatever Starbucks Frank had gone to. Maybe he just assumed there would be one nearby. The girl looked at me, waiting for an answer. *What'sa matter?* Granny Allison said. *Cat got your tongue?*

"I'm here with my coach, actually," I said at last. "He's getting coffee."

"Your coach? You mean for Putt-Putt?" She didn't say it quite the same way Mom did, like she'd just stubbed her toe. The girl just sounded curious.

"Well . . . it's not really Putt-Putt. Not technically."

I had no idea why I said that, it just slipped out. The girl's face squinched. It was the same look some of the kids at school got when I talked. I fully expected her to shake her head and walk away. That's what usually came after a squinch. But this girl just stood there, head cocked, waiting for something. I didn't know what to do, so I just kept talking. "What I mean is, it's not called Putt-Putt unless you're *at* an actual Putt-Putt. Otherwise it's just miniature golf."

I smiled politely.

141

She squinched harder. Why wasn't she saying anything? Why did she keep looking at me that way?

I kept talking, faster than usual, my words tumbling into each other. "It's sort of like saying Kleenex. 'Cause unless, you know, you're blowing your nose into an *actual* Kleenex, then you're really just using a tissue. Yet people still say Kleenex all the time."

The girl finally took her eyes off me, looking down at her pink and silver sneakers. I was sure she thought I was too strange for words, because that's what Granny Allison was saying in my head. *Son, you are too strange for words.* Finally, she looked up, eyes somehow even bigger.

"Coke," she said.

"Huh?"

"Coke" wasn't "freak" or "weirdo" or "loser," so it took me a little by surprise.

"Yeah. You know how people at a restaurant will ask for a Coke, but what they really want is any kind of soda? It's kinda the same thing, isn't it?"

I wasn't sure. When I asked for a Coke, I always just wanted a Coke. "Yeah. Sure. Why not?" I said. I glanced at the clock above the door. Three minutes. This was already the longest conversation I'd had with a stranger in months.

The girl stuck out her hand. Her left hand. "I'm Lex, by the way."

I wiped my left hand on the back of my shorts, afraid it would be sweaty from holding the club. "Malcolm."

"Cool name," she said.

I wasn't so sure. I liked "Lex," though. It reminded me of Lexus. And lexicon. And Lex Luthor. The girl glanced behind her. "I'm flying solo too," she said. "My mother's getting her hair done at that place across the street. It's this monthly ritual, and it takes at least an hour, so she lets me come over here to kill time. I'm allergic to all the hair spray. It makes my skin itch."

That was a lot of information to take in at once. "I don't use hair spray," I said, responding to the last bit.

"Good to know." I wasn't sure if she was making fun of me or not. She was still smiling. But not a smirking smile. Just a normal sunny day kind of smile. "So you must really like miniature golf, I mean if you've got your own coach."

"I do like it," I said, "but the coach was all my dad's idea."

Lex nodded as if that was all the explanation necessary. "Well, you're obviously better than me. I was on hole seven and ended up here. So . . ."

"So . . . you skipped a few."

"Yeah. Sometimes I just smack it and see where it goes."

"Me too," I said. I'd never actually done that. I just felt like agreeing with her. The girl was good at making eye contact. Normally that kind of thing freaked me out. Normally.

A honk from the parking lot made me jump. Lex glanced behind her and waved. "Figures. *This* time she gets done early. Here. You'll have to finish up for me." She handed me her ball and turned to go. "Nice to meet you, though."

What're you doin', dingleberry? Aren't you at least going to say "bye"? Granny Allison chided. Lex was halfway to the exit before I managed to rip the cat off my tongue.

"Why five?" I blurted.

Lex stopped and looked back at me. "What?"

"When you hit the ball, you yelled 'five.' In golf people yell 'fore.' Not even the number four. A different one." Frank had taught me that. Along with the practical advice concerning bathing suits. And balls.

Lex shrugged. "Obviously five is better."

I watched her place her putter back on the rack before heading into the arcade. It was another minute before she emerged on the other side of the iron fence and got into the waiting car. She didn't turn or wave. Not that I expected her to. I was just thinking about it. The possibility that she might.

That was weird, I thought. Not bad. Just weird.

Seconds later Frank came out to the course holding a cup. I could see traces of whipped cream in his mustache. "She seemed nice," he said, following my gaze to the parking lot where Lex's car was pulling away. He must have seen us talking through the fence on his walk back.

"Her name is Lex," I said. "She's allergic to hair spray." And she isn't very good at miniature golf. And she collects buttons. "And yeah. She seems nice."

Frank took a sip of his coffee. "Good, because I gave her your number."

"What?" My stomach seized, that feeling you get when the

car hits a giant pothole unexpectedly. I gaped at him. "How? When?"

Frank pointed at the arcade. "It was your dad's number, actually; I don't know your cell. But I saw you two talking, and I figured you'd chicken out, so I stopped and introduced myself and then gave her your digits. Do they still call them digits? It's probably just jits now. You kids shorten everything. I gave her your jits."

I was flabbergasted, which was another Granny Allison word. This strange girl I'd only just met had my number? *Dad's* number? "I can't believe you did that," I muttered, though it being Frank, that wasn't entirely true.

He tipped his cup at me. "You'll thank me later," he said. "In fact, you can thank me now, 'cause I also got you this." He fished in his pants pocket for a crumpled paper bag. Inside was a smooshed muffin. "It's blueberry." He waved the open bag under my nose.

"I don't like blueberries," I said.

That wasn't true either—blueberry muffins were my second favorite behind double chocolate chip. I just didn't feel like saying thank you to the man who just gave my phone number to some girl I didn't even know.

Or maybe I was just irritated because he was right: I would never have had the guts to do it myself.

"Don't be mad, kid," Frank said. "We all need a little nudge sometimes."

I record another birdie on eight. It's kind of a lucky shot.

I know there's no luck in golf. Since there are no surprises, the mistakes you make are your own. The successes too. But there are still those moments when you feel like you just happened to be in the right place at the right time. When the gods take pity on you and give you a gift.

In my case, it's a whirlpool. That's what I call it. Frank calls it a flusher, because he's Frank. It's when your ball circles the edge of the cup before finally dropping, sort of like those charity funnel things at the mall where you put in a penny and it swirls around until it gets to the bottom.

As soon as I hit it, I sense it's slightly off course, a tiny bit to the left, but still headed toward the hole at the bottom of the hill. It dodges the three frogs and then just catches the edge of the cup and starts its rotation while I hold my breath, waiting to see which way it'll go. In or out.

It circles around once. Twice. Then, *plunk*.

From the fence my mother cheers, a big *"Yes!"* to echo the little one I whisper to myself. If it had been another centimeter to the left it would have missed the hole, and I probably would have ended up with par. A centimeter the other way and it probably would have dropped into the hole without suspense. Lots of balls drop straight into the hole or miss it entirely. But to whirlpool twice like that—that's unusual. Unexpected. And it's always nice when something unexpected turns out to be a good thing, because most of the time it's not. At least in my experience.

I press my hand to my waistband, to the belt loop just above my left pocket and the button that's pinned there. A gift from a friend that I didn't know I needed.

Wondering why I told her not to come.

HOLE #9

Par 2

This T-shaped hole is easy enough to par, provided you hit the triangular stone on the left and don't sail past it. To get a one, however, you have to strike the stone in the exact right spot, getting a rebound that angles straight for the cup. The triangle is large and seems impossible to miss, but looks can be deceiving. And not everything always turns out like you'd expect.

There's a picture of my parents sitting on our piano, right beside the brass lamp and my mother's metronome. They're at a beach in South Carolina. The photo is a selfie—tilted and off-center—but the sunset behind them is spectacular, all pinks and oranges blending around the edges. Mom and Dad aren't even looking at the camera. They are smiling at each other.

I'm not in this picture. I was nearby, throwing clumps of sand or chasing seagulls or jumping waves. There are other pictures from that trip. Me burying Dad in the sand, Mom and me spelling our names out with shells, the three of us posing alongside a giant lobster statue with soft-serve dripping down wafer cones onto our fingers. Those pictures are around the house, too—on the walls, the bookshelves, the mantel—next to others of the three of us in front of a Christmas tree, feeding giraffes at the zoo, standing outside of Wrigley Field. There are a lot of pictures of the three of us, but the one with just them is my favorite. It's one of only two framed pictures in the house that doesn't have me in it.

The other is a photo from their wedding. They look happy in that one too, but it's different. It's posed. They are framed by the altar and their friends and family, the bouquet of lilies perfectly positioned in my mother's hand. They had to smile for that picture. The photographer told them to. The one at the beach is natural. It's like they've just looked into each other's eyes and remembered something important.

Most of the pictures my parents take now get posted on Facebook or just sit on Mom's phone. I don't know the last time Mom printed out a photo to frame it, even though there is still plenty of room on the walls. Maybe she just hasn't gotten around to it. Or maybe there's nothing from the last couple of years that she needs to be constantly reminded of.

I like the picture on the piano, though. I wish there were more like it.

I had to warn him. Just in case.

Not that I thought anything would ever come of it. In the last year I'd only gotten calls from a few people that I could remember: Mom, Dad, my grandparents on my father's side, Uncle Chris and Aunt Shell on my birthday, and the Democratic National Committee, who didn't realize I still had six years before I could vote. Nobody called me because almost nobody had my number.

Lex didn't even have my number. She had Dad's number. Which was why I thought I should say something.

He muted the TV and looked straight at me. "You said her name is Lex?"

"Yes," I said. "I met her today at practice."

Dad took a moment to process this. "And you gave her *my* cell number?"

I didn't think Dad would appreciate it if I told him that Frank was giving out his phone number to strangers. I didn't tell him most things that happened at practice. This was just one more. "I couldn't remember mine," I said. "I was nervous." That part I knew he would believe. "So . . . if she calls, will you come and get me?"

"Sure, bub." He still sounded a little dumbfounded. "Hey, you want watch the rest of the game? Big Ten. MSU versus OSU. The Spartans are smashing the Buckeyes."

A race of legendary warriors versus a tree nut. No surprise. "I'm good," I said. Dad shrugged. I glanced at his phone on the coffee table, trying to see if he had any missed calls from unknown numbers. He didn't.

Of course he didn't.

I went upstairs and lay on my bed for a while, watching the fan spin overhead, throwing shadows against the ceiling.

What are you thinking?

I shut my eyes and listened to the air being split by the fan blades. *Fwip, fwip, fwip, fwip.* It didn't block out the voice though.

Why would she call you?

I threw a pillow over my face. It didn't help.

She came up and talked to me. She said she liked my name.

Maybe she just felt sorry for you.

She seemed friendly.

She was just being polite.

I don't know why I even care that much.

There's no way she's going to . . .

"Malcolm?" Dad's voice right outside my door. "Phone call."

The voice in my head vanished. I bolted off the bed, at the door before he could even open it. "Thanks," I said, snatching his phone out of his hand. Dad winked at me in a cringy way. I shut the door in his face. I opened it back up. "Sorry," I whispered, my hand over the receiver, then I shut it in his face again. I went over to the desk chair that Frank had sunk into two weeks ago and took a deep breath. "Hello?"

"Hi. Is this Malcolm?"

Definitely the same voice that had yelled *"Five!"* at Fritz's that morning. Almost definitely. "Yeah. Yes," I said. "It's me."

"Hey. Hi. It's Lex. We met this morning? At mini golf?"

"Yeah. Yeah. Of course. I remember." Did people normally say "yeah" this many times when they talked on the phone?

"Yeah . . . so you probably think this is strange, but a guy who said he was your coach gave me this number and said it was yours. And, honestly, I wasn't even sure if I should call it or not. . . . I'm not some kind of weirdo who just calls up total strangers. . . ."

"Yeah. No. Of course not."

"But then I came home and started thinking about what you said, and that got me thinking about Band-Aids."

I shook my head. I made her think about Band-Aids. Open wounds. Bleeding. Getting hurt. That couldn't be a good thing. "Really?"

"Yeah, 'cause, you know, Band-Aids are just the name for one *brand* of bandages," Lex continued. "Like what you said about Kleenex. All Band-Aids are bandages, but not all bandages are Band-Aids."

"Huh." I'd never thought about it before, but she was right. We always called them Band-Aids, even though ours were probably made by Target or Walmart. Half the stuff in our house was made by Target or Walmart. "That's cool," I said.

Lex sounded excited. Or maybe relieved. "I thought so too. So then that got me thinking about *other* things like that, and I had to research it and see if they have a name, and they do. They're called proprietary eponyms. But you probably knew that already."

I had no idea what they were called. I'd never looked it up. But Lex did.

And then she'd called to tell me about it.

What did *that* mean?

"So I started digging into it some more," she continued, "and I found out there are a whole bunch of them. Stuff I'd never even thought of before. Kleenex, like you said, but also Q-tip and Scotch tape, Tylenol, Super Glue, Cool Whip. Even the word Escalator was like a brand name, but the company that made it up doesn't exist anymore and the trademark ran out and so now they're all called escalators, you know, except without the capital E. And did you know that Kitty Litter is a brand name? So like, when your cat pees in her litter box, she's probably not peeing on actual Kitty Litter. She's just peeing on litter. For kitties . . . Do you have a cat?"

"A goldfish," I said, my mind spinning with Cool Whip and Super Glue. "His name is Jaws. He pees in his bowl." At least, I assumed he did.

"Great name. I have a dog named Padfoot, but I just call him Paddie."

"Like *Harry Potter*," I guessed.

"Exactly!" Lex said. "Not everybody gets it. They think it's Irish or Scottish or something. Paddie. He's a black Lab, and he makes the best pillow." Her voice sounded like it was winding down, like a golf ball circling the cup, ready to drop. "So anyways. That's why I called. To tell you about the whole proprietary eponym thing. Because I thought maybe you'd be interested. You can look it up when you get a chance."

"Yeah. I will," I said.

There was a long pause and I sensed that Lex was about to hang up. I needed to say something to keep the conversation going. I sifted through the possibilities. Kitty litter. Dogs. *Harry Potter.* Scottish or something. "Speaking of Scottish stuff," I began, "did *you* know that miniature golf was actually invented in Scotland by a dwarf who was banned from playing regular golf courses because he was too short?"

There was another long pause. Then finally Lex laughed. It sounded like cymbals crashing. Loud and brash. "That's ridiculous," she said. "Who told you that?"

Of course Frank told me that. "Remember the guy who gave you my phone number?"

"You mean the guy with the whipped-cream mustache who couldn't stop scratching his armpit?"

"That's him." Clearly Lex was the kind of girl who noticed things. That was one thing we had in common.

It was only the first.

We talked for twenty-three minutes, though she talked most of that. We talked about our favorite Harry Potter characters (Snape for her, Luna Lovegood for me). About the differences between owning a fish and a dog (a fish won't eat your green beans under the table. Or your shoes). About how bad our respective schools were (terrible and *so* much worse than yours). Finally, after explaining how everything served in the cafeteria should either be dipped in maple syrup or ranch dressing, Lex said she needed to go. She'd promised her mom they'd watch a movie together. But before she hung up she asked for my number—not Dad's—in case she discovered any more proprietary eponyms that she needed to share. I hoped there were.

Afterward, I sat in the chair and replayed the conversation in my head. It had felt awkward at first, but the longer we talked, the easier it got. Maybe that's how it worked for everybody, and I just never talked to other people long enough to realize it. Or maybe it was a question of finding the right person to talk to and the right things to talk about.

My hand buzzed and I realized I was still holding Dad's phone.

I found him in his usual spot. Mom was out in the garden; I could see her through the window, trimming bushes. The game was in the fourth quarter and was close—somehow the tree nuts were holding their own—but Dad wasn't paying much attention; he was staring at his laptop instead.

"Malcolm. Hey. Come check this out." He sounded excited.

I set his phone on the coffee table. I'd been expecting him to ask me about the conversation I'd just had, or maybe to say something about getting the door shut in his face, twice, but his attention was fixed on the screen. I sat down next to him and he angled the laptop so I could see.

It was a video of a miniature golf course—much nicer than Fritz's—and a kid close to my age, maybe a little older, sinking putt after putt after putt. The whole video was a montage of what I assumed to be every hole in one this kid had ever scored. It was set to an Imagine Dragons song, the one about the lightning and the thunder. It was over the top, but the kid was definitely good.

"His name's Jamie Tran," Dad informed me. "He's thirteen years old. And he was last year's Junior World Champion runner-up."

On the screen I watched this kid close to my age bank a shot three times before finding the hole. It didn't look like an accident either. He knew exactly what he was doing. He'd mapped out every angle and hit it perfectly.

"He has his own web page *and* his own YouTube channel, all about miniature golf. Can you believe it? This kid has been playing professionally since he was *eight*."

"Wow," I said, though it wasn't that hard to believe. I knew a few kids who had their own YouTube channels. Paul Jenkins posted videos of himself squirting milk out of his nose almost weekly. Chocolate and white. He could even mix them. He probably had more views than this Jamie Tran kid, but Dad wouldn't care about nose squirting. He seemed to care a lot about miniature golf.

"Just look at that stroke," he said. "So smooth."

I watched as Jamie Tran snagged a hole in one on a par three. An eagle. They didn't even have par threes at Fritz's Family Fun Zone. I wondered what Frank would say if he was sitting here watching. *Now that kid's a samurai sword.* Except he would use the word "freakin'." Maybe twice. Freakin' kid. Freakin' sword.

Dad shook his head again. "Says here he practices at least an hour a day every day during the week and then another four hours on the weekend. Here—watch this." He clicked on another video and I watched the shot that earned Tran the second-place trophy at last year's Junior Mini Golf Championship in Tennessee. When the ball dropped, he thrust both fists into the air. It reminded me of all those headbutting football players on TV. "Apparently, he lives in Michigan and goes to tournaments all around the country, so you might even run into him at some point. Wouldn't that be something?"

I didn't answer. The video cut to a man, probably my dad's age, being interviewed by a local news reporter. I guessed he was Jamie's father by the look of him, though he identified himself as Jamie's coach. So there were *actual* mini golf coaches. Not just duct-tape-wielding high school friends who had been good at golf once and needed a little extra cash.

"I'm proud of what Jamie has accomplished so far," the man said. "But this is just the beginning for us. Next year, hopefully, we can elevate our game and take home the championship." The video cut back to Tran holding up a trophy as big as any in the closet upstairs.

Dad let out a low whistle. "That kid's good."

I could tell he was impressed.

"Yeah. He's good," I said.

According to the likes under the video, at least 165 people thought so.

Dad made it 166.

He beats me on nine. He shouldn't have, but he does. There's no way I should have missed that shot.

Nine is a T-shaped green with a triangle-shaped stone hazard that you bank off of to change direction and head for the hole. Just about every miniature golf course in the world has something like it. Hit the obstacle right and the ball caroms sideways toward the cup. It should be simple.

Unless you fail somehow and miss the triangle completely. Then your ball goes into a back corner, and you're basically teeing off again from the other side, except a stroke down.

That's where I find myself, finally settling for a three on what should have been an easy two. Which is exactly what Jamie Tran got, putting him three strokes ahead after finishing half the course.

Mom calls me over to the fence where all the parents are, hemmed in to keep them from disrupting the players. She's holding a bottle of water and a Kit Kat. I guzzle half the bottle and then go for the chocolate.

"You're doing great. You feel good?" She leans in. She can tell I'm upset about the miss. Not about being behind, just about flubbing the shot. She probably wants to fix it, but it's not like she can turn back time and let me play the hole over again. If she could, there would probably be a few other things she'd do over instead. I spy the phone sticking out of her purse. I know she's probably been using it to take pictures of me in these awful yellow shorts.

"He didn't call, did he?"

I wasn't going to ask. I wasn't supposed to. We had an agreement: stay focused and have fun. No worrying, no discussions, just play. That's why my own phone is still sitting in the car. No distractions. But she knows I can't help it. I have to know.

Mom shakes her head. She looks disappointed. Maybe that means she wishes he was here too. Then she squares her jaw and bends down so her eyes are level with mine. Her hands grip my shoulders, tight, but not painfully so.

"Listen. You've got nine holes left. Don't worry about him. Don't worry about Frank. Don't worry about me. You just go out there and do your thing. Okay?"

I know she's not going to let me go until I give her both nods again, and then it's almost my turn to putt. I hand her the empty candy wrapper and she spots a smudge of chocolate on my chin. She digs in her purse, saying she knows she has a Kleenex tucked in there somewhere, but I know it will really just be a dollar-store tissue. She pulls one free of the pack and then wipes away the smudge.

It's just a little thing, but at least it's one problem she can fix. There's not a tissue in her purse big enough for the rest.

HOLE #10

Par 2

The second half of the course kicks off with another bilevel hole, this time shaped like a spiral. The ball starts at the top and then follows the ramp down and around, gaining speed as it rushes toward the cup below. The constant curve coupled with the added velocity makes for a challenging hole for first-timers who simply can't predict the outcome of their shot. One thing is for certain, though: there's nowhere to go but down.

We talked on the phone four more times that next week. On Monday for twenty-six minutes, beating our previous record. On Tuesday for thirty-six. On Thursday for eleven, interrupted by dance practice. Lex had been dancing since she was eight, when her parents stuck her in ballet. She liked ballet, she said, but it wasn't her favorite. Tap . . . now *that* was her *thing*.

So she sounded a little miffed when I told her I'd never seen it before.

It was Friday. Our fourth phone conversation. Lex preferred talking to texting so that's what we did. "Call me old-fashioned. I like to *hear* people laugh, not just see an emoji. I want to know they're really *there*."

So I was *there* when she asked me if I'd ever seen anyone tap-dance before. And I got to hear her gasp when I reluctantly said no.

"Blasphemy," she said. "Tap is . . . it's just so crazy and complex. It's like this fusion of cultures and traditions, you know, like African tribal dances and Irish clogging. Jig and juba. And even though it has this long, dark history, it still grew into this wonderful thing that everyone can appreciate. I mean, think about it, Malcolm: tap dancers create the very music that they're dancing to while they're dancing to it. How cool is that?"

Lex talked like she was afraid to take a breath. She also thought a lot of things were cool. Like stick bugs and meteors and the Human Genome Project. I'd never met anyone so fascinated by everything: where things came from, how they happened, why they mattered. I thought *that* was cool, her fascination with the whole world, but when I told her so, she suddenly sounded concerned.

"You really don't think it's weird?"

"I just told you I think it's awesome."

"Sorry. I know. It's just that some of the kids at school give me a hard time about it," she said. "They call me *Alexa*. Like, 'Hey, Alexa, what's the capital of Zimbabwe?' Or 'Alexa, who was the twenty-third president of the United States?' Or, 'Alexa, what's on my shopping list?' Mom says they're idiots with less than half a brain between them, but she doesn't see the looks they give me whenever I raise my hand."

I could imagine what those looks looked like. I was pretty sure I'd gotten similar looks. But not when I raised my hand. I never raised my hand. "Benjamin Harrison," I said.

"What?"

"The twenty-third president. I had to memorize all of them for a social studies project last year. But I have no idea what's on your grocery list. Cool Whip, maybe? Tylenol? Coke?"

Lex laughed, and I completely understood what she meant about phone calls being better than texts.

"You're easy to talk to," she said.

I was thinking the exact same thing.

Lex got quiet again, and I could tell she was working up to something, but what she said next still took me by surprise.

"So I know you have practice on Saturdays," she began, hesitant, "but what about Sundays?"

If it was a good Sunday I usually hung out with my parents. If it wasn't, I usually holed up in my room or, worse, in the Cove. The past couple of Sundays had been okay—quiet at least. Last Sunday Dad had tried to get me to start watching golf with him, real golf, but I just couldn't get into it. There were no windmills or dinosaurs anywhere and everybody took forever to take a shot. Plus there was no queso this time around. But it was fine. At least we were together.

I was pretty sure whatever Lex had in mind would be better than watching golf.

That Saturday, Frank told me to tee up at number one on the Red Course. At this point I could ace that particular hole half the time. It was becoming automatic, which meant I was improving. Maybe not a katana or even a wakizashi, but at least a steak knife. Something you could cut yourself on.

"Whenever you're ready," he said.

I placed my ball on the middle dimple and squared up, trying to remember all the little things he'd taught me about posture and positioning, thinking he might be testing me on the fundamentals. I kept my eyes focused on the hole, pulled back my putter, and—

"Ouch!"

I slapped at the back of my head with one hand where something got me just as I hit the ball. Not quite like a bee sting or a horsefly bite, not even painful really, just startling. My errant shot careened off the metal siding, making it only half-way down the green.

I looked at Frank, who stood several feet behind me with a blank expression. His left wrist was now braceleted with rubber bands, fully armed and operational. I glanced down to see a yellow one at my feet.

"You *shot* me?"

Frank shrugged, then pointed to my ball. "Sometimes these things happen," he said. "Try again."

I wanted to tell him that things like getting flicked with rubber bands *didn't* just happen. Not here, at least. They happened on the school bus, or in the cafeteria, but only a sadist with a deranged sense of humor would stand around sniping unsuspecting putters in the middle of a family fun zone.

Of course I didn't say that. I just rubbed the back of my head and gathered my ball, glancing back at Frank, who was casually pulling another rubber band from his wrist. By the time I'd teed up again, he had it stretched taut between thumb and forefinger; he wasn't even trying to be sneaky about it. I looked at the hole, back over my shoulder at Frank's hand. Back at the hole. Hand. Hole. Hand. Hole. Twenty seconds passed.

"Are you going to shoot?" he asked.

"Are you?"

He smiled. I clenched my teeth and looked back at the hole. I waited three more seconds. Five. Ten. Maybe he wasn't going to do it this time. I pulled back.

"Hey!"

The club hit the rubber mat as I slapped at the back of my neck this time. The ball I'd barely nudged rolled a few measly inches. I spun around and glared at Frank.

"Your eyebrows slant way down to your nose when you're mad. Did you know that?" he said.

I didn't know that. But it didn't surprise me. My mother's did the same thing. I bent down and picked up the last rubber band that got me. "Are these really necessary?"

"Make you a deal," Frank said. "Soon as you sink a putt, I'll stop shooting you."

Another challenge. I looked at his wrist. He still had plenty of ammunition. I looked at my ball, less than a foot away. Frank's finger was unloaded. I was pretty sure I could beat him.

I snatched the ball and quickly teed up, planting my feet and hitting it before Frank could even pull another rubber band free. The ball zoomed across the green, headed straight for the hole, but I'd hit it too strong and it skipped right over.

"Ouch!"

The rubber band pinged me in the ear this time.

"That's for rushing your shot," he said.

I found the rubber band on the ground, pulled it back as far as I could, my pointer finger aimed at Frank's big nose. I wasn't sure what came over me. I'd never shot an adult with a rubber band before.

I didn't this time either. My shot missed by a foot, sailing high over his shoulder.

"Stick to golf balls, kid," Frank said. "And stop worrying about what *I'm* gonna do. There'll always be distractions. You gotta block out the background noise. You can't worry about everything that *could* happen. Concentrate on what you can control."

I wanted to point out that there was a difference between background noise and grown men standing behind you flicking you with rubber bands, but I knew there was no point in arguing with Frank when he was feeling philosophical. And armed. "Let's give it one more try," he prodded.

How about we just shove those rubber bands where the sun don't shine?

I ignored Granny Allison's suggestion and reset my ball instead. As I lined up, I started to glance over my shoulder again, but Frank chided me. "Don't look back here. Keep your eyes on the green. Concentrate."

I clenched my teeth and stared down at my ball. I didn't know what was worse. Him shooting me or me waiting for him to shoot me. I started my motion, pulling my hands back, but hesitated. I couldn't help it. I glanced over my shoulder, expecting to take one right between the eyes.

His own eyes were shut. Frank's shooting hand was pressed against his sternum, his face redder than usual.

"Frank? You okay? Frank?"

He didn't say anything at first, just took a long, hissing breath. Finally, he opened his eyes wide and shook his head like he had water in his ears. After another second, his face seemed to relax.

"Wow. Jeez. Sorry 'bout that, kid. Been having some heavy-duty heartburn lately." He pounded his chest three times as if that would help.

"Maybe you should go get a drink," I suggested.

Or, you know, eat something with a vitamin in it, Aleck added.

"How about we just take five?" Frank said.

I followed him back to one of the tables. The bright red bursts that had lit up his cheeks were already starting to fade and his breathing had evened out. "Seriously kid, I'm fine," he said, noticing my worried look. "Just indigestion. Let's talk about this tournament coming up. I gotta know: Was that your idea or somebody else's?"

I was pretty sure he knew the answer to that one already. If not, my silence seemed to be answer enough.

"That's what I figured. Your dad's got a bit of a competitive streak, doesn't he? I remember that from our high school days." Frank dug in his ear. "My old man was the same way. He was an arm-wrestler, if you can believe it. Strong as an ox. He could lift me up by my foot and swing me around like a sack of potatoes. He used to go the bars on Friday nights, come home with a couple hundred bucks, minus what he drank, which was considerable."

"So he was good?"

Frank nodded. "Pretty good. He tried going pro once, but the competition was too stiff. Guys who could toss *him* over the table. That's what he said, at least. I didn't believe it, of course. To me there was nobody stronger than my dad."

There was a proud glint in Frank's eyes. It wasn't a look I'd seen on him before. "Does he still do it?" I asked. "Does he still arm-wrestle?"

"Do they arm-wrestle in heaven?" Frank quipped. "Brain cancer got him six years ago."

"Sorry," I said.

"Don't be. You didn't know. Hell, he didn't even know until it was too late. Pinned him quick. Only took three months. Could have been worse." Frank laughed a strangled sort of laugh. "He used to let me win. When I was little. We'd wrestle on the kitchen table after dinner. He'd strain and grunt and pound with his free hand like I was about to break his arm off. I could see the veins in his forehead popping, that's how good he was at pretending. And afterward he'd always say, 'Look at that. Strong enough to beat your old man,' like he was surprised." Frank took a deep breath and scratched at the table with one finger. "For a while there, I believed him."

I wasn't sure what to say. I tried to picture little Frank pinning his father's giant hand to the table, a smile stretching from one ear to the other, David taking down Goliath. "He sounds like a good dad."

Frank nodded. "He was. Some of the time." He straightened up and peeled the rest of the rubber bands from his wrist. "I think that's enough torture for one day, don't you? Let's get back to the green."

I got up and followed Frank back to the hole we'd left off on, snagging a rubber band to keep in my pocket to fidget with. The only orange one in the pack.

That night I challenged Dad to an arm-wrestling contest—right-handed, I offered, so that he wouldn't have to use his bad shoulder—but he was busy catching up on work. "Maybe later," he said. So I arm-wrestled Mom instead.

I'm pretty sure she let me win.

The next day I found myself right back at Fritz's. But not with Frank.

"We're here."

I sat in the parked car with my seat belt still buckled, face pressed to the window. Fritz's toothy smile looked especially menacing today.

"Malcolm?"

Mom's voice pulled me away from the window.

"You okay?"

"Yeah," I said.

"Okay. Well, we're here," she repeated.

"Yeah."

She waited five more seconds. "So then this is the part where *you* get out of the car and go have fun and I drive away."

Mom smiled gently. I'd asked her to take me because I knew Dad would make a big deal out of it. Meeting a friend at Fritz's for the afternoon. And not just any friend. A *girl*. *The* girl. He'd ask too many questions. He'd want to fuss with my hair. Mom would be cool about it. And she had been. But now that we were here, I hesitated. Even though Lex and I had talked for hours already, we'd only spent five minutes face-to-face. And that was by accident.

"You'll be fine. The key to making friends is just being yourself."

I frowned at her. "Really? *That's* what you've got?"

"Okay. Let me be more specific," Mom amended. "Be the self you are when you're just hanging out at home, not your around-strangers self. Because she's not a stranger. You've been talking to her all week. Just relax."

"Yeah, okay," I said. I took a deep breath and reached for the door handle, but now that she had gotten started, Mom couldn't stop.

"But do me a favor, and if you decide to get something

to eat, take small bites, because—and I'm only saying this because I love you—you have a tendency to talk with your mouth full. And try not to look at your feet the whole time; she might get the wrong idea. Oh . . . and compliment her outfit. Girls like that."

"Got it," I said, though I didn't think Lex would care. Then again, what did I know? "Is that it? Can I go now?"

Mom leaned over. I thought she was going to try and give me a kiss goodbye, but she opened my door for me instead. "Have fun. See you in a couple of hours."

I got out of the car, shoving my hands into my pockets. One held the twenty-dollar bill Mom had given me to pay for golf and snacks. The other held five cents. The six-foot-tall alligator leered at me.

Don't look at your feet. Don't look at your feet. Don't look at your feet.

Lex was standing by the ticket booth, waiting for me. She looked much the same as last time. Denim jacket. Stretchy black pants. Dangly earrings that I first thought were dolphins but on closer inspection were sharks. She'd brought her button-covered backpack. I noticed all of these things because I wasn't looking at my feet. Her T-shirt had a picture of Eleven from *Stranger Things* Force-choking Darth Vader. I was about to tell her how cool it was, but she spoke first.

"We're not playing mini golf," she said.

That had been the plan. Meet at Fritz's for a little friendly competition. Winner buys the Cokes. But apparently the plan had changed.

"We're not?" I looked through the back glass doors to see if there was something wrong with the course. An artificial turf fire, a dinosaur tipping, a malfunction with the waterfall causing massive flooding. But Lex had her own reasons.

"For starters, I did a little research, and it turns out mini golf has nothing to do with dwarfs. It was invented because a bunch of chauvinist pigs in Scotland wouldn't let women play real golf because they weren't allowed to lift their arms above their shoulders. It was considered 'unladylike.' So women were told they were only allowed to putt, and courses were made just for that."

"So we aren't playing miniature golf because of a bunch of Scottish pigs?"

"Sexist pigs," Lex corrected. "And no. I just thought that was interesting. *We* aren't playing miniature golf because *you* have an unfair advantage. You have a professional coach. And you practice all the time."

"But it was your idea," I said. I also thought the word "professional" might be stretching it.

"Actually, I only said we were going to play a game. I didn't say *what* game." Lex turned her eyes to the corner of the arcade, straight to the boxy yellow machine half obscured in shadow.

"Pac-Man?"

Lex nodded. "It requires quick reflexes, good hand-eye

173

coordination, and a healthy fear of the supernatural. Plus, it's only a quarter. Golf is, what, seven bucks?" Lex dug in the front pocket of her backpack and produced a handful of quarters. "So how about it? Up for the challenge?"

I nodded. At least we weren't going to the batting cages.

Lex led the way to the machine and dropped two quarters into the slot. The cabinet was ancient. The decals on the console were all peeling and somebody had written *EAT ME* in black Sharpie by one of the ghosts on the side. The handle looked sticky. Everything at Fritz's looked like it was covered in someone's gooey handprints, but this especially.

"You go first," she said. "I like to know what I'm up against."

I squared my shoulders and relaxed my elbows. I'd played versions of this game before. I knew the basics: eat the dots, only eat the ghosts if they're blue, and basically just stay alive.

"You've got this," Lex said. There was the synthesized *beep-boop* of old-video-game music, and my little yellow guy was up and gobbling.

Waka-waka-waka. Gulp.

I concentrated. I tried to block out the noise from the other games, which was easy. I tried not to think too much about the person watching over my shoulder, but that was a lot harder. "Nice," Lex said as I managed to grab the cherry from the center. I made the mistake of glancing at her, to see if the smile I thought I heard in her voice was actually there, but she pointed frantically at the screen. "Look out!"

Too late. The sound of Pac-Man's agonized death emanated

from the speakers. *Wrer-wrer-wrer-wrer—wurp-wurp*. I'd eaten about half the dots on the first level. Not bad for a first life.

"All right. Scoot."

Lex bumped my arm with her shoulder then laced her fingers together, popping her knuckles. It sounded like a string of firecrackers going off. "Good luck," I said. I sort of hoped she would do better than me. I wanted her to have a good time.

I didn't need to worry.

Her Pac-Man zipped around the screen like it was on autopilot, baiting the ghosts and then gobbling them up in a frenzied feeding, getting all four of them every time. Lex cleared stage one and stage two, smiling at me in between levels. But not a gloating smile. A genuine smile. She was having fun.

She was also kicking my butt.

Five minutes later she was still on her first life. "You're really good," I said as she completed stage four. "And I like your shirt." She shot me a funny look, and I wondered if Mom had steered me wrong.

"Thanks. My dad got it for me for Christmas," Lex said, then went right back to obliterating my score.

By the time our first two quarters were spent, I'd made it all the way to stage three, mostly because Lex started coaching me.

She made it to stage twenty-three and got the high score on the game. I watched her type her name into the leaderboard. L-E-X. She looked at me, one eyebrow raised. "Rematch?"

I shook my head. "I think it's pretty clear who the champ is."

"In that case," she said with a smirk, "I owe you a Coke."

We sat at one of the metal tables outside, but not the one with the former slushy stain. Fritz's was hopping, both courses filled with families enjoying a sunny September day. A determined toddler was trying to shove his club up the brontosaurus's rear end. I pointed it out to Lex. "Now we know how they went extinct," she said.

I snort-laughed so hard that soda almost shot out of my nose.

"Sorry," Lex said as I pinched between my eyes, where the fizz still burned. "And sorry about Pac-Man. That wasn't fair."

"You could have told me you were some kind of Pac-Man prodigy," I said.

"Blame my grandpa. He used to fix arcade games for a living. The coin-operated ones. He'd travel all around, repairing busted screens and glitchy boards and jammed change returns. And if a company decided to junk a game for whatever reason, Grandpa would take it off their hands and put it in his basement. That's where I spent a lot of my summers while my parents worked. He had some real classics. Galaga. Centipede. Joust. And he set them all so you didn't need quarters."

I could picture it. An entire basement full of free arcade games. And all the kids playing them. "I bet everybody wanted to come hang out with you during the summer."

"If by everybody you mean my older sister and my grandparents' poodle, Duffy, then yes."

"But not your friends?"

Lex played with her straw, slowly twisting it into a knot. "I guess I've never been real flush in the friend department."

I nodded to let her know that I understood. I turned and pointed to the rack of putters behind us.

"Remember when you asked about a rematch?"

Turned out Lex was better at miniature golf than her previous overshooting of hole seven suggested. We played the Blue Course, which I was less familiar with, passing by the dinosaur (Lex patting it on its rump in sympathy) and pausing for a selfie in front of the windmill. My score was better, but not by much. She could have taken Dad easily.

It was easily the most fun I'd ever had on the course.

We celebrated with nachos this time, and I made a concentrated effort to chew with my mouth closed, only spitting crumbs once. We finished the afternoon with a few games of Skee-Ball, grouping our tickets into one big pile and spending them all on candy. Afterward we sat on the curb next to Fritz, eating Tootsie Rolls and waiting for our rides.

"Chocolate toes," I mumbled.

"What?"

I held up a Tootsie Roll. "When I was little, my mom used to call my toes my tootsies, so I always thought of these as chocolate toes." This wasn't the kind of thing I would say to anyone at school, but it felt safe telling Lex. I knew she wouldn't tease me for it. And even if she did, I wouldn't mind.

"They're named after the inventor's daughter, actually," she said. "He called her Tootsie. And Snickers was named after a horse."

Of course Lex would know that. One of Granny Allison's phrases popped into my head. *I'm so hungry I could eat a horse.* It was funny because Granny Allison seldom took more than two bites of anything. She lived on coffee, cigarettes, and cottage cheese. I glanced at the backpack that was between us, covered with so many buttons that you could barely see the canvas underneath. "So what's with this?" I asked.

"You mean the buttons or the backpack?"

"Both, I guess."

"The backpack's easy," Lex said, settling it in her lap. "You never know when you are going to need something. Or when you are going to find something that you want to hang on to. And most pants pockets are way too small to carry stuff. Especially girls' pockets."

I didn't know girls' pockets were any different from boys' pockets. Seemed a little unfair. "So what's in it right now?"

"You know. The basics," Lex replied. "A notebook. Phone charger. Some pens. A granola bar. A pair of sunglasses. Couple of Band-Aids—actual Band-Aids. A scrunchy. Some hand sanitizer. Bottle of ibuprofen. A hairbrush. A towel—"

"A towel?" I interrupted.

"Yeah. I read this book—*The Hitchhiker's Guide to the Galaxy*? And it basically said the most useful thing you can have with you everywhere you go is a towel. Though mine's just a dish towel, not a bath towel, so I'm not sure it counts. Do you think that's weird?"

It was like the fifth time she'd asked me that. "No weirder than calling Tootsie Rolls chocolate toes," I said. "So then what about the buttons?"

Lex circled one of them with her finger. "I don't know. A couple of years ago my mom and I were at this antique store and there was this big bowl of 'em by the register, only ten cents each. I picked out a few that looked interesting and stuck them on my backpack, and now it's like a hobby. Or a habit. Or a history. Like this record of where I've been and what I've done and the things I like. You can point to any button on here and I can tell you exactly where I got it."

I pointed to a button with a Minion on it rolling his one eye to the back of his torpedo-shaped head.

"Stuart? I got him from a Happy Meal. I didn't even eat the hamburger. I just wanted the button."

I pointed to one of a unicorn barfing.

"That's how rainbows are made. Won it at a carnival."

I pointed to one of the Joker cracking himself up.

"Best villain ever. Got it from a trip to the mall with my sister last year."

I pointed to one with AC/DC in red letters, separated by a lightning bolt.

"One of my dad's favorite bands. He found it in a box of old records and gave it to me. The records, too."

She wasn't kidding—there really was a story for every

button. The story of Lex spelled out across her pack. "How many are there?"

"I don't know. Forty? Fifty? When I started I'd stick just about anything on there, but I've gotten more selective. Sometimes I swap them out. Once I took them all off and carried my backpack around all day button free, just to see what it would feel like."

"And what *did* it feel like?" I asked.

"It felt wrong."

"Like you were missing something?"

"Like I was hiding something," Lex said. She clicked the toes of her sneakers together. "You want to know what my mom said right before she dropped me off today? She told me to just be myself."

I laughed.

"What's funny?"

"My mom told me the exact same thing."

"Yeah. I guess they have to say it. It's like in the manual or something. But they don't know how hard it is. Or they forgot."

"I thought it was going to be hard," I said. "But it wasn't."

I handed Lex my last chocolate toe.

"Thanks, but I should quit. I'm eating over at Dad's tonight. He's making chicken parmigiana. He's a really good cook."

I stopped chewing as something suddenly clicked in my head.

Eating over at Dad's. Watching a movie with my mom. Dad got it for me for Christmas.

In four phone conversations it had somehow never come up—she'd never mentioned it—but suddenly I was 99 percent sure. Lex's parents weren't together anymore.

"Speak of the devil."

A truck pulled up to the curb. The detailing on the side said MIKE'S PLUMBING—WE DO ALL THE DIRTY WORK.

"Ready, pumpkin?" Lex's dad said, staring at us through the rolled-down window, though I felt like he was really just staring at me. Lex stood up and brushed her hands on her stretchy pants. I handed her her backpack, complete with buttons and Band-Aids and dish towel.

"Next time I'll show you where you can hide so the ghosts can't get you," she said.

She waved goodbye and I waved back. She got into her father's truck to drive to her father's house to eat her father's chicken parmigiana. Without her mother.

But I wasn't really thinking about the fact that her parents were separated, because I kept hearing the same two words over and over in my head.

Next time.

I was a little surprised to see my own dad pull into Fritz's parking lot a few minutes later. Mom hadn't actually said she would be the one to pick me up—I'd just assumed. I slipped into the car, quickly preparing answers to questions I knew were coming.

Except Dad didn't seem in the mood to talk. He only asked me if I'd had a nice time and if I had any money left over from the twenty Mom gave me. I told him yes and yes and then fished three dollars out of my pocket, leaving only the nickel, which was mine to keep.

I knew something was wrong when he left it at that and flipped on the radio. When I'd told him that I was meeting Lex for mini golf, he'd grinned like a kid about to blow out his birthday candles.

He wasn't smiling now.

It became even more obvious when we got home and I spotted Mom outside on the front step, smoking. Mom didn't smoke. Not anymore. She'd quit when she found out she was pregnant. She'd always said it was one of the hardest things she's ever done, but worth it. Worth it to have me. To keep me healthy.

As soon as she saw us pull into the driveway, she stubbed the cigarette out, waving her hand in the air, but it was too late. Dad got out first and marched past her into the house without a word. Whatever they'd been fighting about while I was gone, it wasn't finished. Just put on hold.

I trailed behind Dad, putting some distance between us, and approached Mom slowly. The acrid smell of smoke hung in the air. I breathed through my mouth.

"How did it go?" she asked, squinting up at me.

I wanted to tell her how much fun it was. To tell her that I'd complimented Lex's outfit like she said and didn't talk with my mouth full. But for some reason it felt wrong to say these things, not with the mood she was in, so I just said, "Good." Then I looked at the mashed cigarette butt by her feet.

"You don't have to say it. I know," she said. "How about you go inside? I'll be in in a sec to start dinner."

I opened the front door. Inside I could hear Dad already back in the family room with the television going. It was Sunday. There was a game on. Something with winners and losers. Something he could cheer for.

Somewhere Lex was walking into the front door of her father's house—her father the plumber who was a pretty good cook. They would sit down and share a nice dinner together. I'm sure he asked her about her afternoon on the car ride home. I wondered what she said.

With suddenly heavy feet, I went upstairs to my room and immediately ducked into the Cove, flipping on the Christmas lights and sinking into one of the chairs. I closed my eyes, determined not to let everything spiral downward, determined not to let the last ten minutes ruin everything that came before, but I couldn't help it.

I sat there, wondering what they'd been fighting about, if it had anything to do with me.

And if Lex had just been teasing me, or if there really was a place you could go that the ghosts can't get you.

So after nine holes, relative newcomer Malcolm Greeley is only three strokes behind the expected leader, Jamie Tran.

That's right, Jim. Somehow Greeley hung in there for the front nine, but the back nine is where it really gets challenging.

You know it, Bill. And hole ten is not where you want to be if you're looking to catch up. That long spiral makes it difficult to gauge your approach. An easy two, but I think he can forget trying to make it in one.

But Greeley will need to start making aces if he wants to gain some ground. . . . And there he is, so hard to miss in those yellow shorts—really, it's like Pikachu threw up in his lap. And there's his mom waving in the crowd. Total silence among the spectators, though, everyone waiting for his next shot.

Everyone seems to hold their breath when I tee up on ten. Even in my own head, Bill and Jim start to whisper.

Greeley is eyeing his approach. Doesn't take much. Barely more than a tap, then let the ramp do the rest. He adjusts his stance, eyes on the hole. . . .

Focus. Block out the background. Concentrate on what I can control. Because there is so much I can't. So many things are happening—so many things *have* happened—that I can do absolutely nothing about. But this . . . this is different. The ball. The green. The club. The cup. Physics and geometry. Force and angle and acceleration. Just me and the hole. When I first started playing this game, it wasn't about me, but now it is.

Mostly.

I putt. The ball curves downward, riding the outer wall. I'm a spectator now, like everyone else, watching, waiting, praying. It rolls out of the curve and I hear the adults along the fence gasp as it heads for the hole. Gasp. And then cheer.

Amazing! A hole in one to start this second half. And Malcom Greeley is charging right back into this thing!

Yes he is, Jim. Don't count the kid out just yet. I dig my orange ball out of the cup, then turn and wave to Mom, who is giving me two big thumbs-ups. The scorekeeper takes me from a minus one to a minus two. I reach again for the button pinned to my waist. I think about the person who gave it to me, who isn't here because I told her not to come. I think about the man lying in a hospital bed two hours away with a broken heart. I think about Mom and Dad and the miles between them and everything they've been through.

It's all out of my control. But not this. This I can do if I just stay focused. But the ghosts have a way of trapping you.

And they're already in my head.

HOLE #11

<u>Par 2</u>

The long wooden fencing that runs across the center of the green provides the only obstacle on this hole. Two gaps in the fence provide the only thoroughfares, granting players a choice of paths. The one on the right is the wider of the two, promising easy access to the back half and the cup. However, seasoned veterans of the course know that the narrower opening to the left, while trickier on approach, actually provides the optimal angle and is therefore the best chance for a hole in one.

Regardless of which path you choose, getting past the wooden wall is your first priority, and all the nicks and dents in the wood prove that's no easy task.

The calendar on our refrigerator is color-coded. Mom keeps the markers in a cup on top. My upcoming events are in blue, Dad's are in red, Mom's are in green. Whole-family events are in purple. Past events are all crossed out in black, leaving a trail of angry dark blots until the whole calendar looks like a flattened Dalmatian by the end. Then we turn it to the next month and start rainbow fresh.

The morning after the afternoon with Lex, I came down to find the word TOURNAMENT!!! in bold blue letters blocking out an entire Sunday square. The color followed Mom's coding, but it was Dad's capital letters and exclamation points. Everything else was in Mom's usual script: PTA meetings and doctors' appointments and poker games. The Saturday right before the TOURNAMENT!!! said PRACTICE! in blue as well.

And so did the Wednesday before.

I looked again, just to be sure, then ran upstairs to my parents' bedroom. Dad was knotting his tie in the mirror by his dresser. His closet door was cracked open and I could just catch a glimpse of one of his trophies peeking out. Now that I knew where they were hiding, it was impossible *not* to see them. I stood in the doorway and waited for Dad to notice me.

"What's up, bub?"

"The calendar downstairs says I've got practice on Wednesday," I said.

Dad nodded. He adjusted his tie. It looked fine to me, but he was finnicky about some things. "Yeah. I talked to Frank last night and said it wouldn't hurt to get in a little extra before the main event. Something about a samurai sword and a butter knife?"

The main event. I didn't like the sound of that. Just like I wasn't sure "tournament" needed to be capitalized on the calendar. Dad slipped on his jacket and inspected himself in the mirror, fretting with his thinning hair. "The extra practice can't hurt, can it?"

"Not unless he shoots me with rubber bands again," I muttered.

"What's that?"

"Nothing. It's fine." The trophies on the shelf continued to stare at me from on high.

Dad turned away from the mirror. "You still want to do the tournament, don't you, kiddo?" He looked concerned all of a sudden. His fists rested on his hips kind of like Superman. Superman was one of my least favorite heroes. A little too perfect.

"Yeah, sure." *If you want me to,* I thought. And I was pretty certain he wanted me to. Nothing about TOURNAMENT!!! suggested otherwise.

"Good. Because you're going to do great. Frank says you're a natural."

A natural. It should have made me feel good, except I knew Frank's saying so probably got my father's expectations up, as if three exclamation points wasn't expectation enough. Dad nodded and went back to the mirror. End of conversation.

I went back downstairs to the kitchen and stood in front of the calendar again. The word "tournament" filled up the entire square; apparently nothing else was allowed to happen that day. Not that I had anything else in mind.

At least not until Lex called to tell me that she had a dance recital. This coming Wednesday. And asked me if I could come.

There was a way to ace every hole. You just needed the right approach.

Lex said she understood. That it was no big deal. Practice is important—she practiced three times a week—and there would be other recitals. Besides, did I really want to spend two hours watching a bunch of kids in white tights leaping around a high school auditorium to Tchaikovsky?

I said I had nothing against kids in white tights. I just wanted to see her.

"Seriously, Malcolm, don't worry about it. I usually don't dance until the end anyway, so you'd be sitting through a *lot* of Tchaikovsky. Even I get bored sometimes."

I knew that was a lie to make me feel better. "It's just my dad . . . and the tournament . . ." I'd already told her about the exclamation points.

"Believe me. I get it. Maybe next time," she said. She didn't sound disappointed, but she sounded like someone trying *not* to sound disappointed.

"Yeah. Maybe next time," I echoed.

But even after we hung up I kept thinking about it, and the more I thought about it, the more I wanted next time to be this time. Angles and possibilities. Every hole was a puzzle and every puzzle had a solution. I had to try.

I waited until dinner, testing the waters, assessing the mood at the table. Mom seemed okay—I hadn't seen her smoking again, at least. Dad looked tired, but not grumpy-tired. They were at least making eye contact and talking in complete sentences. Yesterday there hadn't been a dinner, not really—Mom made me a sandwich that I ate outside on the back porch while Dad ate leftover pizza on the couch. I don't know if she ate anything or not. I still didn't know what it was they'd been fighting about, but whatever it was, it seemed to have blown over overnight, or at least been temporarily packed away. Nothing was ever packed up for good.

After a few bites, I set my cup down and cleared my throat, getting their attention.

"So I was wondering . . . what are the chances I can skip practice this Wednesday?"

Nothing tricky. Straight up the middle. Just smack it and see what happens.

Dad's hand hovered above his plate. Mom shot me a questioning look. I briefly considered changing course, making up something about having a big school project due, but I stuck with the truth; if I told them why, they would understand. They would see that it was important. "Lex has a dance recital that night, and she asked if I could come."

Dad put his fork down gently, thoughtfully finishing his bite before he spoke. He never talked with his mouth full; I guess I didn't get it from him.

"I don't know, sport. The tournament's this Sunday, you know. And you've only got two practices left. You really think missing one's a good idea?"

Obviously I'd seen this obstacle coming, looming large in the center of the green. I shook my head. "No. Of course not. Which is why I thought maybe I could just practice an extra hour on Saturday instead."

Compromise: the key to effective personal communication. At least according to the internet. I watched his face closely, and for a moment I thought I saw his eyes soften. For a moment I thought I'd made it.

Then Mom said, "It's fine with me."

Dad's shoulders immediately stiffened. I felt the air around the dinner table tighten. It was a mistake.

Mom had joined my side. Which meant that Dad was outnumbered. All the tension from the day before was suddenly back.

"Well personally, I don't think it's a good idea," he said, arching an eyebrow at both of us. "You should go to Wednesday practice."

That's all it took. Mom clanged her fork on her plate. "Jesus, Matt. It's one lesson."

"That's not the point," Dad said. "Malcolm needs to learn you don't just quit something because it's suddenly inconvenient."

Suddenly the dining room chair got harder. Painfully uncomfortable. My parents stared at each other over the basket of rolls. I could sense my mom forming her words, sharpening them, stockpiling them, I could feel Dad steeling himself against the barrage, preparing his own retaliation. It had happened so fast this time. I hadn't meant to start something. I'd only wanted to watch Lex dance.

"He's not quitting. He just said he'd reschedule. What's the big deal?"

"The big deal is he made a commitment."

"I'm pretty sure *you* made the commitment. That's not his writing on the calendar."

I squirmed in my seat. I had already been kicked out of the conversation. I was just "he" and "his" now. I knew there was no point sitting there any longer. "May I be excused?" I mumbled. I'd barely touched my dinner, but I wasn't hungry anymore.

Mom reached across the table and gave my hand a squeeze. Dad didn't say anything, he just nodded, giving me permission. The discussion was paused long enough for me to put my dishes in the sink and then run up the stairs. The house stayed quiet until I reached the top; then Mom went off.

"What is wrong with you lately?"

"Me?"

"Yes, you. It's one practice!"

"It's not just about the practice. It's like this with everything. You always give in, and I always have to be the bad guy."

"I don't *always* give in. It just *seems* like I do because you're always being unreasonable."

"I don't see how this is unreasonable!"

They were loud enough now that I could hear them through my bedroom door, but that didn't stop me from hearing that other voice.

You did this, it said.

"Why do you have to make everything so difficult?"

"Why are you yelling?"

This is your fault.

"I'm not the one yelling."

"No. You're just the one who always has to be right all the time."

Why do you have to make things harder?

"I don't want to talk about it. I just can't deal with you right now."

"Right. Because *I'm* the problem. You never do *anything* wrong."

Be quiet. Be good. Stay out of the way.

I try.

Try harder.

"According to you I do *everything* wrong."

I didn't mean to.

I just wanted to see Lex dance.

"You okay, kid?"

I turned my attention from the vending machine I'd been staring at to Frank, who was standing over my shoulder, a giant gas station soda in his hand. His goatee was scragglier than ever, threatening to explode into a full-grown beard. A beard would look good on him, I decided. It would make him look more like a short Hagrid.

"I'm fine," I said.

It was Wednesday, and I was at Fritz's, right where I belonged. When Dad dropped me off, he said, "Have a great lesson," and "Pick you up at eight thirty." He hadn't said anything about Lex or the recital and neither had I. He hadn't mentioned the argument with Mom either, though it was obvious who won.

I was here, after all.

We had barely finished the first nine holes of the Blue Course before Frank decided it was time for a snack break. He and I were the only ones out there save for a couple of teenagers who seemed more interested in nuzzling than golfing. It was hard to watch. And hard not to.

"Young love," Frank said. "They've got no idea what they're getting into. It starts out so easy, so perfect"—Frank made a fist with his hand, diving it down through the air with a whistle—"and then . . . kaboom!" His fingers exploded.

I thought about poor Starscream. Frank was probably a little biased. "But not always," I ventured.

"No. Not *always*," Frank agreed. "Probably just, like, ninety percent of the time."

The teenagers finally went back to putting and so did we. Blue ten was easy. I just had to avoid the cheerily grinning lawn gnome in the middle of the green and coast downhill to the cup. Except, somehow, I hit the gnome right in the crotch. He was made of metal and let out a hollow gong.

"Nice shooting, Tex," Frank said. "Maybe next time you can get a little more lift on the ball and take the poor guy's head off." He popped the lid off his soda and took in a mouthful of ice, which he crunched as he talked. "You want to tell me what's got your undies in a bunch? Because you haven't hit a decent shot yet."

"I'm fine," I said again. I situated my ball a club head's length from the gnome's boot and tried to concentrate, but before I could swing, my putter was yanked from my hands. I spun around to see Frank had it tucked under his armpit. The leaky one.

"Seriously, kid. Let's have it. I'm not going to watch you mope around here all night, crippling lawn ornaments and sighing like your dog died."

"I don't have a dog," I reminded him. "I have a fish. You've met him. His name is Jaws." Lex was the one with the dog.

Frank stared and tapped his foot. He was back in flip-flops again tonight. I watched his hairy toes bounce up and down. I had three choices. I could go get a new putter and keep swinging. I could stand there and stare back at him until he gave me mine back. Or I could tell him what was bothering me. A few weeks ago, I would have tried to outstare him, but Frank and I had shared a few slushies since then.

"Did you ever have two things that you want to do, but you can only do one of them, and no matter what you choose, you know you are going to disappoint somebody?"

"Hold up," Frank said. "Are you asking me if I've ever made bad choices or if I've ever disappointed somebody? Because I think we both know the answer to *both* of those questions."

"Forget it," I said. "It's not important."

"Nope. Come on, kid. Don't shut down now. You obviously don't want to be here, so what is it? Did you have a better offer on this fine Wednesday evening? A hot date or something?"

I looked down at the gnome and his annoying smile. Frank snorted.

"Hold on. Are you freakin' kidding me? You had a *date*?"

"It wasn't a date," I said. "I was just going to go watch my friend dance."

"Your friend . . ." Frank squinted at me. "This wouldn't happen to be the same girl you met here a couple of weeks ago, would it? The one I gave your number to?"

I looked up. How could he possibly know that? No way was Frank a mind reader.

"Yeah, Claire at the ticket counter said she saw you two here last Sunday," Frank admitted. "She's kind of a Nosy Nellie. So this girl—"

"Lex," I said.

"Lex. Right. So she asked you to come see her dance, but instead you decided *you'd* rather come play miniature golf with a gassy forty-year-old man in six-dollar sweatpants. Am I hearing you right?"

"It wasn't really my decision," I said. I kicked the gnome. He didn't deserve it, but I did it anyway.

Frank smiled knowingly. He looked out across the parking lot. "You know where she dances?"

"I don't remember the name of the studio. The recital's in the high school auditorium, I think."

"Uh-huh. And what time did it start?" Frank had his phone out, keying something in.

"Seven," I said. "But she said she dances at the end. Why? What are you—"

Frank raised a finger, shushing me. "Says it takes twelve minutes to get there. I can make it in nine."

I glanced at the clock above the exit. It was 7:49. Was he serious? "Frank?"

My coach was already walking away, cup in one hand, phone in the other, putter still tucked under his arm. "Priorities, kid," he said.

"Wait. Really?" I jogged to catch up to him. He could move surprisingly fast when he wanted to. "What about the rest of my lesson? The tournament's this Sunday. Dad said I had to practice. He said *you* said I needed the practice."

"We *are* practicing," Frank said over his shoulder. "We are practicing how not to be a total goober."

That *did* seem like a good skill to have. But if Dad found out I'd skipped out, gone behind his back, lied to him . . . "But he's coming here to pick me up."

"So? Text him in the car. Tell him practice is running late and that I'll drop you off myself when we're done." Frank put the putter back in the rack and tossed his cup toward the trash can. He missed, cursing, the last of his ice scattering across the pavement, glittering in the lamplight.

My skin prickled all over and my stomach started to hurt. "But what if he asks me why we ran late? What do I tell him?"

"Tell him the truth," Frank said, picking up his cup and putting it properly in the garbage. "Tell him that golf is all about making the right choice. And that you still have a lot to learn."

I had my second near-death experience that night. No blood was shed, but it could have been.

"You're going to want to buckle your seat belt," Frank said as we got into his old Chevy. There was hardly any room for my feet; the floorboard was covered with empty soda bottles and coffee cups, a few stray French fries, a used ketchup packet, an unused ketchup packet, and one black sock. "Sorry. I don't get a lot of passengers."

We peeled out of the parking lot, the tires actually making that screeching noise you hear in movies during car chase scenes. Frank told me not to look, so I covered my eyes with my hands, peering between my fingers at the yellow lights that weren't quite long enough and the stop signs that were apparently optional. At one point I glanced at the speedometer and saw we were going sixty-five. The speed limit was thirty.

We made it in seven minutes.

Frank pulled up to the door by the high school auditorium. "Don't wait for me," he said. "By the time I park and walk all the way up here, you might miss her."

I nodded and rushed inside, passing by a couple of parents whose kids had probably already finished their routine and were leaving quietly out the back. Even in the darkness I could tell the auditorium was maybe a quarter full. There were still empty seats up front, but I didn't want to draw any attention, so I waited in the back for the current performance to finish. It was a big group of kids of all ages, dressed in tuxedos, moving in sync to something jazzy. They twirled their top hats in their hands as they kick-stepped their way across the stage. A whole bunch of parents crouched in the front aisle, recording on their phones.

I found a seat, about halfway back where no one else was. I

hoped I hadn't missed her. My phone said it was 7:58.

As the crowd clapped off the last group, a woman wearing a red dress approached the mic in the corner of the stage. "Weren't they wonderful?" she said, coaxing even more applause. "Fantastic job, guys. Now our next dancer has been with Art Extreme Dance Academy for nearly three years, which means you've probably all seen her before. She is one of our top performers and is probably the only student here who can even tell you how tap shoes were invented."

Nope. I hadn't missed her.

"Please welcome to the stage Miss Alexis Bauer."

A man in the front of the auditorium let out a shrill whistle, and I wondered if it was her dad. I'm sure he was there. I bet both of her parents were there. The stage went dark again, save for a single spotlight. I felt a shiver work its way through me.

Into the pool of yellow light emerged a girl in black leggings and a black shirt. She had painted raccoon eyes and her long hair was pulled back and twisted into an elaborate knot. Her polished ebony shoes shone in the spotlight. She stood stone still, arms crossed, eyes taking in the audience. I couldn't tell if she saw me or not; her expression didn't change—she'd been smiling from the moment she took the stage.

The music started to thump through the speakers, the deep, thrumming base of a familiar hip-hop song.

And then Alexis Bauer—Lex—my new friend—exploded.

It was as if she'd been jolted to life by a lightning strike. Suddenly her legs and arms were a blur, feet moving so fast they reminded me of old cartoons where the Road Runner's whole bottom half becomes a spinning dust cloud. The bass was crazy loud, causing the whole auditorium to vibrate, but I could still hear the machine-gun staccato of Lex's tap shoes adding a rapid-fire complementary beat. She seemed to fill the entire stage, left to right—a spinning, tapping, twisting whirlwind that made the hairs on my arms stand up.

Just Lex, alone in the spotlight. Drumming and dancing.

And it was incredible, just like she said. Probably—no, definitely one of the most incredible things I'd ever seen.

Four minutes later, she finished with her legs crossed, arms up, face turned toward the ceiling. I stood up, along with everyone else in the audience. Lex bowed and I swear she looked straight at me.

And that look on her face—the joy and exhaustion and exhilaration and relief. I saw it all. And for a split second I was jealous, because I wanted to love something that much. To be as good at something as she was at this. Just once.

Alexis Bauer spun and trotted off the stage, finally giving me a chance to catch my breath.

I got home only fifteen minutes late. Dad was in the kitchen loading the dishwasher. Mom was nowhere to be seen. That wasn't always a bad sign. She could be upstairs in bed already, reading or working on her laptop. She could be out for a walk. She might have run to the store. I didn't always assume the worst, but these days it was hard not to.

"How was practice?"

"Practice?" I repeated, wrapping my head around the suddenly unfamiliar word. "Yeah. No. It was good. Really good."

"*Really* good?" Dad sounded skeptical. I should have used the word "fine." He was used to "fine." "So does that mean you're ready for this weekend?"

"Totally ready," I said, trying to sound confident. I didn't like lying, and not telling the whole truth felt like a lie; it made the same sickening hole inside of me. I looked for a way to change the subject. "You want help with the dishes?"

"No. You've obviously worked hard tonight. Go relax. I'm almost done here anyways."

Dad dropped a handful of utensils into the basket, the forks sitting with their tines up even though Mom always told me to put them tines down so I didn't poke myself. I thought about reminding him about the rinse aid but reconsidered—it might just make him mad, like I was taking her side. I ran upstairs, thankful to escape, and noticed that the door to my parents' bedroom was closed.

That *wasn't* a good sign. Another night I might have knocked. Just to tell her I was home, and to say good night. But not this time. I didn't want to ruin this feeling I had.

When I got to my room, my pocket buzzed. Lex only texted when she couldn't get away to talk, but I knew it couldn't be from anybody else.

Thought you said you couldn't come.

I hadn't stuck around for the rest of the recital. I knew I was pushing it in terms of time and I didn't want Frank to have to wait any longer for me. She'd seen me, though. She knew I was there. My phone buzzed again with a follow-up message.

So how was it? How'd I do?

I thought about all the things I might text back, tried to think of something clever or witty, something having to do with dancing or tapping, a pun or a joke. Instead I just texted back:

You were amazing.

It was the first honest thing I'd said since I walked in the door.

There are lots of ways to cheat at miniature golf. You can move your ball when no one's looking. You can lie about your score when your mother asks you what you got. You can push the ball rather than actually putt it, shimmying it along with your club. If you're stuck against the wall, you can move it out more than the regulation club-head's length, maybe reposition it so you have a better shot. If you're really gutsy you can "accidentally" kick the ball with your foot, then put it back "more or less" where it started, but closer to the hole.

Doing any of these in a tournament is cause for instant disqualification.

And so when my shot on eleven sticks in the corner, still a couple feet from the cup, I carefully place my club head against the green railing and put my ball at the very tip of it—not an inch farther. There are people watching. Parents, and other competitors, and the scorekeeper. But even if I thought I could get away with it, I wouldn't try. I don't want anyone accusing me of being dishonest.

I line up my putt. If it weren't for my awkward positioning straddling the boundary wall, it would be a cinch. Two feet, no slope, straight shot. But I'm boxed in, forced to take an unusual stance, unable to hold my club the way I always do.

It's frustrating, being backed into a corner. But you have to work with the lie you're given. You have to suck it up and make the best of it and try not to be a total goober.

I take my shot.

This time I don't miss.

HOLE #12

Par 2

The obstacle that graces hole twelve, known locally as "The Crossing," is more decorative than challenging. The oaken bridge the hole is named after spans a skinny, pebble-strewn stream, but the high sidewalls ensure that most putts stay on the green. Once you cross the water, a gentle downhill provides the extra momentum needed to get to the cup in the center of the circled green, making this a comparatively easy hole to one-putt. As you stroll across the bridge, take note of the etchings in the wooden railing, as this is the most popular spot for high school sweethearts to engrave their names and proclaim their undying love.

The sentiments are fleeting, however: the bridge is repainted every spring.

When Frank greeted me the Saturday after the recital, his hands were suspiciously snack free. He waved to Dad in the car and then turned to me. "He suspect anything?"

I shook my head.

"Good. What happens at Fritz's stays at Fritz's. And what happens when you're *supposed* to be at Fritz's also stays at Fritz's. Now come on: you've got your first tournament tomorrow and we've got some practice time to make up."

We walked through the arcade—Frank waving to Claire, Mini Golf Gossip Queen—and out to the greens. He pointed to a wire basket of golf balls he'd set on the table. "This basket has ten balls in it. That's ten shots for each hole."

"What's the catch?" I asked. This was Frank—there had to be a catch. I looked for duct tape, rubber bands, handcuffs, a squirt gun, superglue, whatever. He seemed unarmed. But I was still right.

"One of those ten shots has to be a hole in one. If it's not, you go back to the beginning and start over."

I looked at the basket, at the greens, at Frank. "You mean the beginning of the *course*?"

"You think ten tries is too many?"

I shook my head. Better than baseball, where you only get three strikes before you have to shuffle back to the dugout and the row of hard stares from your teammates.

"Then let's get started."

I took the basket and grabbed one of the worn rubber-handled putters from the rack. There were a few holes that I'd never birdied on the Red Course. Hole seven, with the mine field of stone obstacles dropped at random along the path. Hole fourteen, with the crazy slope that caused your ball to angle unpredictably. And hole sixteen, the one with the killer plateau. The Mountain, Frank called it. I was lucky if I could *par* that one. There was no way I was going to get birdies on all eighteen, even with ten tries apiece, and Frank knew it.

Frank positioned himself near the cup on hole one, ready to retrieve my missed shots. His T-shirt had a picture of a cat eating a taco on it. Taco cat. A palindrome. I bet Lex liked palindromes. I made a note to ask her the next time we talked.

My first shot missed the cup by less than an inch.

"Golf is as much mental as it is physical," Frank said. "You have to go in believing you'll ace every hole. You have to know in your heart that it's possible. You think Kris Bryant ever steps up to the plate and thinks, 'Nope, forget it, not getting a hit this time'?"

I knew who Kris Bryant was. Dad talked about him too, though not quite the same way he talked about Ryne Sandberg. I gave Frank a dirty look.

"Right. No baseball," Frank said. "How about this: you think Frodo Baggins was ever like, 'Screw this, I'm not taking this stupid ring all the way to Mount Doom'?"

Finally he was speaking my language. "Yeah. I'm pretty sure he says that at least three or four times." I changed my voice, making it whinier and whisperier. "*I can't do it, Sam. It's too heavy. This lava's too hot. The lembas bread is stale. The*—"

"All right, fine," Frank interrupted. "He *complained* about it, but he still *did* it."

"Technically, Gollum was the one—" I began, but Frank cut me off again.

"Forget it. I shoulda known better than to try and talk nerd with you. The point is, you have to know you can do it. Whether you do it or not. Now try again."

I took the next ball from the basket and sank it easily.

"In your face, Frodo Baggins," Frank said. I glanced at Frank's hairy toes and grinned.

We moved on to hole two and three and four, and as the morning went on, I felt myself slipping into a kind of trance. The sound of Fritz's waterfall crashing, the satisfying *plink* of the ball dropping into the cup, the feel of the club in my hand and the autumn breeze cooling my back, the little nod from Frank every time I birdied a hole. The course was still empty by the time I got to hole sixteen. Empty and peaceful and perfect.

I took all ten shots on that hole, emptying the basket. Not a single one of them went in.

Frank pointed to the start of the course. "You know the rules," he said.

His rules. My rules. Same rules. I went back to hole number one. But it was okay. I was still having fun. Dad was right. Things are more fun when you're good at them, but mostly it was just being here where it was comfortable, where I didn't have to watch where I stepped or what I said.

With five minutes left in our lesson, Frank called last shot. "We've got one more thing to take care of before you leave," he said. He told me to have a seat at the nearest table and then disappeared into the arcade: slushy time.

It had become a tradition. It was my reward for getting through the lesson. Always red for him and blue for me, brain freezes free of charge. Frank was funny when his brain froze; he always did a little dance, tapping his feet and pounding on his head as if he could knock the cold out of his ears.

He didn't come back with slushies this time, though. Only a long, skinny cardboard box that he set on the table in front of me.

"What's this?"

"What does it look like?"

Obviously it was a present; I could tell because along the box in black marker Frank had scrawled the words "WRAPPING PAPER." In the center he'd written the word "BOW." I had a pretty good idea what I would find inside the box. I used my thumbnail to peel up the duct tape he'd used to seal it.

I slid the putter out of the box and held it in both hands.

"You know what that is?" Frank asked.

I hesitated. "My arm?"

"Your ar . . ." Frank shook his head. "Smart aleck. *That*, my young apprentice, is a Ping Anser. One of the finest putters ever made. That baby was revolutionary in its day. The freakin' *king* of putters."

Its day must have been a while ago, judging by the look of it. I would have expected the king of putters to be shinier. Yes, it was much nicer than all the cheapo clubs lined up along Fritz's racks, with their gummy handles and bent shafts. This one was heavier, its head more substantial. But it was obviously . . . *extensively* . . . used.

"That baby was invented by an engineer who also made jet fighters," Frank explained, beaming. "Now tell me *that* ain't cool."

That was pretty cool. I rubbed my finger along the letters etched into the club's head. "Anser. Was that the name of the engineer?"

"No. It's actually supposed to be the word 'answer,' you

know, like 'the answer to all of your putting needs.' But the whole word wouldn't fit, so they took out the *W*."

Answer. Without the *W*. The king of all putters had been misspelled, on purpose. "Huh," I said.

"Just huh? I'm not sure you realize what you are holding there, kid. That was the putter I used all throughout my high school days. I once sank a forty footer from the edge of the rough going uphill in the middle of a—"

"Hurricane?" I offered.

"I was going to say a rainstorm," Frank said, "but you're right. Hurricane is better."

I held the putter in both hands. I sensed something significant was happening, like that moment in every fantasy novel when the hero opens the chest to find his father's hand-me-down sword, the same one used to slay the dark lord the first time around. Except my sword was a putter. With a typo. And something red caked on the edge of the head. I flicked at it with my fingernail. "That's not blood, is it?"

Frank leaned over to get a good look. "Naw. That's just paint," he said. "I may have used this baby to knock the side mirrors off my neighbor's Camaro a few years back."

This didn't surprise me. I ran my finger along the head of the putter, feeling the smooth metal. It certainly had some weight. And some history.

"I can't take this," I said, handing it back to him. "I mean, it's awesome. Really. But it obviously means a lot to you and I think you should keep it."

"It does mean a lot to me," Frank said, pushing it back. "That's why I want you to have it. I want to see it get some use again."

The answer to all of my putting needs was being thrust back in my face. I remembered that first moment in my room, Frank's fist suspended between us. *Don't leave me hanging.* I didn't have a habit of saying no to adults. I didn't start now.

"Thanks," I said. I stood up and took a few practice swings. It was a little long, and it would take a little time to get used to the difference in weight, but it felt good in my hands. Like it belonged there.

"So what are you going to call it?"

"Call it?"

"Yeah. You have to give it a name. Something flashy, like Clutch or Eagle Eye or Birdie Boy or Hole Seeker." Frank and I looked at each other. "Okay. Maybe not Hole Seeker. But something."

"What did you call it?"

Frank scratched at his bushy chin. "Yeeeahh . . . I called it Danielle," he said. "Which is why you need to call it something else."

He was right. I couldn't name my first putter after my coach's ex-wife, even if she did know how to swing it. I thought for a moment, and then it came to me. "Katana."

Frank looked a little confused at first, but then he remembered. "Katana," he said. "I like it." He pointed again to the basket of balls at his feet. "How about you go give ole Katana a few more swings before your dad gets here. Get used to it a little bit before the big dance tomorrow."

The big dance. And me with a brand-new chicken stick. At least new to me.

I took the bucket in one hand and Katana in the other and started off for the Blue Course, just for something different. I got two steps before stopping and twisting back around.

"This is great, Frank. Really," I said.

Frank gave me a weak smile. "Take better care of her than I did."

"What's that?" Dad asked when I got into the car fifteen minutes later.

"That's Katana," I said.

"Katana, huh. Did Frank give that to you?"

I shrug-nodded. "He said he didn't have much use for it anymore."

Dad looked again at the old, paint-scarred putter resting on my lap. "Looks a little beat up, don't you think? I could take you to Golfer's World. We could pick out a new one."

"I don't think I need two putters," I said. Of course I didn't think I needed a new baseball bat every summer either.

"No. I guess not."

I could hear the thread of disappointment woven into his voice. He'd wanted to take me shopping himself. Maybe he'd planned on going this afternoon. Maybe it was supposed to be a surprise. A chance for us to spend a little extra time together.

213

He'd been busy at work with the promotion, and between homework and lessons and Lex . . .

"We could always go and look," I said. "I mean, it couldn't hurt."

Dad threw the car into gear. "No. You're right," he said. "Nobody needs two putters. I'm sure that one's good enough."

We didn't say anything else about it the whole drive home.

That night, while Mom was playing the piano and Dad was on the couch checking his email in between innings, I left Katana on my bed and crawled into the Cove to call Lex. She picked up on the first ring.

"Whatever you do, don't say the word 'tournament.' Or 'golf.' Or 'putt' or 'ball' or 'birdie' or 'bogey' or anything related to *any* of those things. Or anything related to anything *related* to those things."

"Nervous?" she asked, after I'd finished.

"Yeah, maybe," I admitted.

This wasn't just nerves, though. I would get nervous before baseball games too. And tests at school. And waiting while the teacher paired kids up for group projects. And sometimes while standing in line at the McDonald's wondering if they were going to put pickles on my cheeseburger even though I asked them not to. This was different. It *felt* different. Bigger.

"I get nervous before recitals too," Lex admitted. "I seriously just want to puke my guts out."

"You couldn't tell," I said, remembering her whirlwinding

across the stage. "You made it look easy." In the pause that followed I imagined Lex smiling on the other end, crooked teeth and all.

"Okay, so what do you want to talk about?"

"I don't know. Anything. Tell me something interesting."

"Well . . . ," she began. "Did you know that the microwave oven was only invented because some scientist studying radiation accidentally melted a chocolate bar in his pants? I'm saying this because I'm currently microwaving a bag of popcorn as we speak."

"Who keeps a bar of chocolate in their pants?" I asked.

"Right? And can you imagine what the other scientists said when they saw the stain? I mean, the poor guy is bombarding himself with radioactivity *and* he gets called professor poopy pants?"

"It's terrible," I agreed. "But he *did* invent the microwave, so now *you* can have popcorn."

"Everything comes at a price," Lex said. She got quiet for a second. When she started talking again her voice was serious. "I'm sorry I can't be there tomorrow," she said. "You know. For *the thing that will not be named*. I begged my mom, but she says I'm not allowed to miss my cousin's birthday party, even though he's turning ten and only cares about fart jokes and Fortnite."

I knew this already. And she'd apologized already. But Lex believed in multiple apologies, which was refreshing when you lived with two grown-ups who refused to admit they were ever wrong. "It's okay," I insisted.

"No. It's not okay. You made it to my recital. I should be there. But I promise I'll come to the next one."

I didn't tell her that I wasn't even sure there would be a next one. It probably depended on how this first one went.

"I'm afraid I'm going to mess up," I said.

"You'll do great," Lex insisted. "Just remember to shout 'five' as loud as you can before each shot, in honor of your good friend who taught you not to keep chocolate in your pants."

I told her I would. Maybe not shout it, but at least whisper it.

I wasn't a fan of shouting.

I recover from the messy first shot on hole eleven and manage to get a birdie on twelve, skipping easily over the bridge and bounding straight for the cup. I stand awkwardly at the tee, staring at the red smudge on Katana as people in the crowd clap. Applause makes me uneasy. It means I'm the center of attention. I feel my shoulders relax when it stops.

On my way across the wooden bridge to retrieve my ball, I wince, feeling a sudden sharp prick in my thumb. A pinhole of bright red blood bubbles up around the miniscule sliver of wood sticking out of the pad. I tweeze the splinter out with my fingernails and then suck on the sore spot, making it throb more but somehow hurt less.

If Lex was here, she'd probably explain why we instinctively suck on our thumbs after we cut them or slam them in car doors. If Frank was here, he'd probably look at the tiny hole in my thumb and tell me they might have to amputate and that I'll never putt again. If Dad was here . . .

If . . .

Standing on the bridge, I see all the graffiti that's been scratched into the wood. One etching claims CHRIS RULES. Another says EAT ME, just like the ghost on the Pac-Man machine back at Fritz's. But most of the scratches are pairs of names drawn together with hearts or plusses. If my parents had lived here thirteen, fourteen years ago, if they had come to this place for a date, would they have carved their initials into this bridge? If they had, would you still be able to see it? How long do these inscriptions last? The paint didn't look that old.

Behind me, Grace Xin is already teeing up on this hole, which means I need to get off. I pull my thumb from my mouth and inspect the wound. The bleeding has stopped. In fact, you can hardly even tell where the splinter got me. No need for a Band-Aid.

But it still stings.

HOLE #13

<u>Par 2</u>

The thirteenth hole at Putter's Paradise earns its unlucky numerical designation with its frustrating gauntlet of hazards, starting with two logs, angled and staggered like crooked fangs, giving golfers no other choice but to play it off the walls. To make matters worse, the off-center hole sits at the top of a hill, making a hole in one a nearly impossible feat. Even the most skilled golfers will be thankful to break even, and regulars at Paradise will soon get used to disappointment.

The morning of my first ever miniature golf tournament I was jitterier than a june bug, as Granny Allison used to say. Too nervous to eat the chocolate-chip waffles that Dad made for me, even with all the Cool Whip he'd piled on top. Instead I forced down a glass of orange juice and went back up to my room to get ready.

"You can't wear that," Dad said, appearing in my doorway. I looked down at my Nike shorts and ZOMBIES LOVE BACON T-shirt.

"Why not?"

"Because that's not how golfers dress."

"Maybe it's how *miniature* golfers dress," I suggested. At least, miniature golfers who liked zombies who liked bacon. But Dad wasn't having it. He rifled through my drawers, finding a pair of shorts with an actual button and zipper and a white polo shirt that I didn't even know I owned.

"I'll look like I just got out of some hoity-toity private school." "Hoity-toity" was another one of Granny Allison's phrases.

"You'll look professional," Dad corrected. He licked his hand and tried to slick down some of my unruly hair.

Mom was already waiting by the door when we came down. "You look nice," she said. The shirt felt tight around my neck. I didn't feel like me. I thought about what Lex said about her backpack and the one day she'd taken all the buttons off. Backpacks were better with buttons. Shirts were not. I grabbed Katana from the closet and followed my parents to the car.

It wasn't until we were halfway to Fritz's that I remembered I'd left my grandpa's lucky nickel in the other shorts. I almost asked Dad to turn around and go back, but I knew that would only irritate him. There's no luck in miniature golf. That's what Frank said. I was about to test that theory.

Fritz's was busier that morning than I'd ever seen it. The parking lot was packed, forcing Dad to find a space in the back row, which made him grumble. There was already a crowd of competitors and parents scattered across the greens. There had been no official announcement as to which course we would play, but Frank said it would probably be Red because it was harder and would more easily separate the players from the pretenders.

I wondered which one I was. I had an imaginary friend once. And voices inside my head. I was a pretender in most things, but hopefully not this.

Claire the Nosy Nellie was running the sign-in desk by the entrance. She'd gotten a new lip piercing since yesterday, a little gold ring, which immediately brought to mind Frodo and Mount Doom. My stomach felt like the inside of Mount Doom, bubbling and seething. She pointed to a piece of paper on the desk and instructed me to put a check by my name.

The top of the sign-up sheet read "Junior Golf Tournament" and had the minimum and maximum ages listed as eight to fourteen. Below that it listed the prizes. Third place would win a ten-dollar game card to spend in Fritz's arcade. Second place got two free rounds of golf for a family of four. And the grand prize: one free chicken sandwich a week for a year from Leroy McClucker's, the local restaurant that was sponsoring the whole thing. There was no trophy to be seen, though there was a stack of certificates printed on cardstock. It looked like there was one for everyone who participated.

My name was third on the list. There were only thirteen players total. I didn't recognize any of the other names. Until I got to the last one.

"Really?" I whispered to myself.

"What?" Mom asked.

I pointed at the name on the sheet.

"What? I don't get it. Who's Jamie Tran?"

221

"Wait. *He's* here?" Dad asked, looking over Mom's shoulder.

"Seriously, who's Jamie Tran?" Mom repeated.

"That certainly raises the bar a little bit," Dad said.

"Will someone *please* tell me who Jamie Tran is?" Mom asked a third time.

I scanned the course, then pointed across the concrete and artificial turf with the tip of Katana. "*That's* Jamie Tran," I said.

I recognized him from the videos, but I think I could have picked him out of the crowd regardless. It wasn't just the bright red Adidas polo and khaki pants that looked good on him, even if it reminded me of every trip I'd ever made to Target. Or the fact that he actually had a golf bag beside him with three different putters in it. It was something about his demeanor. The way he walked the course by himself, crouching down by each hole as if to get a sense of the turns and slopes. He was the only kid here wearing sunglasses, even though it was overcast, the sun feeling shy. He just *seemed* intimidating. He moved with purpose. His hair had clearly been heavily gelled.

"He's one of the top junior mini golfers in the country," Dad explained. "He travels all around playing in big tournaments. And local ones too, I guess. I certainly didn't expect him to be *here*."

"Maybe he really likes chicken sandwiches," Mom said with a shrug.

"Did someone say sandwiches?"

I spun to see Frank standing behind me, cup of coffee in

one hand, sprinkled doughnut in the other. He nodded to my parents. Dad said, "Good to see you, Frank." Mom didn't say anything.

"Jamie Tran is here," I told him.

Frank's eyes blew up like birthday balloons. "Shut the front door. *The* Jamie Tran? Oh my god, I think I'm going to faint." He took a bite of doughnut and his eyes relaxed again.

"You have no idea who that is, do you?" I asked.

"Somebody's ex-boyfriend?" Frank said, winking at Mom.

"He's one of the best junior mini golfers in the country," Dad explained.

Frank blinked.

"He's nationally ranked. Just like you are . . . or were."

Frank blinked some more. Then he polished off the last bite of his breakfast and snatched the sign-up sheet from off Claire's desk. "Wait a second. You know who *else* is here?" he said, spraying doughnut crumbs on the paper.

"Who?" Dad asked, sounding worried.

"Malcolm. Freakin'. Greeley," Frank said, pointing repeatedly to my name on the list. "*That's* the guy you should keep your eye on." He looked at me with a raised eyebrow. Claire smirked. Even Mom smiled this time. Frank bent over so that we were nose to nose. "Remember, kid. This isn't football. It isn't soccer or tennis or, god forbid, baseball. This is golf. It's just you and the course. You hear me?"

I nodded. Then I looked over at Dad, who seemed to be biting his tongue. Or chewing on it.

"Just you and the course," Frank repeated.

Just me and the course. And I could beat this course. I knew I could.

But apparently, so could Jamie Tran.

Some things are not all that they are hyped up to be. Like filet mignon. The one time I had it, I was told by Dad to prepare myself because I was about to taste the food of the gods. It was good, but I think I would've been just as happy with a cheeseburger from the kids' menu.

There are others. Things that you think are going to be so much better than they really are. DC superhero movies. Hatchimals. The Indianapolis 500. They seem awesome, but it's hard not to be a little disappointed when you finally get around to them.

Jamie Tran wasn't like that. He completely lived up to expectations. He finished the day at five under par. Even on my best practice days I'd never scored so low. It was impressive. He aced the first three holes to take the lead and then never looked back.

He was a putt-making machine, a samurai sword and a chainsaw rolled into one. He never put himself in a corner or miscalculated the angle on a bank—at least not that I saw. And I watched him all morning, out of the corner of my eye, when I wasn't sizing up my own shots. He made it look easy. I sensed Dad watching him too. When he wasn't watching me.

It's easy to keep your eyes on someone when you are always one step behind them.

After hole fifteen, Frank called me over to the fence. He'd been quiet all afternoon. No pep talks. No pointers. Just go out and putt, he said. Tran, on the other hand, went back to his coach after every hole, the two of them always locked in intense discussion.

"Told you he was good," I said.

"You're good," Frank said. His shirt collar was damp. So was mine. "Don't worry about him."

"He's got his name on his balls," I said. It was true. I'd snuck a peak as Tran teed off at the last hole. It wasn't his whole name. Just his initials, JRT, etched in gold against dimpled black.

"Probably because he doesn't want somebody else playing with them," Frank said with a sly grin. I didn't laugh. Not even a nervous laugh. I was way past that. "Come on. Lighten up, kid. You're doing great."

I actually was. Tied for third place. Three under par. On pace to beat my lowest score. I'd heard Dad clapping and hooting all morning just like he was now. Frank saw me looking at Dad and tapped my forehead to get my attention.

"Listen. Forget the crowd, all right? Forget the score. Forget Jamie Tran. Just go out there and relax. Have fun. Play the course, remember?"

"But what—" I started to say before Frank cut me off.

"No buts. Just pretend like it's practice and you and me are the only ones out here."

I nodded. Play the course. Tune out the noise. Don't worry about the score.

And don't look at the crowd.

But as I walked back to hole sixteen, Dad called out from the fence, "Go, Malcolm. You're still in it. This is *your* game."

He smiled and I smiled back. Imagine how ecstatic he would be if I somehow managed to come from behind and win this thing. Forget free chicken for a year. It would be worth it just to see the look on his face.

I put my ball—a boring white one with nobody's name on it—on the center pip and eyed the cup at the top of the Mountain, adjusting my stance and taking a practice swing. I'd never birdied this hole—not even with ten tries. Now I only had one. I tightened my grip on Katana. Just you and the green, I thought. Nothing else. Nobody else.

Except the voice in my head.

You can't do it, it said.

I licked my lips. Replanted my feet.

You're not good enough.

Cold sweat sheened the back of my neck. I shut my eyes tight for a moment and then opened them again, focusing on the top of the plateau, imagining the path my ball would take to get there, but the moment I thought I had it, the voice started in again.

What if you miss?

What if?

I willed myself not to look back at the crowd, but I still sensed everyone's eyes on me. My arms and legs stiffened. I wiped my forehead on my shirtsleeve. I kept my eyes pinned on the ball by my feet. I forgot to take one last look at the hole to confirm the distance. I knew it the moment I hit it: too tentative, too soft. The ball made it halfway up the hill before rolling back down, coming to rest nearly three feet from the incline.

I took in the muffled groans from the line of onlookers. The collective *aww* as they watched the ball come back. I saw Dad's head drop, as if his neck had just snapped.

It's all right, I told myself. *You can still make par.* Jamie Tran had only made par on this hole. But as I squared up to the ball again I noticed my hands were shaking. I felt dizzy. The voice in my head was gone, but it didn't matter. It had been branded onto my brain: I wasn't good enough.

My follow-up shot was too soft again, failing to crest the hill. Frustrated, I hit the third shot too strong, skipping over the cup and coming down the other side. With each shot, the reaction from the crowd grew quieter. Dad had both hands behind his head now, fingers intertwined. Mom's hands were clasped under her chin. My fourth shot finally rested at the top of the plateau, though it didn't drop in the cup, and I finished with a five. Three over par.

A triple bogey. Any shot I might have had of winning this thing was gone. I stared at the ball sitting in the cup, knowing I had to pick it up and go on to the next hole, but I couldn't move. It felt like I was stuck to the green.

This was supposed to be my game.

In that moment, I wanted to vanish. To teleport back home, straight into the Cove, where there were no more downcast eyes, no more hanging heads, no more disappointed groans. I couldn't bring myself to look back at the fence, afraid of the looks on the faces I would find there.

I bent down and got my ball and stuck it in my pocket where my grandfather's nickel should have been. There was no luck in miniature golf.

This was all on me.

Angela Rauschbaum was ten years old and had pigtails that fell well past her shoulders. She wore a flowery rose-colored dress and had pink-banded braces to match. I'd congratulated her on an awesome birdie back on ten.

She overtook me after sixteen, ultimately snagging second place and two free rounds of golf. A kid named Jonathan Everholm finished in third, scoring the ten-dollar game card.

There was no prize for fourth place.

After the announcement of winners and runners-up, Jamie Tran stood by one of the wrought-iron tables next to his coach, accepting his prize from the owner of Fritz's and some corporate relations girl from Leroy McClucker's. Claire took their picture, presumably to post on Fritz's website. Then the PR girl requested a picture with all of the competitors. Jamie stood in the middle, beaming. I stood on the far end in the back, holding my certificate down by my side. I was right. They had printed enough for everybody.

Mom asked to see it, said she was going to put it on the fridge. She lassoed me with one arm, hugging me tight. Frank offered me a fist bump and the last of his gummy bears.

Dad said, "A lot of good shots out there." I wasn't sure he meant mine, even though I'd made a few—right up until I didn't. He didn't look disappointed, exactly, but his smile looked thin and forced, like it hurt. He patted me once on the back and said he'd go pull the car around.

Once he was gone, Frank leaned over, his bushy chin close to my cheek, his fruity gummy breath in my ear. "You did good today, kid."

But you know what being good gets you, I thought, remembering one of the first things Frank ever told me. I looked down at the certificate in my hand. Frank gently lifted my chin.

"We'll get 'em next time," he said.

Dad pulled up to the curb and honked the horn.

The whole drive home I waited for it. For him to ask me what happened out there. How I folded so fast. Five strokes on a par two. On a course that I'd been practicing on for a month. On a course that he *paid* someone to coach me to play.

What would I tell him? Do I tell him the truth? That I got frustrated? That I couldn't stay focused? That I was so afraid of losing that I lost?

Or do I tell him what the voice told me: that I just wasn't good enough?

He caught my eye in the rearview mirror as we pulled up to a stoplight. This was it. He would say something, and then Mom would get defensive and say something back, and the whole thing would go downhill from there. I squeezed Katana between my knees. *Here it comes.*

"Personally, I think Leroy McClucker's chicken is a little *too* greasy. Don't you?" He winked at me through the mirror.

Mom laughed. A little snort that probably came with a roll of her eyes.

And the knot in my stomach loosened just a little.

We made it all the way home without incident. No one said anything more about my fourth-place finish. Dad made it to the couch in time for the Bears to kick off. Mom insisted on magneting my certificate to the fridge. But I was still right. The fight was unavoidable.

It was just waiting until dinner.

It started with the tater tots. I asked Mom if she could make them crispy because the ones at school were always mushy little lumps of still half-frozen potato shreds, and Dad told her to broil them because that was the easiest way. Except she

230

forgot she'd turned the broiler on and they ended up burned on one side, still soggy on the other. We sat at the table with our canned green beans and our BLTs and our half-blackened tots, eating in silence until Dad said, "You should have set the timer."

A dark look crossed my mother's face. "I didn't see you making dinner," she shot back.

Dad held up one of his tots and frowned, like a jeweler inspecting a flawed diamond. "I'm just saying. You set the timer for two or three minutes to get one side crispy and then you flip them and crisp the other side. That way they don't burn."

My teeth clenched. There was only one way this could possibly end.

Mom put her sandwich back on her plate. Then she calmly raised the middle finger of her right hand.

"Flip this," she said.

I stared at Mom's finger for a moment, then glanced at Dad, waiting for the sigh. *Real mature, Nicole. Nice example to set for our son.* Somehow or other, I knew it would come around to me. I would be put in the middle.

Dad took in Mom's brandished finger with a nod, then wordlessly pierced one of his crunchy-soft, black-and-beige tots with his fork.

He pulled it back like a catapult.

He let it fly.

The tot hit my mother in the chest, leaving a grease mark on her red blouse before tumbling into her lap.

I stared, lips tight, eyes wide. Dad cocked his head to the side as if to say, *Now what?*

This was new territory. Before it was words. Always words. But Dad had picked a new kind of ammunition. Mom raised an eyebrow at him. Then she grabbed her fork, carefully stuck two tots on the tines, one right beside the other, and fired. One potato landed ineffectually in the tub of butter, but the second smacked Dad right in the glasses, smearing the left lens.

He didn't make a sound. Nobody made a sound. Neither of them smiled. I was afraid to even set my glass of milk back on the table—I just held it in both sweaty hands. Dad carefully removed his greasy glasses, clearing the smudge with his napkin, but as he did, I caught the sidelong glance, the dart of his eyes in my direction. Mom nodded ever so slightly, and I sensed what was happening, what was *about* to happen, but by then it was too late.

Tots flew at me from both directions, hitting my cheek and neck.

And then the air was suddenly filled with greasy, burned potato.

It was war.

The forkapults were quickly abandoned, as dinner instantly devolved into a full-out food fight, the three of us pelting each other with tots first, and then moving to the green beans, one of which somehow slunk down my shirt, leaving a wet, slimy trail. In my head a marine sergeant barked out orders: *Incoming! Get down! Fire! Fire!*

I went after both of them, careful not to aim for faces if I could help it, though I managed to accidentally get Dad in the nose with a green bean. He just gave me a wicked grin and tossed four tots at me rapid fire, all of them hitting home, bouncing off my chest. Food caromed off the table, smacked against the wall, dropped into our drinks as we ducked and dodged and laughed.

We laughed. Through the whole thing. Mom. Dad. I laughed so hard I couldn't breathe.

When it was finally over, Mom had shredded potato in her hair. There were bloodred streaks on the wall behind me, remnants of a tot that had been dabbed in ketchup before it was thrown. A green bean floated in Dad's iced tea. The battle had probably lasted only a minute, maybe two, but the carnage was total. We all three stared at the mess we'd made, our laughter thinning out, turning to sighs, the moment slipping away.

There was no indication who won. It didn't seem to matter for once.

Afterward we sat and finished our sandwiches quietly, which were pretty much the only things left on our plates worth eating. At one point, Dad told Mom the bacon was cooked perfectly.

I could tell he really meant it, and maybe she could too, but she gave him the finger again anyway.

The next morning, Dad came up to my room to deliver the news while I was feeding Jaws: there was another miniature golf tournament coming up in less than three weeks, this one actually sanctioned by the Junior Mini Golfers Association. It took place in Williams Bay, Wisconsin, only two hours away. First place was awarded three hundred dollars—in cash, not sandwiches—and an automatic bid to compete in the national tournament in the spring. "So whaddya think?"

I watched Jaws gobble up his little floating flakes, darting to the surface to grab one before diving back down, as if he was afraid to stay at the top too long. "I don't know. What do you think?" I asked back.

"Well, I thought yesterday went pretty well, minus a couple of bad breaks. And Frank said he'd be happy to keep going with the lessons. Plus this is kind of *it*, you know—the whole reason you practice. To get better and better and see just how far you can go. I mean the national tournament *would* be pretty cool." He paused, probably letting all of that sink in.

I kept watching Jaws. That fish never seemed to get full, and I felt bad for only giving him a pinch of food, but Mom warned me not to overfeed him. She said he would probably just eat himself to death. That he wouldn't know when to quit.

I glanced at Dad standing in the door. "So you're saying you think I should do it."

"Well, yeah," he said. "But it's not about what I think. You do what *you* want to do."

Don't worry about what he thinks. Do what I want. I didn't tell him that the first part was impossible, had always been impossible. Or that that it sometimes made the second part impossible too.

I just told him to mark it on the calendar. Exclamation points and all.

After every hole, Jamie Tran goes and talks to his coach, the stern-faced man with the thin mustache and crisp-looking clothes. He stands apart from all the other adults, and every time Jamie goes over, he seems to get an earful of advice. Sometimes two earfuls. Whatever his coach is telling him, it must be working. Tran rips through hole after hole, one- or two-putting each one, keeping his spot at the top of the leaderboard, just as uncatchable as the last time we met.

I'm guessing my coach is probably unconscious right now.

Even though I manage to squeak out a par on an incredibly tough hole thirteen, I make no headway, because Tran gets the same. But I keep going, because at least Mom is watching, and I need to show her that even when something seems impossible, you don't quit. You line up your next shot and you try again and see how far you go.

With the hope that, eventually, somehow, things will get better.

HOLE #14

Par 2

Two stone hazards stand in the way of a direct shot here, the first rock big enough to cast its shadow over its smaller sibling. Once you make it past the twins, the second half of the green consists of a long, uphill climb that finally levels out after fifteen feet. If you fail to make it past the rocks on your first try, it could be hard to recover and make par. Hard, but not impossible.

There was a little spot of dried ketchup on the wall that we'd missed, a reminder of flipped fingers and floating green beans. I didn't tell anyone about it, and I didn't wipe it off. I liked seeing it there. Like the picture of my parents on the beach, it made me smile. It was something to hang on to.

None of our other dinners were ever like that. Most were quiet. Some so quiet you could hear yourself swallow. But when you're afraid to say the wrong thing, quiet is better.

When it's quiet you can feel the tension. Sometimes it's like walking through an open, grassy field with a giant bomb sitting right in the middle. You can see it from a mile away, and you know if you touch it, it will blow, so you make the choice to go around. More often, though, it's a field littered with a hundred little mines, buried underground so you can only guess where they might be, and you don't know you've found one until it's too late.

Someone forgot to switch over the laundry.

Boom.

Someone forgot to pick something up after work.

Boom.

Someone didn't bother to call to have the pipe fixed and now there's a water stain on the ceiling.

Boom.

Someone never listens.

Someone always does this.

Someone can't admit when they've made a mistake.

When it triggers, the force of the explosion can be felt throughout the house.

The important thing was to step softly. To keep your eyes open and look for clues: the creased corners of mouths, the slanted, sideways looks. To not step on anything, or spill anything, or say or do *anything* to make things worse. Because if you trigger one mine, it might trigger the rest, causing a chain reaction that brings the whole place down.

I tanked my math test.

Nearly a week after the tournament at Fritz's.

And not just a C minus kind of tanking, but a full-out 55 percent failure. I'm not sure how. I'd always earned As or Bs in math before, but for some reason, this one unit threw me. I nearly cried when I got it back. Mr. Caudill calmed me down after class. He said he knew it was a fluke, and that I could easily make it up, but I still had to get the test signed by my parents. School policy. I thought about just forging their signature, but they probably would discover it eventually; all our grades were posted online. Better if I was up-front about it. But I was still afraid.

Dad didn't explode when I showed him at dinner. Not at first. He frowned, though, which was enough. More than enough.

"I know you can do better, bub," he said, but in such a way that *can* really meant *will*. Starting immediately.

I spent the next two hours at the dining room table with him leaning over my shoulder, going over the test problem by problem. His hovering made me nervous and I started making silly mistakes, misadding numbers or forgetting the order of operations. After the fifth or sixth miscalculation, Dad's tone shifted, his patience gone.

"Focus, Malcolm. I know you can do this. You're not concentrating."

"I'm trying," I mumbled. My eyes found the splotch of ketchup on the wall in the corner. Someone who didn't know better might think it was marker or paint or maybe dried blood. I could feel Dad's hands on the back of my chair, knuckles brushing the hairs of my neck.

"Well, you're obviously not trying hard enough," he said.

Mom appeared from the kitchen, rubbing her neck, looking exhausted.

"How many problems do you have left?" she asked, her voice strained, her eyes only on me. I held up three fingers. She bit her lip, and I could see she was doing some mental calculations of her own. Finally she said, "Okay. How about you go on upstairs and get ready for bed and I'll help you with the last three in the morning before I leave for work."

It wasn't a question. It wasn't a suggestion. It was an order. She was setting me free.

I couldn't see Dad's face, but I could still sense him standing behind me. I counted to five in my head, waiting for something—the sigh, the comeback, the counter-order—but Dad stayed quiet. I gently closed my math book and set my test on top of it, the 55 percent circled at the top, calling attention to my failure. The sound of the chair scraping against the laminate floor made me cringe. I didn't dare look at him. Either of them.

Go softly. Watch where you step. Don't say anything.

I made it to the foot of the stairs before it started.

"Why do you have to do that?" Dad's voice. Hurt. Frustrated.

"Do what?" Mom's voice. Tired. Short.

"Undermine me like that. Make me seem like some kind of ogre when *I'm* the one trying to help him."

"Yelling at him is not helping him."

"I wasn't yelling at him."

"Yelling at me is not helping either."

"I'm not yelling!"

Up the stairs to my door. I paused, one hand on the knob.

"Maybe if you didn't push so hard, I wouldn't *have* to say anything."

"Come on, Nicole. You and I both know I'm not asking him to do anything he's not perfectly capable of. There's no reason he should fail a math test. He's good at math. He's a smart kid."

"You don't need to tell *me* how smart he is. *I* know how smart he is."

"What's that supposed to mean?"

"Nothing. Forget it."

"No. Tell me. What did I do this time?"

"I said forget it. I don't want to fight about this right now. Not again."

"Who's fighting? *I* don't see what the problem is. I don't see what's wrong with wanting Michael to work to his full potential."

Silence.

The quiet only lasted a few seconds, but it felt longer. I held my breath, waiting, not sure I'd heard right, pretty sure I couldn't have. But I had. Because Mom heard it too.

"Malcolm," she said.

"What?"

"You said Michael." Her voice was softer now, almost too soft to hear.

"Well, obviously you knew who I meant," Dad said quickly. "Let's not turn this into something it's not."

"No. We certainly wouldn't want to do that."

There was another pause, and then I heard Mom's steps moving down the hall, coming toward the stairs. I ducked into my room and quietly shut the door, then retreated to the Cove, dropping into one of the beanbag chairs, hands in fists, fists tucked under my arms, repeating the name Dad had let slip. Asking the question that Mom hadn't bothered to ask, maybe because she knew the answer already.

Who on Earth was Michael?

I waited until the next day to ask. It was a Friday, so I knew Mom and I would have a couple of hours alone after school. Better to ask only one of them, just in case.

Last night the name had put an end to the argument, but Dad had still gone to sleep on the couch with the television on—I could hear it through the floorboards—which meant it wasn't really over. Which meant it wasn't something I wanted to bring up with both of them in the room.

I managed to make it through the school day, spending more minutes than usual staring out the window waiting for the last bell to ring, and held it in until we'd pulled out of the parent pickup line on our way to the library. I thought I could at least wait until we'd checked out our books and gotten to the park, where we were supposed to read them under a canopy of red and gold, but I barely made it to the first red light.

"Who's Michael?"

I watched Mom's expression carefully: she blinked four

times as if waking up. The light turned green, but she just sat there, staring straight ahead. I was about to say something when the car behind us honked; Mom shook her head and mashed down on the gas, darting through the intersection with a screech.

She glanced at me, frowning. "Who told you about Michael?"

"Last night. I overheard you," I admitted. "Dad said the name Michael, and then you two just sort of stopped arguing."

"We weren't arguing."

I waited for her to look at me again.

"Okay. Yes. We were arguing. But I didn't think you heard us."

"I hear you all the time," I said.

Mom frowned. I could tell she was having a conversation in her head, deciding how to approach this. I can usually tell when someone else is talking to themselves. She quickly changed lanes, then took a sharp turn into a shopping center.

"Where are we going?" We were nowhere near the library.

"If we are going to talk about this, I'm either going to need a cigarette or some ice cream," Mom said. "And neither of us needs to be smoking."

Five minutes later, we sat in the Wendy's parking lot with the windows down, Frosties in hand. Mom was a shoveler, digging with her spoon. I was a sucker, even though it took some effort getting the thick shake up the straw. I waited for her to talk first. I was good at that.

"Okay," she said finally, setting her empty cup down and swiveling to face me. "Michael . . ." Deep breath. "Michael's your brother."

The word gut-punched me, taking my breath away. Impossible. She was lying. I didn't have a brother. It had always just been us. Mom, Dad, and me. There were pictures of the two of them, of all of us, of just me, but never more than three. "I'm confused."

"I know . . . it's a doozy. But that's the truth. He would have turned fourteen just last week," Mom continued. "He would have started high school next year, in fact, which is just . . . just so *strange* to think about. Except, he didn't, obviously. He couldn't. Because . . ." She took another yoga breath, clearly doing her best to hold it together. "Your brother was premature. You know what that means, don't you?"

I nodded. It meant he'd been born too early, before he was ready.

"He was six weeks early, which is a lot, but there were other things. Complications. There was something wrong with his lungs. He had difficulty breathing. And he had a heart defect."

"Defect?"

Mom cleared her throat. Stumbled through her words. "His heart . . . it hadn't formed quite right. So the doctors kept him in a special room, in this special enclosure, so they could treat him and monitor him, you know. But he was too small, too weak for surgery. So we could only wait and hope that he would get better."

"But he didn't," I whispered.

Mom shook her head, sniffed. "No. No, he didn't. He lived for seventeen days. Seventeen days and never left the hospital. Never even left that room." Her voice started to shake, which made my own throat tighten. "But your father and I still got to see him and talk to him and sing to him. We got to sit next to him and watch his tiny fingers make tiny little fists. And then, at the end, we were allowed to hold him . . . you know . . . to say goodbye."

One of Mom's hands covered her mouth, trapping some sound before it could get out. I reached out and grabbed the other one, squeezing it as hard as I could.

"He never came home. We never got to show him the crib your father built or give him his first bath. We never got to eat ice cream with him or build Legos with him or teach him how to ride a bike. We didn't get to do any of those things. Not with him." She smeared her tears on the back of her free hand.

"I'm sorry," I said.

"Are you kidding? You of all people have nothing to be sorry about. Nobody has anything to be sorry for, but least of all you."

Because of course I wasn't there. I wasn't born yet. I didn't even know about him until just now. But I still felt sorry.

"I know. I blamed myself for so long. When you have a child, the moment you see him, you suddenly feel this . . . this *weight*. It's not a bad thing, but it's there, this overwhelming need to protect him, to *fight* for him, and I just *couldn't*. I couldn't do anything. I couldn't even hug him. My own kid. My baby. I could only watch. And it made me mad . . . *God*, it pissed me off. But also, just sort of broken, you know? Like there was this giant crack, right down the center of me."

I looked at her: my mother who was broken, or had been broken once. I felt myself break a little. "What about Dad?"

Mom wiped her eyes again. "Your father was just as devastated. But he . . ." She hesitated. "We're very different. He wanted to fix it, to make it better, the only way he knew how. Within a couple of months, he was ready to try again, but I just wasn't. I just couldn't. I was afraid. What if it happened again? I couldn't bear the thought."

And yet, here I was, sitting next to her, holding her hand. She must have seen the look on my face. "Yeah, well. Eventually he convinced me," she sob-laughed. "And I'm so glad he did. Because we had you. And you're perfect."

Mom looked at me with a quivering smile. It was too much. I had to look down. I wasn't perfect. Not even close. But in that moment I wanted to be. Like Dad, I wanted to fix things. To make them better. "Do you still think about him?" I asked.

"Of course. Even though I hardly even got to know him, I still miss him. Especially now. This time of year."

Michael would have turned fourteen last week. That's what she said. We would have been celebrating his birthday. He would have gotten to make a wish.

So many would-haves. In another two years he would have

been driving me around, taking me to the movies, telling me what music to listen to and what kinds of clothes to wear. Maybe it would have been him and not Mom who taught me how to whistle. And how long you could hold an Oreo in milk before it crumbled in your fingers and dropped to the bottom of the glass. He could have taught me how to ride a skateboard. He could have taught me my first cuss word. He would have been older and stronger and faster and wiser than me.

I would have called him Mike. Or Mikey. Or just big brother.

Everything would have been so different.

I tried to add it all up in my head. One hundred thumb-wrestling contests. Two hundred Mario Kart races. At least a dozen pillow fights and Nerf gun wars in the backyard. I could have asked him about zits. About growing up. About being weird and feeling out of place. About how to make friends and how to keep them. About how to stop worrying so much about what other people think. About what to do when Mom and Dad started to fight.

I could have talked to him about everything, instead of talking to myself.

I wondered if that was what Dad thought too, every time he looked at me. If he thought about the things he never got to do with his other kid, the one who came first. Maybe Michael would have loved baseball. Maybe he would have been a runner. Maybe he would have known how good the Pittsburgh

Steelers were. Maybe he would have been left-handed.

Maybe.

I looked down at my empty cup. "Is that why you and Dad fight so much?"

"We don't . . . ," Mom started to say, but she stopped herself. "I don't know. Probably not. Your father and I have always had our differences. But going through that . . . it changed us. It changed the way we look at each other sometimes. And I think it changes how we both look at you. It's not fair, I know, but it's true. I'm just so thankful to have you, but your father . . . he wants to give you the world, Malcolm. He wants you to see everything, be everything, do everything."

"And what do you want?"

"I just want you to be happy," she said.

She looked at me, her hazel eyes full of tears and expectation. I knew what she needed to hear, and I knew that sometimes you say those things, even if they're not entirely true.

"I'm happy," I said.

Mom smiled. I could tell she didn't believe me. "We should have told you. We were waiting for the right moment. But I guess there really is no right moment. Some things are just hard no matter what."

I leaned across the seat and rested my head against her arm, staring out the window at the passing cars. "The ice cream helps."

"Yes," she said, stroking my hair. "It does a little."

We sat quietly, leaning into each other, me thinking about

all the things I missed out on, wondering if she was thinking the same.

Jamie Tran is still in the lead. Unstoppable. Looking a little like a miniature Terminator with his sunglasses and spiky hair.

I catch him out of the corner of my eye, coming up behind as I'm placing my ball on fourteen. We haven't said a word to each other all day. I'm not even sure he recognizes me from the competition at Fritz's. I'm not famous; I don't have my own Instagram account devoted to my mini golf career. I've only got the one club.

It's not just me, though. He avoids everyone. The other junior golfers gather between holes to complain about lip outs or bad banks, compliment each other on nice shots, or whine about annoying parents who cheer too loud and embarrass them. But not Jamie. He sinks his putt, pumps one fist, and then goes straight to his coach.

He doesn't even look at me now, even though he's less than five feet away, trailing his bag behind him. But just as he's over my right shoulder, I hear a whisper.

You can't win.

I spin around. "What?"

Jamie looks at me, startled. "Huh?" It's the first word he's ever spoken to me. His voice is soft. Unassuming.

"What did you say?"

Jamie shakes his head. "I didn't say anything," he mumbles, then shuffles away.

I know he's right. I know that it wasn't him, but I can't help it. I look at him and I can't help but wonder if things would be different if I were more like him.

If you had to choose between Malcolm Greeley and Jamie Tran, who would you pick? What if there was a better version of me who never got the chance to show the world how good he was? What if I was born a runner-up?

What if I'm just not good enough? What if I never will be?

HOLE #15

Par 2

Another rocky outing; the field of solid stone hazards scattered at seemingly random intervals across the green like a Plinko game makes planning your route a necessity on this frustrating par two. Only a carefully orchestrated series of banks can lead to a hole in one.

Alternatively, you could just say a prayer, hit the ball hard, and watch it pinball unpredictably off the rocks. Maybe you'll get lucky and your ricocheting ball will find the hole. Just don't be surprised when it doesn't.

The next day I found myself in the car headed to Williams Bay to get a little on-site practice in. It was Frank's idea. "You can't play the course unless you know the course, and you can't know the course until you've played it." This sounded like convoluted logic. But it was also Frank, so I did what I usually did and just nodded along.

There were only three of us. Dad drove. Frank rode in the passenger seat. I had the back to myself. Mom stayed behind; she said she wanted to get the garage cleaned out before the weather changed, but I suspected she just wanted to be by herself. I could tell by the extra-long hug she gave me before we left that our conversation from the day before was still on her mind. Mine too. Now that I knew about him, I couldn't get Michael out of my head.

Dad didn't mention it. I was pretty sure she told him. She must have. I'd heard them having a discussion behind their closed bedroom door late into the night, their voices just loud enough for me to know they were talking but not loud enough for me to make out what they said, even standing right outside with my ear pressed to the wall. Some days I could make out every word from half a house away, but this wasn't that kind of talk. He didn't say a thing about it to me in the morning over breakfast or on our way to pick up Frank, and I didn't ask. It had gone unspoken for twelve years. It could stay that way awhile longer.

We drove north with the windows down and the radio off. I sat in the back, eating peanut butter–filled pretzels and texting Lex pictures of the changing trees—a collage of yellows, oranges, and pinks—while Frank and Dad reminisced over their high school days: pranks they pulled, teachers they despised, friends they'd forgotten, and awkward first dates. It was clear that Frank Sanderson and Matthew Greeley remembered those years differently. Every time Dad mentioned something he'd done on the baseball diamond—which was every ten minutes or so—I expected Frank to counter with some story of his success on the golf course, the kind of "oh yeah, well get this" bragging I overheard all the time at school. But Frank didn't take the bait. Maybe because he thought there was no way he could compete. Or maybe because he didn't care. The closest he got was when Dad proclaimed that high school was the best, and Frank replied, "For some of us, maybe."

Eventually the crackle-leafed trees lining the highway were replaced by quaint stores advertising souvenir knickknacks and fresh-baked sweets, until finally we saw a brightly painted sign that said *Putter's Paradise* with the equally vibrant picture of a toucan on it. A tropical bird in the middle of Wisconsin. No different from a brontosaurus in Illinois, I guess. "We're here," Dad said.

I pulled myself out of the car, one foot tingly from falling asleep, and froze, leaning against the door.

"Wow."

We definitely weren't at Fritz's anymore. There were no giant potholes in the parking lot. No broken lampposts. No overflowing trash cans. No cheesy alligator statues. There was no arcade. No go-karts. No ticket exchange for cheap plastic prizes. The whole place was devoted to miniature golf.

The course was just as impressive. There were no rickety windmills or loop-de-loops. There was no giant toadstool sitting in the middle of worn fake grass. There were no rusty letters to push your ball through or torn-up pieces of turf in the middle of the green that you had to avoid. There was just one course at Putter's Paradise, and it was pristine, lined with thick ropes and wooden posts that made me think of pirate ships. All the hazards were natural, real rocks and logs that stood like sentinels in the middle of the greens. Evergreens provided patches of shade and meticulously manicured hedges guided you from hole to hole. The only thing that seemed unnatural was the too-blue stream trickling from the center waterfall and running under a wooden bridge. That, and the bank of vending machines lining the back fence. Pepsi again. And Powerade.

"It's beautiful," I said.

"It's no Pebble Beach, but it will do," Frank said. "Lots of hills. Lots of curves. This is what a real miniature golf course looks like. Not all of that little kiddie stuff."

I frowned at that. I kind of liked the kiddie stuff. I liked hitting my ball through the barn door and hearing it strike the cowbell as it exited. I liked that there was a rocket ship at Fritz's that you could pretend to ride. There was something quirky about the run-down props and haggard greens. On second glance, this place was almost *too* perfect. The grass was so green and thick, I was afraid to step on it.

"Maybe this isn't such a good idea," I said, meaning the tournament. Meaning driving all the way out here. Meaning a lot of things.

"Looks expensive," Dad replied.

Frank had a different response. He reached into the pocket of his joggers and produced a tape measure. "Do me a favor, Malcolm. Go over to that hole over there and measure how far it is across." He pointed to the first on the course, a down-hill with just one stone hazard blocking the way.

I stepped hesitantly onto the green and knelt down, spanning the hole's width with the tape measure, trying not to think about how silly I looked. "Just over four inches," I said.

"Four and a quarter," Frank replied. I looked again. Four and a quarter exactly. "I believe you'll find that is the exact same as the size of the holes back in Falls Point." Frank stared at me, waiting. "Oh c'mon, kid. *Hoosiers*? Gene Hackman? The Huskers?" I shook my head. I had no idea what he was talking about. Frank turned to my father in desperation. "You've never shown this kid *Hoosiers*?"

"Malcolm doesn't really like basketball," Dad answered. "Or movies about basketball. Or movies about most sports, actually."

I wasn't sure I'd ever *seen* a movie about basketball, but even not knowing what the heck a Hoosier was, I got the point. The greens at Putter's Paradise might look different, but the goal was the same: get the ball in the cup. It should fit just fine.

"So are we going to play this thing or just measure it?" Dad asked.

"Sure, but I'm a little short on cash," Frank said.

Dad didn't look surprised. Annoyed. But not surprised.

We made a threesome the first time around. We didn't officially keep score, but Frank said he was keeping track in his head and that I beat them both. The second time I played by myself while Dad snapped pictures and Frank took notes in a little spiral notebook. Later, Frank said, we could print out the pictures and use a marker to trace the best approach. It felt like we were a team of anthropologists cataloguing the remnants of some lost civilization.

Hole #3: Bank off the right.
Hole #8: Beware of frogs.
Hole #14: Hit it a little harder than you think you need to.

By the time we finished, it was late in the afternoon. The three of us stood on the edge of the course, admiring its emerald slopes and cobblestone walkways, its picturesque bridges and artificially colored streams. I felt a prickle of excitement mixed with a surge of pure terror. In one week I would be competing right here against other members of the Junior Mini Golf Association. I wondered if this was how Dad felt when he took the mound back in his pitching days. Did he ever get butterflies beforehand? Did the fans cheering in the stands make him nervous or just give him an adrenaline rush? Was he ever afraid to throw a pitch? Worried that he would give up the big hit that would cost him the game?

I didn't have to ask, though, because I already knew what he'd say: that it didn't matter if he was scared or not. His team was counting on him; he couldn't let them down. You show up, you do your job, you get the win. Simple.

Dad threw his arm around me as we looked across eighteen

holes. "I know you are totally going to *own* this course," he said.

I knew he was only trying to make me feel better.

I wondered if *he* knew it wasn't working.

On the way back from Paradise, Frank suggested stopping for dinner. There was a place called Romero's about an hour out of town, made the best Chicago-style pizza. "Crust full of butter and big chunks of tomatoes camped out on top and so much cheese you won't be able to poop for a *week*." It sounded good to me. Dad said we could just wait and eat at home.

"Ritz and Cheez Whiz it is," Frank said with fake enthusiasm.

By the time we dropped him off—at his rust-fenced apartment complex with its dented dumpster—it was well past dinner, but Dad said he still had one more stop to make. We drove to the mall in the center of town and parked outside the two-story sporting goods store. I'd gotten my first mitt at this store nearly four years ago. "Do I have to come in?" I asked.

"Yeah. It really shouldn't take long, but you never know."

I stayed on Dad's heels as we walked by the shoes and weights and racks of sweat-wicking shirts. Dad strode right past the baseball section with its rows of bats hanging like swords in some medieval armory, not even glancing at the display of new gloves sitting on the endcap. Normally he would have wanted to stop and admire them, touch them, smell them. Not this time.

He led me to the counter in the golf supply section. The kid working there was fiddling with his phone behind the counter. "Can I help you?" he asked, finally looking up.

I had no idea why we were there. Dad had already made it clear that you don't need more than one putter, even though Jamie Tran had three.

"Yeah. I've got a special order ready for pickup," Dad said. "The name's Greeley."

The counter clerk consulted his computer and rummaged through a cabinet, finally coming up with a small box no bigger than a carton of Girl Scout cookies, sleek black with fancy silver lettering. It reminded me of Putter's Paradise: elegant and professional. In other words, not something I was used to.

"You want a bag for that?" the clerk asked.

"Not necessary," Dad said. He grabbed the box and headed back for the exit with me trailing behind.

"What was that about? What's in the box?" I asked, but Dad ignored me until we were back in the car. Before I could even buckle my seat belt, he handed it over.

"Go ahead. Open it," he said.

"What is it?" My palms were sweating already.

"Just open it."

The lid slid off with a satisfying whisper.

Inside were golf balls. Three of them. Each in its own little foam nest, snugly cuddled side by side. All of them pumpkin orange, and all with my name on them. My first name, not just my initials. Printed in regal-looking blue letters, all caps.

I pulled one out of its nest and held it up to the vanishing sunlight.

"The guy at the store said these were the best for pure putting. I know that the pros probably use different ones for different situations, but they at least have to be better than the cheap ones you get at Fritz's."

I turned the golf ball around and around, fixed between thumb and finger, spinning it like a globe, watching the letters pass by with each revolution. MALCOLM.

I set it gently back into place next to its siblings. They fit so perfectly. All three of them. Together.

"Wow," I said.

"These are especially designed for artificial turf," Dad continued. "The dimpling's different from a regular golf ball. And something about the core composition. I don't know. I didn't quite understand everything the guy was saying, but I figured, what the hey—try 'em, and if they don't work, we'll turn them into Christmas ornaments or something. So how about it, bub? You like 'em?"

I stared into the box, trying to figure out how to say what I wanted to say. Right there, right then, sitting in the car with this unexpected gift in my lap, this unexpected and wonderful gift, I wanted to talk. To open up about everything. About miniature golf and baseball. About him and Mom. About Michael. About me. I wanted to ask him if he was happy, and if not, if there was anything I could do to make things better.

Anything at all. Because I would do it. Or at least I would try.

But even with all of that bottled up inside, all I managed was "I love them. Thank you."

"I'm glad," Dad said. He started the car but took one last look into the box himself. "Not my *favorite* color, honestly, but at least nobody's gonna grab your balls by mistake."

Dad turned to me and winked.

And I laughed. Because it was better than crying, which, for reasons I only half understood, I also wanted to do.

That night Lex called, all excited. "I have something to tell you."

I was glad to hear her voice. I had a lot to tell her too, though I wasn't sure I could tell her everything. Or that I should.

"Are you ready? Listen carefully, here it comes. . . . Is it crazy how saying sentences backwards creates backwards sentences saying how crazy it is?"

"Um . . . ," I said.

"You don't get it?" Lex scoffed. "It's a palindrome. Except made with words instead of letters. I found it online and now it's kind of my new favorite sentence." She said it again, slower this time so I could fully appreciate it.

"That's pretty awesome," I admitted.

"I know, right? A whole lot better than *taco cat*."

Our friendship had evolved from proprietary eponyms to palindromes over the last week or so, ever since I brought up

Frank's T-shirt. I was right. She loved them. Her favorite was rotator, which, when rotated, spelled rotator. But now she had a new favorite.

"I got your pictures, by the way. How was Wisconsin?"

I told her about Putter's Paradise. How pristine the grounds were. How real the grass looked. How much harder the course seemed. "They have sand traps with actual sand in them."

"Can't wait to see it," she said.

I sort of froze in my beanbag chair. "What?"

"The tournament. It's next weekend, right? I was hoping you could give me a ride."

She wanted to come. Of course she did. She'd missed the last one. I started talking quickly, Lex-like. "Honestly, I wouldn't worry about it. The course is almost two hours away, which means we're going to have to leave early in the morning, and I know you usually spend Saturdays with your mom. Plus there are more golfers this time, so it will probably take forever. A lot of time just standing around, twirling our clubs. Even I'm going to be bored." I knew I was just parroting her own words back at her. I wondered if I'd overdone it.

Lex went quiet for a moment. Then she said, "Malcolm, if you don't want me to come, just say so."

"No, it's not that. It's just . . . I don't want to make a big deal out of it, you know?"

Which was true. It was already in all caps on the calendar. I didn't tell her the other reason I didn't want her there, the

262

real reason: That I had seen her dance, and it was perfect. That I'd heard the crowd go wild and been a part of her standing ovation. That there was no way I could ever match something like that.

There was already enough pressure.

Lex didn't say anything. I could sense her dissecting my excuses, trying to decide whether to push it or let it go. I needed a diversion, a change of subject. "Okay. Forget taco cat. Taco cats are lame," I said. "But what about a *dog god*?"

For a moment I thought she was going to push harder, to insist on coming, or at least insist on knowing why I didn't want her there; Lex wasn't the kind of person who flinched at finding the truth. But she decided to let me off the hook.

"The Egyptians had one of those, you know. A dog god. His name was Anubis. He was the god of mummification and embalming. Have you ever read a description of embalming? It's pretty sick."

We spent the next twenty minutes wondering how it would feel to have your brains tweezed out through your nose and deciding what sized Tupperwares you'd need to store all your organs when you died. She didn't mention the tournament again, and neither did I, which I hoped meant I hadn't hurt her feelings. Though sometimes it was hard to tell with her; for as much as she talked, she still kept a lot to herself.

We had that in common too.

🌑 🌑 🌑

Grace Xin's ball takes a wrong turn, her decision to go left coming back to haunt her as her shot rebounds off the wrong face of a rock and comes rolling right back, resting a foot away from the tee. I can see the disappointment in her sagging shoulders. The frustration in how she holds her club. I want to say something, to tell her that it will be okay, that she can recover, but if she's anything like me, she doesn't want to hear it. Not right now. So I keep my mouth shut. She plays it safe, giving up on making par and concentrating on not making another mistake. She finishes with a four, dropping her in the overall standings.

Golf is a game of choices. And each choice contributes to the path. And each path represents a hundred other paths you *didn't* take. And those paths start to multiply—a hundred times a hundred times a hundred—until it's hard to know where you might have gone wrong, what you might have done differently. Especially with all those obstacles in your way—the rocks and the water hazards and the sand traps, put there just to lead you astray.

Apparently, I choose wisely, remembering the picture of hole fifteen folded with the rest in Mom's purse, the bright red arrow predicting the path I should take. I bank it off the right siderail and then off the third stone, right in the sweet spot, just the angle I need for my monogrammed ball to drop for a hole in one.

I turn and wave to Mom, who is literally jumping up and down, pumping her fist. She never got this excited during three full summers of baseball. It's much more the kind of thing that Dad would do if he was here. But he made a choice too.

He loves me. I know that. Some days, I wonder if maybe he loves me too much. I wonder if it hurts him to love me on days like that.

And he loves her too. Maybe not in the same way he loves me. Maybe not even in the same way as before, but he does. In a way that just can't be stashed away in the top of a closet or packed into a duffel bag. You don't stop loving someone because it gets hard, do you? When that happens, can't you just learn to love them harder?

Can't you at least show up?

HOLE #16

Par 2

Known as "The Fountain," this highly challenging yet beautiful par two starts narrow and then expands to accommodate its primary hazard: the three-tiered fountain at the hole's center. There is no fear of soaking your ball unless you happen to have switched your putter for a pitching wedge. However, the bubbling ivory tower does force you to go around, making banking a necessity.

You can always drop a penny in the fountain if you're feeling lucky. Just don't waste it wishing for a hole in one.

The Wednesday before the tournament in Wisconsin, I had my last lesson with Frank.

The night everything fell apart.

Mom dropped me off and Frank met me by the door, like always. This time he and Mom actually talked, though it was only the small kind. How are you? How's Matt? Enjoying the cooldown in the weather? How are lessons going? My own conversations with Mom had been a lot like that the last few days too: How was school? Did you get your homework done? Did you remember to put on deodorant? Have you talked to Lex lately? Two-minute conversations followed by an hour of interim silence.

The whole house had been quiet, in fact, Mom and Dad keeping their distance. If he was in the family room, she was outside. If he went upstairs, she came and read on the couch.

Once, when she was playing the piano and I was sitting in the papasan listening, Dad appeared in the entryway, hands in his pockets. Mom had her back to him, but I saw him, saw the look on his face. It wasn't the look he gave her in the picture sitting on the piano. This time he just looked lost, like he couldn't remember what he came in the room for. He left without a word.

There hadn't been any shouting, but I could still sense the mines scattered everywhere—enough to make me walk through the house on tiptoes. Enough to make me appreciate being here, at Fritz's, where the traps were much easier to spot.

We passed the concessions stand but Frank didn't even slow down. He was popping antacids like they were Pez. "Shopping mall hot dogs are not to be trusted," he informed me. I added that kernel of wisdom to the list.

We spent the first half hour sitting at our table—the one with the faded but still visible blue slushy stain underneath—reviewing notes from our scouting trip, examining the pictures Dad had printed out for each hole, tracing the optimal paths from tee to cup with red marker. I tried to remember the contours in the turf, the banks and drops, the little things that made each hole different, but it was a lot to process. I could draw every hole of the Red Course at Fritz's down to the dents in the rusted metal siding, but I'd only been to Putter's Paradise once.

When we finished going over the eighteenth and final hole,

Frank tidied the papers and handed the stack to me. "Look 'em over before bed, but don't just memorize them . . . visualize them. Pretend like you're there."

I was good at pretending. "Then I'll be ready?" I asked.

"Ready enough," Frank said.

I realized that wasn't the right question and tried again. "I mean, do you think I can win?"

Frank scratched at his armpit. "You want me to be honest?"

At that moment I realized you always *want* someone to be honest until they *ask* you if you want them to be honest. Then you realize you probably shouldn't have asked. But it was too late now. I nodded.

"Okay . . . and I'm being honest, here . . . you *can* win. Definitely. You see the angles, you've got a smooth stroke. But it's not always up to you, is it? If life has taught me anything, it's that no matter how good you are, there's always somebody better."

"Like Jamie Tran?"

"Like Ernie Els," Frank countered.

"Tiger Woods," I said, exhausting my repertoire.

"Rich Somersby."

I'd never heard of Rich Somersby. "Another golfer?"

"Danielle's new fiancé," Frank replied. "He's a podiatrist. They met over a bunion and now they're apparently getting married."

I could tell by the sour look on Frank's face that he wasn't a fan of Rich Somersby. I rested my chin on the table and looked out at the pink horizon. "Okay, but what if I *have* to win?"

Frank gave me a sideways look that said *Why?* And I gave him a look back that I hoped contained all the answers: Because I'd actually come pretty close last time. Because I'd seen the top of Dad's closet and heard Mom play the piano. Because for the first time in my life, I'd found something that I liked *and* was good at.

But mostly it was because I wanted to make things better. Because I wanted to do one thing that might make everybody forget about all the other things that made them unhappy, even if it was only for a day. One day to remind them of how good it could be.

That's what I hoped the look said.

Frank leaned back on the bench, hands on his head. "Wanna guess how many tournaments I won in college?"

I shrugged. I really wasn't in the mood for guessing games, but Frank gave me the answer, making an *O* with his fingers.

"Wait. None?"

"Zilch," he said.

I knew he was only trying to make me feel better. "No way. You're lying. Dad said you were nationally ranked. Like, the nine-hundreth-best golfer in the world." You don't become ranked, even nine hundredth in the world, without winning *something*.

Frank snorted. "Actually, *that* was the lie. I just made the whole ranking thing up. He said you needed a coach and remembered that I played golf in college, so I embellished a bit. Twenty bucks is twenty bucks, kid."

So Frank had padded his résumé to land a gig coaching me at miniature golf. Not a huge surprise. But I still couldn't quite believe he'd never won a tournament. "But you're good. I've seen you putt. And you got to play against Ernie Els. *The* Ernie Els. Or was that a lie too?"

"Nope. That part's true," Frank confirmed. "But it wasn't a competition; it was just a charity event at school. There were dozens of other golfers there, and he smoked the whole lot of us. The truth is I was just barely good enough at golf to get a scholarship and make the team. I was never good enough to win. Not when it counted."

I squinted at him across the table. "Why are you telling me this?"

"Because I want you to know that *I* know what it's like. For the longest time it drove me crazy. I'd wake up at four in the morning and go to the driving range. I'd practice my putting in the dorm hallway while my buddies were out partying. I obsessed over it. I busted my butt to get better, but I still couldn't win, no matter how hard I tried. Then, at some point, I realized I was chasing the sun."

I gave Frank my what-the-heck-are-you-talking-about look. That was one look he was used to by now.

"Okay. Imagine there's a road that goes clear across the middle of the Earth, sort of like the equator," Frank began, paving the air in front of him with one hand. "You're on this road, sitting in your car, and you see the sun making its way across the sky above you, and you think, 'Know what? I'm going to catch that sucker.' So you race down the road at full speed, staying right behind it, following it as it makes its way around the globe. You drive all day, and then the next day, and then the next day, except there really are no days because you're right on the sun's tail, see? You don't let it out of your sight. And you're exhausted by now. You keep chasing it and chasing it and chasing it, but you never catch it. Because it never stops. It just keeps going, around and around and around." Frank made circles with his hands.

I made a circle with my eyes. "That's ridiculous," I said. "The Earth spins at a thousand miles an hour. No car can go that fast. And even if you could, you'd run out of gas within hours and be forced to stop anyway."

"And then what would you see?" Frank asked.

I thought about it for a moment. "I don't know. The sunset, I guess?"

Frank popped another wintergreen Tums and smiled.

The gears in my head turned, thinking back to the first time we'd met, me nervously drumming my fingers against my bedsheet, him squeezed into my desk chair, telling me what golf felt like, how perfect it was. The dew on grass. The whistle of wind as the ball flew over the trees. It wasn't the weight of the trophy in your hands or the year-long supply of greasy chicken sandwiches. It was just being there, in the moment, doing what he loved.

"But what if you're afraid to stop?" I asked.

He shrugged. "Like you said: you'll run out of gas eventually. Play the game, kid. Just make sure you're playing it for the right reasons." Frank slapped his knees and stood up. "Ready for tonight's lesson?" He didn't even give me a chance to answer; he vanished through the door and back into the arcade, leaving me at the table alone, thinking about what he'd said. About chasing the sun.

I watched as a family of four came outside and selected their putters: a mother and father and what looked like twins, maybe first or second grade. The girls had the same hairstyle and wore the same shirt—white with a big red ladybug stitched on it. The clubs they chose were almost as tall as they were.

I wondered if one of them was better than the other at miniature golf. And if so, what was the other one better at? Drawing? Doing cartwheels? Math? One of them would always have an edge. One of them would learn how to blow a bubble first; would that make the other one jealous? Would they have different taste in music? Would they go to the same college just to be close to each other? Their parents would probably love them equally, but would they love them *differently*?

Suddenly, I had an overwhelming urge to be home, curled up on the couch between Mom and Dad. It didn't matter what was on TV. It could even be a baseball game, just so long as they were both there beside me. I looked over at the clock hanging above the entry to the arcade to see how close it was to eight.

That's when I saw Frank. Or some version of Frank. He was wearing a black cape and a hard plastic mask, the kind you might get as part of a cheap Halloween costume. He still had on his blue sweatpants and green T-shirt, but from the neck up he had transformed. Into Darth Vader.

"Um. Are you okay?" I asked as he approached the table, walking more purposefully than usual. He stopped by the rack of clubs to snag a putter—one with a red handle—then came and stood right in front of me. From behind the mask I could hear him breathing heavily, but he often breathed like that.

"The Force is with you, young Skywalker," he said, making his voice deeper than usual. "But you are not a Jedi yet."

I pointed at his cape, which was so long that it dragged on the ground. "Is that a bedsheet?"

Frank held the putter down by the head, pointing its red rubber grip at me. "You are unwise to lower your defenses," he said.

He raised his putter menacingly as if he was really going to hit me with it, and I scrambled for Katana, which was leaning against the table, barely grabbing it in time to parry Frank's first blow. He made a sound as he swung. The lightsaber sound. *Vwom.*

Our clubs met between us, *ping*, and stayed there, crossed at the handles, Frank making crackling noises now—*kssshhhhhzzk*—until he reared back for another strike.

It was so on.

I scrambled up to the top of the table, brandishing Katana in both hands. I didn't have time to look around and see if the other golfers were watching us. Frank drove forward, swinging his putter in telegraphed strokes so I could block them. He slashed low, his weapon parallel with the tabletop, and I leaped over it, landing in a crouch and spinning around just in time to deflect his follow-up. I countered with a quick blow of my own, striking him lightly on the arm with the end of Katana. Frank growled pseudo-menacingly and lunged again.

I jumped backward, meeting his club blow for blow and then shifting to go on the attack. I backed him onto the start of the Blue Course, headed toward the brontosaurus, swinging and twisting and making sabery sounds of my own. *Vwom. Vwom. Crrrrsssh.* Everyone was definitely watching us now. A posse of teenagers was laughing and taking pictures. The two little girls were already copying us, dueling with their own clubs. Maybe we weren't setting a great example, but I didn't care. Frank was going down.

He ducked behind the windmill, jabbing at me from between its slowly revolving arms. "You are using Bonetti's defense against me, eh?" I said.

"What?"

"Come on. *The Princess Bride*? Don't tell me you've never seen it."

"You seen *Hoosiers* yet?" Frank countered.

I rounded the windmill and renewed my attack.

We slashed and jabbed and parried and feinted, across the first nine holes of Blue, climbing up and then leaping dramatically off obstacles, balancing on the metal sidewalls, scrambling in and out from between the dinosaur's legs. Once Frank almost tripped over a stone hazard and I reached out to help him. He took advantage of my guard being down to poke me in the ribs. He went back on the offensive, forcing me onto the bridge near hole eleven where our clubs clashed again against the eerie red-and-blue glow of the soda machine.

"Now, my young apprentice," Frank said, "You. Will. Die."

He drew his putter back slowly, his motions exaggerated. I understood. This was the grand finale. He was letting me win.

I made my own slow-motion maneuver, ducking and spinning before thrusting the handle of my club at Frank's chest. He stepped sideways just at the last moment and leaned forward, the putter sinking into his armpit—the one that oozed—and sticking out the back so that, from the side at least, it looked as if I'd run him through.

"Nooooooo!" he bellowed, dropping to his knees and looking up at the darkening sky.

The teenagers applauded, one of them whistled, the crowd more or less going wild. Frank reached up to pull his plastic Vader mask off, revealing a face like a turnip, his forehead beaded with sweat. He didn't look good. He held out a clammy hand. "Help me up, kid," he huffed.

Back on his feet, Frank put both hands on his knees, bent over, catching his breath, his face still bright red.

"You okay?"

"I'm fine. Just . . . you know . . . haven't been in a duel to the death in a while." He looked over at me and smiled. "Already know you. That which you need." Then he wiped his face off on a corner of his bedsheet and pointed to the arcade with a wink.

The wink meant slushies.

Which meant our time was almost up.

I didn't think much of it when Dad picked me up fifteen minutes later than usual. I sat on the curb with the Vader mask in my hand—a gift from Frank, who told me to use it for trick-or-treating. I figured I'd at least hang it up in the Cove as a reminder of my triumph over the Dark Side during what was probably the best mini golf lesson ever.

Dad didn't comment on the mask. I'm not sure he even saw it. He was staring straight ahead, mouth pulled tight. My own smile vanished the moment I got in the car, the high from my victory dissipating. I looked out the window at Fritz's. The overhead lights made overlapping pools along the courses, but out here in the parking lot most of the bulbs were burned out and it was already dark. The sun had set already.

"Malcolm, we need to talk," Dad said.

The seat belt seemed tighter all of a sudden, pinching my neck and pressing in my on chest, making it hard to breathe. My fingers started to tingle.

The voice crept in.

You should have seen this coming, it said.

"Malcolm? Are you listening?"

I wrapped both hands around the handle of Katana, just to have something to hold on to. I nodded. I was listening. I was always listening.

"Malcolm, your mom and I . . . we haven't really been getting along. . . ."

Except I knew I wasn't ready to hear this. I didn't want to be here. I wanted to jump out of the car.

"And I'm sure you've noticed how tense it's been at home. . . ."

Run back out to the course. Back on the green where it all made sense. Where I knew what I was doing.

"We've been arguing more, which isn't good for us . . ."

Start at the beginning. Hole number one because it was easy. Straight shot.

". . . or for you."

See the angles and breaks. The climbs and drops. The obstacles and traps. Easy to avoid because you know how.

"So we talked. . . ."

Back on the course, where there are no surprises or excuses.

"And your mom and I have decided it would be best . . ."

And you can always go back to the tee and try again.

". . . if we spent some time apart."

I shut my eyes. It felt like I was falling, spiraling downward, even though I was still strapped in my seat. The voice in my head was louder, more insistent. It sounded angry. *You should have seen this coming.*

278

I did. I did see it. The big one, sitting right in the middle of the field.

You didn't stop it, the voice said.

But I tried. Be quiet. Be good. Stay out of the way. Find a way to mend the crack. To fill the hole. To make things better.

"Talk to me, Malcolm," Dad pressed. "Please."

He's leaving you.

What did he want me to say? I stared at the tip of Katana, flecked with rusty red paint. I thought about the spot of ketchup on the dining room wall. The curved scar on Dad's shoulder. The blue stain on the cement under the table. Little reminders. Even things that happened a long time ago can stick with you.

"Is this because of Michael?"

Dad didn't look surprised at the mention of my brother's name. "That was a long time ago." He sighed. It was his defeated sigh, eyes closed, head tilted back. "I'm sorry that we never told you. But that's not what this is about."

"Then is it because of me?" I asked.

You always want the truth until somebody asks you if you want the truth.

Dad frowned. I turned back to the window, locking eyes with the alligator standing guard, feeling this hole getting bigger and bigger inside me. I thought I might throw up.

"Malcolm, look at me."

I looked. I had my father's eyes. I could feel the tears

threatening. I tried to hold them back. I'd never seen my father cry. Not once. Not ever.

"It's not you. Okay? This is just something your mom and I have to work out between us. We just need a little space."

You're not enough.

I wasn't enough. I couldn't hold it together.

Dad reached across the gap between us, putting a hand on my back, starting a slow circle the way he did when I was little and got scared of the dark or fell off my bike and scraped my knees. Back then it calmed me. This time I flinched, drawing myself into a ball and moving closer to the door. Dad took his hand away, put it back on the wheel. "I'm sorry, Malcolm," he said. "Really I am."

In my head I said, *Me too.*

Out loud I asked if we could please go home.

When Dad pulled into the driveway fifteen minutes later, we both sat silently in the car for a minute. I was waiting for him to turn the engine off. Then I realized he was waiting for me to get out.

I stood by the open door and caught Dad's reflection in the dashboard lights. "It's only temporary," he said. "A couple days. Maybe a week. But I'll still see you. We'll still talk."

"What about Saturday?"

It wasn't meant to be a question. No way would he miss the tournament. It was his idea, after all. His writing on the calendar. His exclamation points. His insistence that this was something that mattered.

Dad took a deep breath. "I don't know, bub. We'll just wait and see, okay?"

I wiped my nose on my sleeve, Katana still clenched in both hands. I looked through the back window and saw a big black duffel bag in the back seat, only half zipped, clothes haphazardly shoved into the top. Apparently that was all he needed. At least, it was all he was taking.

Maybe that meant he would have to come back.

"I love you, Malcolm," he said.

I softly shut the door.

As soon as I stepped inside the house, I heard Mom's voice call out from the living room. "Malcolm? Is that you?"

I didn't answer her either. She would know it was me by the quick thump of my shoes on the stairs, taking them as fast as I could. I knew she would follow me, so I immediately ducked into the attic and closed that door as well, pressing my back up against it. Seconds later I heard Mom's knuckles tapping, heard her voice through the walls, pleading with me to come out and talk to her. I put my hands over my head, trying to block her out, to block them all out, but there was still one voice, impossible to escape. The one that, three years ago, said, *They left you. They're gone. You're alone.*

Now it just said, *I told you so.*

Hole sixteen is tougher than it looks. The gurgling fountain in the center takes up most of the green. It's pretty to look at, but it makes getting to the hole a pain. Because of the way the green curves around the fountain and the shape of the bricks that line them, it's almost impossible to bank a shot for one, so I don't even try. The goal here is just to break even. If I can make par on this, I'll only be two strokes out of first.

I pass by the fountain to take my second shot and my eye catches the glitter of coins throwing back the sunlight. The pennies don't shimmer much, and they far outnumber the nickels, dimes, and quarters, but the water still sparkles. I wonder what kinds of wishes are in here. I'm sure some people just toss in a coin to hear the splash. Maybe they forget to make a wish at all, or they think it's pointless to try. There are a lot of coins.

I reach into my pocket and touch my grandfather's lucky nickel, the one that's worth fifty bucks. Does that mean it could pay for fifty wishes? Or five thousand? I figure I would only need three.

Granny Allison's voice croaks in my head: *Wish in one hand, poop in the other, see which fills up faster.*

I press the edge of the coin against my thumb but keep it in my pocket. Maybe there really isn't any luck in golf, but I know there's no such thing as magic. And I'd rather hang on to what I've got.

HOLE #17

Par 3

The penultimate hole of this beautiful course is perhaps the most difficult. Two long, consecutive slopes lead to a small plateau with a cup at its center, but a sharp downhill just on the other side means you don't want to overshoot the mark, or you'll roll down and be stuck against the back wall, forced to make another ascent. The vast number of bogies brought on by this infuriating hole has earned it the nickname "Heartbreaker."

Every turtle has a shell, but they all can't hide inside them.

Lex didn't tell me this, though it sounds like something she would know. I actually learned it from Dad. On our trip to the South Carolina coast—the one immortalized in the framed photo sitting on the piano.

We happened upon a nest, just the two of us. It was late June, and the loggerheads had come ashore to lay their eggs. We'd seen nests like this already, but those had been staked off, the area encircled with caution tape. This one hadn't been discovered yet, and I would have walked right through it if Dad hadn't pointed out the tracks leading out to the ocean and where he suspected the egg chamber was buried. I asked him if the unborn baby turtles growing inside the eggs already had shells of their own, shells within shells.

That's when I discovered the truth: that sea turtles can't pull their heads or fins inside their shells, and suddenly I felt terrible for the babies about to hatch. The best thing about being a turtle was being able to duck inside when danger comes, taking shelter inside your keratin armor. Impenetrable. Safe. A common box turtle that you could buy for ten dollars at the pet store could do it, but the poor loggerhead babies would emerge from their sandy nest defenseless, their jaws not strong enough to fight back, their heads and flippers exposed. What was the point? What was the point of having a stupid shell if you couldn't use it to escape?

"She'll come back, though, right?" I asked. "The momma turtle? She didn't leave for good."

Dad frowned and shook his head. "I don't think so, bub. Pretty sure these little guys are all on their own."

Alone. I looked out to the ocean, feeling sick to my stomach, thinking about all the untold dangers that awaited the turtles if they even managed to make it that far. The cool air coming off the water made me shiver. Dad noticed and wrapped an arm around me.

"Don't worry," he assured me. "We'll make sure the babies are safe, all right? You and me." He got the number for the Department of Natural Resources and called to tell them what we'd found so they could come and rope off the nest. To protect the poor creatures who had no one else to look out for them.

Standing on the shoreline with my father holding me, I knew exactly what kind of turtle I never wanted to be.

I retracted.

In the morning, coming downstairs to silence instead of the pounding of Dad's feet on the treadmill. Sitting at the kitchen table across from no one, burying my face as much as I could in my bowl of cereal, answering my mother's tentatively probing questions with mumbles and grunts.

In the car on the way to school, shoved against the door, face against the cold window, backpack pressed against my chest like a shield.

In class, hunched in my desk, tucked behind a computer screen, or peeking out over the cover of a book.

At lunch, sitting beside Samantha Diggs, who asked me if I was okay and gave me one of her Oreos because she could tell I was lying.

In the bathroom, scrunched into a stall, door locked, determined not to cry.

In the car on the way home from school, asking if I could sit in the back seat instead, ignoring my mother's question and doing it anyway. Keeping my eyes closed. Pretending to be asleep. Only once, at a stoplight, cracking them open to see her staring at me in the rearview mirror.

Hunch your shoulders. Tuck your chin down. Put your hands in your pockets. Draw your knees up to your chest. Don't say a word. That's how to make a shell.

Mom let me stay that way until dinner, not protesting when I went straight up to my room after school. But at about six o'clock she coaxed me out. With the peppery scent of takeout from our favorite Thai restaurant down the street.

I slunk to the dining room table, my head peeking out just enough to nibble on my pad kee mao. Mom took advantage of some fleeting eye contact, seeing it as an opening.

"Malcolm, I know this is difficult," she began.

Eating pad kee mao with chopsticks was difficult. I couldn't get the hang of it. I always ate my noodles with a fork. I stabbed at pieces of pork while Mom kept talking.

"It's hard for me too. But sometimes you have to take extreme measures to make something work."

I could probably use the chopsticks if I practiced more. I could use them to pin the peppers and chunks of meat, but not the noodles; they always slipped off, and they were meant to be eaten together.

"Am I making any sense?"

I didn't want to talk with my mouth full. I took another bite before the first one was completely down.

Mom tried again. "Okay. You know how sometimes your computer freezes up completely and you have to shut it off and wait a few seconds? Then you turn it back on and everything sort of clears out and gets back to normal? Like a system reboot?"

I twirled a noodle. Stabbed a piece of pork. Added a pepper. Chewed slowly. It didn't taste as good as I remembered.

"Well that's sort of what's happening with your dad and me. We're taking this time to reboot, you know?"

I waited until I'd finished my bite. I glanced over at her. "And then everything will be back to normal?" I asked.

Mom hesitated. "Yes? Maybe? To be honest, Malcolm, I don't really know what normal should be at this point. But I'm hoping it will be better. That's the goal. I just want it to be better."

I could tell her exactly what normal looked like. Normal—*my* normal—was having both of your parents sleeping in the room across the hall, not having one of them sleeping in a friend's apartment five miles away. I wasn't sure what better would look like. Normal would be better. Normal would be enough.

"But he's definitely coming back," I ventured.

Mom hesitated again.

The doorbell rang.

I stared at her, waiting for an answer. The bell rang three times in a row. Insistent.

"Are you going to get that?" she asked. "I think it's for you."

Dad.

I put down my fork and went to the door, stopping with my hand on the knob, second-guessing myself. Dad wouldn't ring the bell. This was still his house too. Which meant . . .

"And this is what happens when you don't answer my texts or return my calls."

Lex stood there with her hands on her hips, head cocked, eyes squinting behind her glasses. She looked me over before waving at the Mike's Plumbing truck pulling out of the driveway. She had her backpack on, of course, and she was wearing the same shirt as last time. The one I'd said I liked. The one that now reminded me of Frank dressed up in his bedsheet.

"You must be Lex," Mom said, coming up behind me, not looking surprised at all to see this girl she'd only heard about and never met standing at our door.

"Thanks for having me over, Mrs. Greeley," Lex said. "I brought dessert." She set down said backpack and pulled a box of Little Debbie Zebra Cakes from the pouch. She pointed to the happy, redheaded farm girl on the box. "Not sure if you know this, but that's the original owner's granddaughter, Debbie. The cakes were named after a family member, just like Tootsie Rolls." She looked down at my bare feet and then gave me a knowing wink.

"Lex knows a little something about almost everything," I said to Mom, catching the look on her face, something between confused and impressed.

"The internet and I spend a lot of time together," Lex admitted.

Mom smiled and suggested I give Lex a tour of the house while she cleaned up the dinner I'd only half eaten.

"Sorry to just show up like this," Lex said as we made our way upstairs, "but when you didn't get back to me, I texted your dad, who gave me your mom's number. She said you might like some company."

I'd retracted. From everyone, including Lex. From the

moment I'd gotten out of Dad's car, I'd wanted to be alone, to shrink down to nothing. Now that she was here, though, I realized that wasn't what I really wanted at all. "It's been a rough couple of days," I said, as if that explained everything. Then I opened my door and ushered her in.

Lex scanned the room. "Yup. Absolutely spotless. Just like I expected. Mine's a total disaster. At least at Mom's house. Dad's sort of a neat freak, so I try a little harder there. Is that . . . ?" She pointed to the attic door.

Lex knew about the Cove because I'd told her during one of our many phone conversations. But only Mom and Dad had ever been invited in. The few times that other kids came over to the house were spent out in the backyard or downstairs in front of the TV. It had been a while since I'd had visitors of any kind.

"You want to see it?" I pulled on the handle and flipped the switch. The overhead bulb blinked on along with the strings of Christmas lights that hung from the rafters. Motes of dust appeared like the world's smallest snowflakes. "Watch your head," I said, scrunching. Lex followed, her eyes perfect circles.

"I feel like Lucy Pevensie right now," she said.

I didn't know who that was, but I assumed it was a good thing by her smile. "Don't go over to that part. The insulation will make you itchy," I warned.

Lex crouch-walked over to the shelf that held my favorite books—basically all the ones I'd read more than once. All of the Harry Potters were there—hardbound, no less—so I knew she would approve. "So, what, you just sit in here and read?"

"Read. Draw. Talk to my friends."

"Your tons of friends," she said, but not in a mean way, more with the wink and nod that comes with an inside joke. She ran her hand along one of the heavy beams above. "I think it's amazing."

"Amazing" seemed like a strong word for a cramped attic alcove with two leaky beanbag chairs, a bookshelf, and a dusty box fan. "It's really not anything."

"Are you kidding me? I have *two* bedrooms and I still don't have anything as cool as this." Lex collapsed into the closest beanbag chair and the floor protested with a loud creak. "Is that supposed to happen?"

"It does sometimes," I said as I sat in the other one. It felt strange, having her there. Not bad—it just made me see the space differently. It was perfect for one but a little cramped for two. Suddenly I wished there was more to it. That there was more to show her.

Lex didn't seem bothered, though. "This is a good place for a clandestine conversation," she said, settling more firmly into her chair. "So how about you tell me why you didn't answer any of my calls."

"You really wanna know?" I asked.

"Malcolm, it's me. I want to know everything."

So I told her. Because I needed to tell someone. And because it *was* her; I knew she'd been through some version of this already. I told her about how Dad dropped me off last night and didn't come in. About the bag of hastily packed clothes in the back seat. About the frozen computer and the reboot and how I wasn't even entirely sure he was coming back because my mother didn't answer my question. Then I went back and told her about everything building up to last night: the bursts of shouting and the quiet spells between them, the sidelong glances and the slammed doors. I still didn't mention Michael, though. Or the voice inside my head. Even here, tucked safely inside the Cove, I kept those two things to myself.

Lex sat and listened, nodding thoughtfully, waiting for me to finish. Afterward, she sat quietly for a few seconds. Then she reached for her bag. "I know just what you need," she said, tearing open the box of snack cakes she'd been holding and tossing one to me. I thought about my last Friday conversation with Mom—ice cream or cigarettes. I wasn't supposed to eat in the Cove. Odds are I wasn't supposed to have a girl in there either. I figured exceptions could be made in both cases.

"So what's it like, having two rooms?" I asked, no longer worried about taking tiny bites or keeping my mouth shut.

"Just because your parents are spending some time apart doesn't mean you're going to have two rooms."

"But it could."

"Could doesn't always mean will," Lex countered. "Just like tissue doesn't always mean Kleenex." She licked the cream filling from her fingers, then pulled one of the strings of Christmas lights close, pressing a yellow bulb against her fingertip. It glowed a little. Like E.T. "You know, when my parents split, I was actually kinda glad. I mean, not at first, obviously. At first, I was seriously ticked. And then sad. And then angry again. Sort of back and forth between those two for a while, probably that whole first year. But then I saw how much happier they were *not* together, and . . . I don't know . . . I just decided to go with it. You can't be mad at someone for wanting to be happy. At least, you can't *stay* mad."

I wasn't mad at my parents for wanting to be happy. I just didn't see why they couldn't be happy together. "So why did they split up?" I asked.

"I think they just realized they weren't right for each other."

"But they got married," I said. "So they must have been right for each other at some point."

Lex continued to play with the string of lights in her hand, touching one bulb after another, turning her index finger different colors. "You can love someone and not want to spend the rest of your life with them. Heck, you can love someone and not even *like* them half of the time. My older sister and I used to fight constantly. But now that she's away at college, I miss her constantly. It's weird."

I wondered if Dad missed Mom yet. He'd been gone less than a day, but it was possible. I wanted him to miss her. "She's your sister. It's different. You can't divorce your sister. Even if you can't stand her, you're still family."

"So are you," Lex said. "That part doesn't change."

"Why does *any* of it have to change?" I sank even farther into my chair. I could feel the tears coming again, but this time I didn't try to stop them. "It's not fair. I wish there was something I could do to fix it, but it's like it's all out of my control, like nothing I could do will ever be enough to make them happy. I hate it."

Lex let go of the lights so that she could reach over and grab my hand. It was the first time I'd held hands with someone my age without being told to. Her hand was colder than mine.

"It's not your job," she said.

We sat there quietly for a moment. Then she let go and pulled her backpack into her lap again, carefully undoing one of the buttons from the front pocket. "Here. I want you to have this," Lex said. "It's one of my favorites, so you'll have to promise me you'll take good care of it."

I took the button and studied the image of the big yellow Pac-Man against the black background. Underneath in white letters the button read WAKA WAKA.

"One dot at a time."

"What?" I sniffed.

"Waka waka. It's the sound he makes as he gobbles them up. It means take it one dot at a time. At least that's what *I* think it means. You can't go in all directions at once. So pick a path and start chomping and get as many as you can."

"Easy for you to say," I told her with another sniffle. "You get all the dots."

"Yeah, well—I've played the game more than you."

I ran my finger along the outside edge of the button and then closed it in my fist. Lex slid a couple more Zebra Cakes out of the box, handing one to me. She unwrapped hers, took a bite, and nodded at the picture of Little Debbie. "She looks a lot different now, though she still has sort of curly hair. She's also like a millionaire and is vice president of her grandfather's company. You know what that means?"

I shook my head.

"It means everything works out in the end."

We spent the next hour in the Cove, talking and eating and even messing with the Rubik's cube she found on my shelf, though she didn't reach for my hand again. Afterward we washed down our Debbies with Dr Peppers in the kitchen while Lex told Mom everything she'd learned about the history of miniature golf. She made my mom laugh, a sound I hadn't heard in days, and by the time her dad picked her up, I had almost started to believe her, about how things were destined to work out somehow.

But for as hard as she tries, even Lex doesn't know everything.

In miniature golf, most courses have a six-shot maximum. After six shots you're allowed to just pick up your ball and move on to the next hole. Otherwise, on some holes, you could be there forever.

But that's miniature golf.

The night Dad left, I thought things couldn't get any worse.

But life doesn't put a limit on how much it can suck.

The day after Lex's visit, Mom picked me up from school like always. It was the Friday before the tournament in Wisconsin and the second day without Dad. We were supposed to go to the park if the weather was nice. Mom insisted that we still go. We didn't have to talk, she said. Not unless I wanted to. We could just quietly admire the trees and try to spot snakes along the stream that ran through the woods. But when I got in the car that afternoon, Mom's forehead was pinched. She turned the wrong way out of the parking lot.

"Isn't the park that way?"

"We're not going to the park. We're going to the hospital."

The hospital? My mind scrambled, imagining car accidents, a fall down the stairs at work, a burst appendix. "What? Why? Is Dad okay?"

"Your father's fine," she said. "It's Frank."

"Wait, what's wrong with Frank? Is he hurt? What happened?"

"Deep breaths," Mom said, putting her free hand on my knee. "He's not in any danger. He passed out at work this morning, and an ambulance took him to the ER to get checked out. He's okay, really, but your father said we should stop by this afternoon if possible. I guess Frank wants to see you."

"But if he's okay, why is he still in the hospital?"

Mom shook her head. She didn't know. Or maybe she just didn't want to tell me.

Which meant he wasn't so okay after all.

The hospital smelled like the school cafeteria. Hospitals should smell clean, like a freshly mopped floor or lemon dish soap, but this one smelled like microwaved chicken nuggets. Frank was in a room on the fifth floor, no longer in the ER at least. Mom said that was a good sign.

He smiled as soon as we walked in.

"And this, ladies and gentlemen, is what four decades of double bacon cheeseburgers gets you." Frank opened his arms wide to show us the wrinkled, mint green hospital gown. A big bruise shone on one arm, and an IV line snaked out of the other. Another bundle of wires escaped through the top of his gown, winding its way across his shoulder to a monitor that blipped in time with his heartbeat. When he moved, the tubes and wires moved with him, sort of like a marionette. "Come on in," he said.

I followed behind Mom. There were two chairs, but she stood, so I stood. "How are you feeling, Frank?" she asked.

"Okay, I guess. Got a raging headache. Apparently when I blacked out, I hit my head on the counter. Managed to bruise my arm in the landing too." Frank winked at me. "Bet you wish *you* were that talented."

For once, no, I thought.

"And what did the doctors say?" Mom pressed.

"Eh . . . you know doctors. They called it a minor heart attack," Frank replied with a shrug.

Minor heart attack. I didn't know there was such a thing. I assumed all heart attacks were major. That's why they were called attacks and not heart scuffles or teasings. "It's no big deal. My right coronary's plugged up a little," Frank explained. "They put me on medication and they've already got me scheduled for some plumbing work tomorrow morning. Little Roto Rooter to clean out the old grease trap and get the pumps back up to full speed again."

Mom frowned at him the same way she frowned at me when she could tell I was trying to pull a fast one on her.

"Where's Matt? He not with you guys?"

Not with us. That was a good way to put it. I pretended to suddenly take an interest in the TV, which was tuned to experts in suits discussing the upcoming World Series. I knew which teams had made it. Dad had been talking about it all week. Right up until he left.

"He said he'd try to stop by later," Mom answered.

Even staring at the TV, I still caught Frank looking at me. I tried to keep my face still, but what followed was one of those silences that give everything away. Frank scratched at his chest. "Mrs. Greeley, I hate to bother you, and I know you just got here, but would you mind sneaking over to the nurses' station and seeing if you can rustle up an apple juice or something? I could press the button again, but I'm pretty sure they're sick of me already."

Mom got the hint. "Sure," she said. "I could use a cup of coffee. You want anything?" she asked me. I shook my head.

"I'm pretty sure he wants a cookie. Or a muffin. He likes muffins. Blueberry if they got 'em," Frank added as Mom ducked into the hall.

I stood in the corner, hands in my pockets. A nickel in one, a half a pack of Starbursts in the other. Lex's button was currently pinned to my own backpack, which was sitting in the car. I hadn't been this nervous around Frank since our first lesson together. Then I'd had no idea what was going to happen. I felt sort of the same way now.

Frank waited until Mom was gone, then pointed to the chair stationed right beside the bed. "Have a seat."

I shuffled over, noticing the white surgical tape around his hand holding his IV in. *What goes around comes around,* Granny Allison said. On the TV, a bald guy was picking the Dodgers as the clear favorite to win the championship. Dad always hated the Dodgers. Funny that I knew that, but he couldn't remember what Quidditch was.

"So . . . let's have it," Frank said.

"Have what?"

"C'mon, kid. I know a troubled face when I see one. Especially when it's your troubled face. Let me guess: parental problems. That's why your mom looks so wrung out and your dad's not here and you're all clammed up and mopey like your fish just died." Frank was apparently the kind of guy who noticed things too.

"Jaws is fine," I told him.

"And your parents?" he pressed.

"Rebooting," I said.

"Rebooting?"

"You know. Like a computer. At least that's how Mom put it. Dad said they are just taking some time to think about things. He's staying with a friend from work."

Frank nodded. "Rebooting. Right. Danielle and I skipped over that part and went right to smashing things with a nine iron."

"Starscream."

"May he rest in pieces," Frank said. "So that kind of tells me where *they're* at. How are *you* doing?"

How was I doing? Do you tell your miniature golf coach that you've only known for a month that you've woken up sweaty the past two nights with your covers kicked to the floor? That you snuck into your parents' room when your mom was downstairs just to sit on the edge of the bed and stare at your father's old trophies? Do you tell him how you spent the first half of third period in the nurse's office feeling like you might throw up? I looked at the man lying in the hospital bed wired to a heart monitor and sucking fluids through a bag.

"I'm okay," I said.

Frank stared at me.

"All right, fine. It kinda sucks."

"Of course it sucks," Frank said. "Nobody likes landing in the rough."

I knew what the rough was: the long, thick grass off the fairway where balls get lost. If you're in the rough it means everything did not go according to plan. My parents were definitely in the rough. I was in the rough. Next to me, Frank's little heart monitor machine blipped and whirred. It seemed like there was nothing *but* rough.

"I'm sorry. I didn't mean to dump this on you. You just had a heart attack, and all I do is come in here and complain."

"*Minor* heart attack," he corrected. "And you don't have to apologize. I get it, kid. We're both having a crappy day. But there's always tomorrow. You *are* still planning on doing the tournament, right?"

The tournament all the way up in Wisconsin. The one Frank had planned to attend; that is, before his pumps clogged up, sending him here.

"Mom's taking me," I said.

"*Just* Mom?"

I shrugged. That's all I knew for sure. The last I'd heard from Dad was *We'll see.* So that's what I told Frank. "We'll see."

"Well, I'm sure he's not going to miss it," Frank said. "Wish I could be there. Helluva lot more fun than what *I'll* be doing, that's for sure. You nervous?"

He meant about the tournament. Or Dad showing up. Or the reboot. Maybe everything. The answer was the same, regardless. "Maybe. A little. You?" I nodded at his chest with the disks and wires attached and the broken heart beating underneath.

Frank waved it off. "Nah. It's just a stent. These guys do this kind of thing in their sleep. It's all muscle memory."

"They're heart-fixing machines," I said.

"Something like that."

I returned Frank's smile, but I could tell he was lying. He wasn't just nervous. He was scared. We both were.

"To be honest, I'm not even sure I still *want* to go," I admitted.

Frank frowned and glanced toward the door, then leaned closer to me, pulling all his cords with him. "Tell me, kid. How many holes on the Red Course at Fritz's?"

"Eighteen," I said. There are eighteen holes on every golf course. I wasn't sure why. It would be a good question to ask Lex. Even if she didn't know, she would probably love to find out.

"And how many strokes to make par?"

There were no par threes at Fritz's, so eighteen times two. "Thirty-six."

Frank nodded. "So assuming you make par on every one, that's thirty-six shots you've got to take, right? Which one is the *most* important?"

"I don't know. The last one?" I guessed. Because if you had a score of thirty-five with one more putt to make, you'd be mad if you missed it. At least I would be. You'd at least want the chance to break even.

Frank shook his head.

"The first one, then?"

He shook his head again. "It's the next one," he said.

"You mean the second one?"

"No, I mean the next one. Doesn't matter what it is. It could be a tee-off. It could be a gimme. It could be a shot past the barn or through the dinosaur's legs. It could be uphill or downhill or around the bend. Out of the bunker. Right by the cup. First or last. Doesn't matter. Whatever shot you're squaring up on, *that's* the only one you've got to worry about. And the moment you make that shot, no matter if the ball drops or not, you move on to the next one. You don't let anything hold you back. You get me?"

I thought about Lex's pin, the one fixed to my backpack. "But some shots are harder than others," I said.

Frank took in his ugly green hospital gown. "Tell me about it. But that doesn't mean they're impossible. Not for guys like us." He looked back up, and for a second I saw that glint again, the one that he got when he told me the story of his father the arm-wrestler, only this time he was looking at me.

Then his eyes darted over my shoulder and I realized Mom was standing in the doorway. She had a cranberry juice box in one hand and a steaming Styrofoam cup in the other. "You boys okay?" she asked.

"Just talking shop." He took the juice from Mom with a nod of thanks. His eyebrows furrowed. "No cookie?"

"The nurse said you were on a restricted diet."

Frank looked crestfallen, as if this was the worst news imaginable.

"Does that include Starbursts?" I asked, pulling the half pack out of my pocket.

Mom frowned. Frank winked at me again and took a lemon one off the top. "Malcolm Greeley comes through in the clutch," he said.

But in my head, the crowd stayed silent.

There are eighteen holes in a round of miniature golf. This is because there are eighteen holes in regular golf.

That's because the first-ever golf course, known as the Old Course in Scotland—home of women who once weren't permitted to raise their arms above their shoulders—had eighteen holes. I know this because I looked it up. That's what awesome people do when they are curious about something; then they call their best friend and tell them all about it.

Eighteen holes. But it only takes one to screw up your day.

With two holes to go, I'm third on the leaderboard. I honestly don't know how. I've parred plenty more than I've aced, plus the bogeys on two and nine and the screwup on fourteen. But even on the bad shots, I kept my cool, just like Frank taught me. I never flipped out and threw my putter on the ground.

Jamie Tran can't say the same.

It's a straight shot, maybe four feet from the hole. No bumps. No curves. No hazards. No way he misses it. Not Jamie.

But he does. The ball skirts past the hole on seventeen, nicking the edge of the cup before rolling down the slope on the opposite side, ending up in the right corner. A tough putt, no matter how good you are. And that's when his club hits the turf. He doesn't throw it so much as drop it, completely frustrated. Jamie glances at his father, his coach, just as quickly looking away as he bends over to retrieve his putter and take his next shot. Golf is a game of composure, and Jamie quickly tries to regain his, knowing everyone is watching.

I know how it feels to miss a shot like that.

I know how it feels when he misses the next one too.

Jamie's ball crests the hill but then just crawls toward the cup, settling right on the edge like it's having second thoughts. I can see the pained look on his face. Finally, he taps in the fourth putt, and what probably should have been a birdie turns into a bogie, turning what looked like a foregone conclusion into something suddenly up for grabs.

Because I'm right on his heels now, and I have yet to play this hole.

Jamie takes his ball and stalks off toward his coach, who wears the same frustrated expression but twice as intense. They're mirror images. Like one of those apps that take your picture and show what you will look like in twenty-five years. Jamie's dad is already lecturing him from ten feet away. I can't quite hear it but I don't need to. I can imagine it well enough. *What just happened out there? You had this one in the bag!*

I hold Katana with both hands. The clock on the post in the center of the course says it's almost noon. Frank's probably out of surgery by now, provided everything went according to plan. I look back at the fountain on the last hole and wonder if I should have tossed my grandfather's nickel in anyway. Fifty bucks is a small price to pay for a fixed heart.

"Up next on seventeen, Malcolm Greeley."

I set my ball on the mat, picking the center divot, making sure my name is faceup. Big blue letters. All caps. An unexpected gift. I take one last look over at Jamie, but he's off to the side still getting whisper-shouted at by his father.

It's not my concern. Just another distraction. I need to stay focused. This hole's even harder than it looks. I think back to the notes that Frank and I took. Seventeen: the longest on the course at thirty-eight feet. No rocks or logs or water hazards, just hills and banks and enough breaks to make anything resembling a straight shot impossible. The kind of hole that requires constant practice. You could start with a bucket of a hundred balls and never get a hole in one. In fact, it's a lot like number sixteen back at Fritz's. And I won't let myself forget how that one turned out.

I take my stance, squaring my shoulders. I study the curves of the green, imagining my bright orange ball barreling along. If you know which path to take, I think, then maybe the ghosts can't catch you.

But it's no use. I can sense it creeping up inside of me, that voice, *my* voice. I already know what it's going to say. *You can't. You won't. Why even try?* There's no escaping it. The feeling you will never be enough. I can hear it saying my name, over and over again. *Malcolm. Malcolm. Malcolm.*

"Malcolm!"

I freeze. That's not my voice.

And it's definitely not inside my head.

I look over at the line of spectators and spot him slipping through the crowd, coming to stand beside my mother. My legs so soft. My heart, already at a full gallop, hammers even harder. I don't believe it, not at first, because I'd almost given up. But I'm not imagining it. He's right there.

Dad sees he's gotten my attention and makes circles with his hands, putting them up to his eyes. The gesture has always been Mom's and my thing—*I've got you in my sights.* This is the first time he's ever done it.

I blink three times as another familiar face comes up behind him, thick-rimmed glasses, dark hair, button-covered back-pack.

Lex waves at me. I give a little wave back.

Standing off to my right, the scorekeeper on seventeen clears her throat. *C'mon kid, are you putting or not?*

I resume my stance, trying to focus on the ball, but I can't help it, I keep glancing at the crowd for confirmation. They are still there. Mom. Dad. Lex.

"As soon as you're ready," the scorekeeper says.

My head feels like it's going to explode, still so full of questions and doubts, can'ts and won'ts, all the things I don't know and can't control. I can't seem to keep Katana steady.

Then Lex—who doesn't know the no-shouting rule of golf, or maybe, just chooses to ignore it—booms out over the crowd: "Go Malcolm! You've got this!" which is exactly what I imagined she'd say."

Her voice is so loud it drowns out all the others.

And I realize, right then, I've won.

HOLE #18

Par 2

The final hole at Putter's Paradise provides a picturesque conclusion, curving around the cascading waterfall and following a stone-edged pathway to a gentle downward slope. Putters have commented that the last hole is too easy compared to the one before, though that is undoubtedly because the owner wants players to leave on a high note, feeling good about themselves. There are worse ways to end a day on the links.

The shot itself, putting putter to ball, only takes a second. But a second can seem like forever. In a second you can turn around and find the people who love you are gone.

But it works the other way too.

I whisper the word "five" under my breath because five is better than fore, and then I sink it. Drop it like a nickel in a wishing well. It is probably the greatest putt of my life. A hole in one on a par three.

In real golf, that's called an eagle. Impossible at Fritz's, but not here. And it's beautiful. The sound of the ball clinking into the hole reminds me of my mother's fingers dancing along the piano keys.

And the crowd—the real crowd—actually goes wild. A standing ovation. Because there's nowhere for anybody to sit.

I quickly pocket my ball and walk over to the fence. Mom

is first in line with big eyes and a high five. "Wow," she says. "Just. Wow."

I whisper a thanks and look over her shoulder. She turns to my father and raises her eyebrows. An invitation? A warning? I'm not sure which. He's dressed in his usual weekend getup, blue jeans and a button-down shirt, though the circles under his eyes have darkened, maybe a sign of a couple of rough nights on a friend's stiff sofa.

"I didn't think you were going to make it," I say.

"I had a feeling you would," he replies, nodding toward hole seventeen. "That was a heckuva shot."

"He's had a few of them today," Mom says. It's a quick jab— the kind that could easily start an argument—and part of me wishes she hadn't said it, but the rest of me knows he had it coming.

He knows it too. I can tell by the sigh. It's not his exasperated sigh or his angry sigh or even his defeated sigh. This is something new.

"Listen, Malcolm . . . I screwed up. I should have been here from the start. With everything that's going on . . . I just thought it might be easier on everybody if I didn't come." He glances at Mom when he says "everybody," but then he looks back at me. "I was selfish and stupid. And I'm sorry."

I just stand there for a second. I've never heard my father admit he was wrong before.

Mom is speechless—maybe she's never heard it before either—so it's up to me to tell him what he needs to hear.

"We all screw up sometimes," I say. And I hug him, which is my way of also saying it's okay.

Dad points at the whiteboard with my name sharing space at the top. Greeley and Tran. Tied for first. "So this is it," he says. "Last hole."

Next hole, I think to myself, but that thought triggers another. "Have you heard anything about Frank?"

Dad shakes his head. "I'm sure he's fine. I don't think he'd want you worrying about him *now.* He'd want you to hustle back out there and finish this thing."

I know he's right. Frank would say pretty much the same thing if he were here. But I'm not doing this for Frank.

"What about you?" I ask. "What do you want?"

Dad looks at Mom again. Back at me. "I already got what I wanted," he says.

I stand there, clutching Katana, seventeen holes behind me, but in my head I'm back on the beach at the edge of the turtle's nest, feeling the weight of his arm around me, promising me everything would be all right.

Mom makes a little movement with her head, indicating the girl waiting patiently behind Dad. He steps back, making room. "Right. I brought a friend."

Lex takes that as her cue to grab my arm, dragging me several feet away.

"What are you doing here?" I ask. "I told you you didn't have to come."

"Right. You told me that, and then I decided to anyways, because that's what friends do. Besides, it's Mom's hair day, and I wasn't about to spend the morning at Fritz's by myself."

"So—what? You called my dad and asked for a ride?"

"Actually I called him because you wouldn't answer your phone again. When he said he wasn't with you, put two and two together. I told him how my parents came to every one of my dance recitals. How they even sat next to each other to cheer me on. Then he volunteered to bring me. I didn't have to ask."

I glance at Dad, who is talking quietly to Mom. Just talking. "He wanted to be here, Malcolm," Lex continues. "He just needed a little nudge."

A nudge. Sometimes, when you're sitting right on the edge of the cup, a little push is all it takes. "Thanks," I say.

Lex nods. "You know if you win this thing you owe me a Coke, right?"

I point to the Pepsi machines along the back fence. "Sorry. You're out of luck."

"You know what I mean."

The announcer calls my name. "Up next on eighteen, Malcolm Greeley."

I take a deep breath. My hands are trembling. Lex notices. Of course she does. "You still have that button I gave you?"

I lift my shirt just high enough to show her the Pac-Man pinned to the hem of my screaming yellow shorts. For the first

313

time I realize how well they match.

"Waka waka," she says.

One dot at a time.

On the last hole of the tournament, Jamie Tran makes par. They put a box around his score, meaning his day is finished. All he can do now is sit and wait.

It's easy math, even for someone who bombed his last test: I can beat him with a one, tie him with a two.

I step up to the tee, Katana under one arm, shirt damp, sweat stinging my eyes even though it's really not hot out. By my father's own definition, miniature golf is a sport. At least for me.

This is it, Bill. Malcolm Greeley comes into eighteen with a chance to put this thing away.

That's right, Jim. We have battled through seventeen grueling holes and seen some marvelous putts and a few near disasters, but really, it all comes down to this.

I try to remember everything Frank taught me. I can see the forest. I can trace the path with my eyes. I know what I have to do. Beyond the cup I can see everyone watching me.

And as Greeley gets ready, we take a look at the fine crowd that's gathered here today. There are both of Greeley's parents now, looking even more nervous than him, if such a thing is possible, and his good friend Lex cheering him on. And there's our current leader, Jamie Tran, apparently getting yelled at by his coach—

The running commentary in my head suddenly stops as I

watch the sharp exchange between Jamie and his dad. They are back by the vending machines again; Jamie's eyes are fixed on the cement, absorbing whatever his father is saying. Finally, Jamie speaks, but he must not say the right thing, because Mr. Tran grabs his son's chin forcefully and wrenches Jamie's head up to face him, pointing a finger repeatedly at Jamie's chest.

The finger says *you, you, you*.

You did this.

You messed up.

You're responsible.

I feel sick again. I know I shouldn't be watching—Jamie's probably embarrassed enough—but I can't help it.

And in that moment, I wonder what would happen if he lost. Would the car ride home be cold silence or a painful recounting of every missed shot? Would he sit and suffer quietly through it all, waiting until he got home to drag himself up the stairs and slam his door? Would he punch his pillows or maybe his wall? Or would he just bury himself in his covers and will himself not to cry?

What would I do if I was him?

I look at the crowd . . . at *my* crowd, now triple in size. Mom has her fingers crossed again. Dad has his laced behind his head. They aren't shoulder to shoulder, but they are at least standing together. No one's pointing fingers at me. Even the voices in my head are quiet.

I think I can win this thing, but one more trophy in the

house isn't going to change anything.

The scorekeeper motions for me to take my shot. I take one last look at Jamie, then back at the hole, squinting, contemplating the angles, considering the possibilities.

In miniature golf there's more than one way to make a putt. Lots of times the hole will have an intended route. If there's a giant barn in the center of the course with a tunnel running right through its center, you can bet it will lead you straight to the cup. But you don't have to follow the path that's laid out for you. In fact, some holes force you to make a choice— do you take the high curve up and around or do you try to bank it off the wall? Do you go between the stones or try to navigate around them? And every choice just leads to more choices, a hundred times a hundred.

The trouble is you don't know if your choice was right or wrong until you make it.

I line it up, visualizing my approach.

In miniature golf there's usually a dozen different ways to make a shot.

But there are a million ways to miss one.

When it's over, the scoreboard officially reveals what everyone already knew.

Jamie Tran finishes in first with a score of thirty-five. Malcolm Greeley, the relative newcomer out of Falls Point, Illinois, finishes two under par with a score of thirty-six, tied with Grace Lin for second place.

Thirty-six is a really good score. At Fritz's it would only amount to breaking even, but on a course like this, it's something to be proud of.

"That was freakin' great," Mom says, pulling me in for a hug. Clearly Frank has rubbed off on her somehow.

"You were fantastic," Lex agrees.

Dad looks like he's about to say something too, or maybe just pull me into another hug, but before he can, I feel a tap on my shoulder. Jamie Tran stands there, his cheeks ruddy, eyes red. Without his sunglasses he looks a lot less intimidating. Nothing at all like a thirteen-year-old Terminator. Just a normal thirteen-year-old.

"Nice job today," he says. He extends his hand.

"You too," I say. We shake. It's good sportsmanship. Like the high-five line at Little League. Except so much better than Little League. I figure that's it, but Jamie keeps talking.

"Sorry, I guess it's probably not polite to ask, but I just gotta know. That second-to-last shot. Did you . . . you know . . ."

I know what he's asking. My second shot on eighteen, the one that could have tied me for first place. A two-footer on flat turf with nothing in the way. The kind of putt that some golfers I know could make with their eyes closed in a rainstorm with rubber bands plunking them in the back of their head. But I missed it by half an inch, forcing me to settle for second place.

"Did I what?" I ask.

Jamie shakes his head. "Nothing. Forget it. Good match."

"Good match."

I watch him go back to his coach, who is being interviewed by a reporter from the local newspaper, standing by the awards table holding up his son's trophy as if he'd won it himself. Mr. Tran is all smiles now. I hope that means Jamie will get to enjoy his car ride home.

I know I will. Mom says that Lex and I can ride back with her, and I've got a few classic arcade games downloaded to my phone to keep us occupied. I'm guessing Lex is an expert at all of them and will beat me soundly. I don't really care.

Before we leave, a woman from the JMGA hands me my consolation check for fifty dollars and the newspaper takes my picture standing next to Grace Lin, my fellow second-place finisher. Afterward Grace gives me her number, saying we should keep in touch. It's my second set of jits this year, though Frank technically got the first set. I guess I still owe him one.

Thinking about Frank makes my stomach rumble, of all things. I look at the check in my hand, then over to the three people waiting for me by the exit.

Fifty bucks is fifty bucks, and I know exactly what to spend it on.

Romero's Pizza is situated right off the highway, about an hour out of our town, just like Frank said. It looks like a dump—a run-down brick building with dark windows and only half-lit neon signs—but my mouth waters the moment we walk in, the air saturated with smells of fresh garlic and baked dough. The hostess seats us at a booth, and I quickly slide in next to Lex on one side, forcing my parents to sit next to each other on the other. It's a cheap shot, but I wanted to sit by Lex anyway. Mom's purse is wedged between her and Dad like a stone hazard in the center of the green, but I'll take what I can get.

I text Frank a picture of my second-place certificate along with a selfie of Lex and me standing in front of the sign for the restaurant. I figure he's probably in recovery, maybe still knocked out from anesthetic, but he surprises me by texting back immediately.

Knew you could do it! he replies to the first picture.

I hate you now is his response to the second.

An enormous wave of relief rolls over me, like the feeling of making a hole in one times a hundred. "Frank's out of surgery," I tell everyone. "Don't know about his heart, but his sense of humor's intact."

"Looks we have two things to celebrate," Dad says.

After we order drinks, there is a moment of awkward silence—everyone fidgeting, waiting for someone else to start talking. Finally, Dad grunts as if he's remembered something interesting. I figure it's going to be something about the tournament, and I'm suddenly afraid he's going to ask about that second-to-last shot too, the one I really should have made. Instead he looks across at Lex.

"So Malcolm says you're into tap dancing. What's *that* all about?"

Lex grins. A cat in a roomful of canaries, as Granny Allison would say.

And just like that, the awkwardness falls away. For the next hour, we don't talk about golf, miniature or otherwise. No mentions of birdies or bogeys or balls of any kind. Instead we talk about dancing and music and movies and how good greasy breadsticks are. At one point, Dad makes a corny joke and Mom elbows him for it, a little nudge right in the ribs. It doesn't escape me; I've spent half my life noticing things like this. When the pizza comes, he serves everyone a thick slice but gives her the one with the biggest chunks of tomatoes because he knows she likes them. I notice this too.

In the middle of my second slice, Frank sends me a picture of himself sitting in his bed, staring at a cup of lime Jell-O. **This is what I get for lunch,** the text says, followed by the fuming red emoji.

I wonder when I will see him next. If he will still want to coach me. If Dad will still want him to. I hope so. I would miss the time on the green. And hearing Frank's stories. And the reward at the end. I hope minor heart attacks don't exclude you from drinking slushies, though knowing Frank, he'd drink them anyway.

As the pizza steadily disappears, I also start to wonder if Dad will follow us home tonight or take a different turn and head back to his friend's apartment. I wonder what Mom will say to him after we've paid the bill and are standing by the door.

If their reboot will take another day or another week, or if it will even work at all.

Sitting there, I can't help but wonder about these things, but I don't worry about them. Because Lex is laughing next to me. And Frank is sending me grumpy texts. And Dad is picking at the olives scattered on Mom's plate while she bats his hand away.

And because I'm sitting by the window—my favorite spot— and I'm looking out at the sun, which has already peaked and is starting its slow descent. I'm not going to chase it. Not today, at least.

I want to watch the sky change.

ACKNOWLEDGMENTS

I honestly don't know how miniature golf courses get made. Like Malcolm, I suspect it is the work of gnomes or fairies. I do know how novels are made, however—at least enough to know that they are the work of many incredible individuals with Jamie Tran–level talent . . . and perhaps magical powers. I also know I am indebted to them for their efforts.

My thanks to Josh and everyone else at Adams Literary for helping an amateur go pro and supporting me for almost a decade now. To Tiara Kittrell for managing the greens, Amy Ryan for laying out the course, and Vaishali Nayak for finding the right angles and pitches. To Christina MacDonald and Renée Cafiero for their eagle eyes and endless patience in keeping the aim of my sentences true. To Rafael for visualizing my approach. To Debbie Kovaks, Donna Bray, and Suzanne Murphy for cheering me on, one shot to the next.

And to Jordan Brown—the Frank to my Malcolm. Somehow you turn bogeys into birdies. That is your gift.

Finally, many thanks to my friends, fans, and family for supporting me whether I make it or miss it. I couldn't do it without you.

TURN THE PAGE FOR A SNEAK PEEK
AT JOHN DAVID ANDERSON'S *STOWAWAY*.

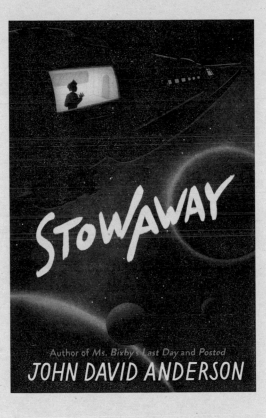

Our posturings, our imagined self-importance, the delusion that we have some privileged position in the Universe, are challenged by this point of pale light. Our planet is a lonely speck in the great enveloping cosmic dark. In our obscurity, in all this vastness, there is no hint that help will come from elsewhere to save us from ourselves.

—*Carl Sagan*, Pale Blue Dot: A Vision of the Human Future in Space, *1994*

Never judge a planet by its crust.

—*Aykarian proverb*

PROLOGUE

CHASING GHOSTS

THEY WERE PLAYING TAG WHEN THE FIRST TORPEDO HIT.

In the narrow hallways of the crew quarters, the clomping of their standard-issue Coalition boots echoing down the corridors. Gareth chasing Leo, gaining, cornering him at a dead end, reaching out to make the tag.

Only to find his hand pass right through his brother's chest.

Hologram. Again.

"Cheater!"

The holo flickered, the prerecorded video of a sprinting Leo finally timing out, the illusion dissolving into pixelated bits. Leo laughed, and Gareth turned to see his brother in the flesh, standing right behind him.

A moment's hesitation, muscles tensing, traded smiles. The one saying, *You'll pay for that.* The other: *You'll have to catch me first.* Then Leo turned and bolted back the way he came, Gareth launching himself in pursuit.

Leo knew there was no way he could outrun his older brother; Gareth had been a middle school track star back on Earth, now a tall, wiry seventeen-year-old. It wasn't a matter of winning for Leo. It was a matter of holding out as long as possible. A question of survival. They'd played this game a hundred times before.

He turned a corner, headed toward the commissary, conscious of Gareth's feet pounding on the steel grating. Louder. Closer. Maybe if he could make it to the door he could duck inside, find somewhere to hide, delay the inevitable.

But he wasn't fast enough. Gareth's hand whipped out, grabbing Leo by the shoulder, not so much tagging him as lassoing him, pulling him to a stop.

"Gotcha."

Leo spun around, hands on his knees, sucking in recycled air.

"You okay?"

"Fine," Leo huffed. "Just . . . catching . . . my breath."

"You cheated again. I told you you aren't allowed to use that thing."

That thing was Leo's watch. A gift his parents had given him years ago. A hybrid of human and Aykari technology—like so many things nowadays—it could be used as a data viewer and a communicator. It kept track of his vitals (his heartbeat was currently 142 beats per minute). It could tell you where it parked your car. Almost incidentally, it told time.

But the watch's most advanced feature was its miniaturized holographic generator, capable of creating three-dimensional projections of prerecorded vids. Like the one of Leo running, recorded with the express purpose of fooling his brother in games of tag or hide-and-go-seek. The projections looked real enough until you got up close and could start to make out the digital imperfections. Their parents had given Gareth the same watch, but he'd lost his long ago, left somewhere in the house they grew up in. On the planet they'd left behind.

"Dad says technology is the tool that allows us to overcome our limitations and sets us free," Leo reminded his brother.

"Except you're not free. I still caught you."

"Because your legs are twice as long as mine."

An exaggeration. At one time it might have been true, but a couple of growth spurts since they'd come on board and Leo was no longer the scrawny runt whose head fit underneath Gareth's armpit. Not so easy to boss around, though Gareth could still wrestle him to the ground and rip the watch from his wrist if he wanted. Not that he would. Leo knew Gareth would never hurt him; he just wanted to give Leo a hard time. That's what big brothers were for. . . . That and pretty much everything else. Especially out here, on this ship, where Gareth was the only real friend he had.

Besides, as long as they played nice, their father wouldn't interrupt to badger them about their studies. As important as it was to Calvin Fender that his two sons learn how to balance chemical equations or calculate the masses of nearby stars, it was more important that they got along. And chasing each other around the *Beagle* was always preferable to reading a chapter of galactic history.

Leo's breathing finally evened out. He brushed the brown mop out of his eyes, his bangs hanging like curtains, in sore need of a trim. The *Beagle* didn't have a barbershop, just Leo's father, whose DIY haircuts often resulted in disaster. Cosmetology was one of the few things his father wasn't good at.

"You have to give me at least a ten-second head start," Leo said. "And you have to count loud so I know when you go."

"Fine. Ten seconds. But seriously, no more cheating. If I catch you—"

"You won't," Leo shot back with mock confidence.

"Right."

Leo coiled, ready to sprint down the corridor as soon as his brother started counting. But Gareth never even made it to *one*.

The explosion nearly threw them off their feet as the *Beagle* lurched sideways. The steel beams shuddered. Leo's ears rang. The lights blinked off, on, then off again, triggering the fluorescent yellow emergency lighting that ran along the floor. Leo put a hand on the wall to steady himself. His brother's eyes shone like moons. "What was that?"

The question was answered with a second explosion, the ship quaking again. Every alarm screamed at once. Leo stumbled, falling into his brother's ready arms. From down the corridor he could hear the crew of the *Beagle* shouting to one another, though it was impossible to make out what they were saying. It was impossible to hear anything over the ship's wounded bleating until the captain's voice echoed over the coms.

"Attention crew of the *Beagle*. We are under attack. Security personnel report to the bridge immediately. Engineering to the drive chamber."

Leo looked up at his brother, still holding him tight. "Did she just say we're under attack?"

Gareth nodded, then looked sideways, startled by the sound of boot heels clomping down the hall.

Leo knew the sound. He'd learned to recognize the rhythm of his father's footfalls. Like the sound of his brother's snoring or his mother's pensive sighs. Leo spied his father turning the corner, his eyes falling on him and Gareth, pressed together. Dr. Calvin Fender's face softened, then hardened again. He spoke in a whirlwind. "What are you two doing out here? Didn't you hear what Captain Saito said? You need to hide. Hurry!"

Their father pointed to the nearest door, leading to an empty bunk room barely half the size of the one the Fenders shared. He hustled Gareth and Leo into a corner, his white lab coat flapping on both sides like broken wings. Leo could tell he was scared—he could see it in his father's eyes, even if he couldn't hear it in his voice.

His father was seldom scared.

Dr. Fender tipped over a metal desk, making a barrier,

concealing the boys from anyone passing by the door. "Stay right here. Do not move. Understand?"

"What's going on?" Leo asked. "Are we really under attack? Is it pirates?"

"Worse," their father said.

Worse than pirates? *The Djarik*, Leo thought. And from the look on Gareth's face, he knew it too.

"They've knocked out our engines and navigation systems," Dr. Fender continued. "Communications too. I believe they intend to board us."

"You mean they're coming on the ship?" Leo felt his chest tighten, a coil wrapping tight, working its way up to his throat. He wheezed in a painful breath.

"Dad, I think he's about to have an attack," Gareth said.

Dr. Fender bent over, patting down Leo's pockets. Leo reached for it as well, finding what he needed, fumbling with the cap of his inhaler, squeezing the trigger and hearing the familiar hiss of medicine, the cool sensation as it snaked its way into his lungs, loosening the noose. Leo took a shuddering breath.

"You're okay," his father whispered, hands on Leo's shoulders. "It's okay. Just breathe. I'm right here. We're both right here." Leo closed his eyes and took in his father's voice, the hint of coffee on his father's breath, the feel of his father's hands. And for a moment, he was somewhere safe. He imagined himself back at home. *Home* home.

Until another, smaller blast caused the ship to shiver again, bringing Leo back. In the corridor, even the emergency lights started to flicker. The *Beagle* was wounded, limping, its engines disabled. The Djarik were preparing to board.

Dr. Fender leveled a finger at his sons. "Whatever happens, you two stay here, understand? Gareth, you're in charge. You keep your brother safe. I will be back as soon as I can."

Gareth nodded, but Leo reached out for his father's coat. "Wait—where are you going?"

"To engineering. To see if I can do something to help with the navigation system. Hopefully the security team can hold off the Djarik long enough for us to break free and make a jump. Stay here. Keep yourselves hidden." Dr. Fender gathered his sons in an embrace that lasted all of ten hammering heartbeats.

"I love you both. More than anything."

And then he was up and out the door, letting it whisper closed behind him, leaving Leo and Gareth huddled together, trembling in the dark.

"Gareth?"

"It's okay, Leo. I'm here. And Dad will come back. He's going to get us out of this."

Leo felt his brother's hand smoothing his hair, working his way from front to back. It was something he remembered their mother doing whenever they got sick, running her forked fingers through their sweaty bangs, softly blowing on their foreheads to cool them. *Her* breath always smelled like mint from the gum she chewed. *Everything's all right*, she would say.

Everything's going to be just fine. He always believed her.

But Leo knew it wasn't always true. Of all the things that could happen—of all the things that *had* happened—this was as bad as it could get. The Djarik were sworn enemies of the Coalition, a plague on the universe. Brutal and bloodthirsty, with little care for humanity—or any species other than their own. They had no qualms attacking an unarmed ship, stripping it of its fuel and leaving it to drift, its crew to suffer and starve. Leo had heard all the stories, but he didn't need them to know what the Djarik were capable of. He'd seen it first-hand.

Leo tried to take deep breaths, but they still hitched and sputtered. "What will they do . . . if they find us?"

"They won't find us," Gareth whispered.

"What will they do if they find Dad?"

Gareth didn't answer at first. Their father was one of the highest-ranking science officers in the Coalition. That alone made him valuable. "Dad's smart," Gareth said at last, understating it by a mile. "He'll think of something."

A final explosion drew a whimper from Leo as the alarms abruptly shut off, making it easier to hear the muffled chaos from the other side of the door. Shouting. Gun blasts. The *Beagle*'s limited security forces making their stand against the Djarik boarding party.

It didn't last long.

Leo pressed even closer to his brother as the sounds of battle gave way to silence. The room was bathed in an eerie yellow glow that made the shadows loom large against the wall. He wanted to call out for their father. Why couldn't he have just stayed with them? Why did he have to leave them here, alone? Leo knew the answer, of course: Calvin Fender would do everything he could to save the ship. The crew. As many as possible.

The silence was interrupted by voices from beyond the closed door. They weren't ones Leo recognized. They certainly weren't human.

"Gareth? What's happening?"

His brother clamped a hand over Leo's mouth, but a moment too late.

The door slid open softly and Leo nearly jumped, giving them away, but Gareth held him, both arms knotted around his chest. Leo peeked through a slit in the metal desk that provided their only cover and barely choked down his scream.

It was one of *them*.

He had seen them before—in pictures, vids, but never so close. Close enough to see the skin of diamond-shaped scales stitched together, hard as a sapphire but ashen gray in color. The ridge of spikes running along the jawline, mirroring the rows of serrated white teeth inside. The gill-like slits along their necks, rippling with each breath. Scalies. Lizzies. Gray devils—the nicknames given to them by humans to degrade or diminish them, to make them seem less scary than they were.

It didn't work.

The Djarik's giant, lidless black eyes swept the room. Like a spider's eyes, a glossy black mirror that gave away nothing, showed no sign of pity or fear. The soldier's spindly arms held its rifle at the ready. It was said that the Djarik were somewhat humanoid in shape, with their straight spines and short necks, their splayed, unwebbed fingers, their prominent skulls, but to Leo they looked as far from human as possible.

The creature raised its chin, giving a sniff through two thin slits. Its eyes came to rest on the desk and on the two boys cowering behind it. It made a sound, a clicking from some-where behind its pointed teeth. A warning. A call to others. Or maybe just some note of satisfaction at having discovered such easy prey.

Tag, you're it.

Leo wondered if they should make a run for it. Try to squeeze past the Djarik marauder, slip into the corridor, make their way to engineering. To Dad. But his limbs were stiff with fear. The Djarik's rifle swept across the room, those black, unblinking eyes reflecting everything in miniature. Leo thought of his mother and a hot anger surged inside him.

The alien's head whipped sideways, the sound of more gunfire from farther down the corridor catching its atten-tion. With another click of its tongue, it slipped back through the entry, leaving the door open, the brothers still bunkered behind the desk.

Leo felt his brother's breath on the back of his neck, the one

Gareth had been holding. "Okay," Gareth whispered. "It's okay. He's gone."

But he wasn't. He was out there somewhere. They were inside the ship. There was no safe place. No matter what Leo's father said.

The brothers huddled in their shadowy corner for five minutes, ten, thirty, their legs cramped, afraid to stand up to even activate the switch on the door, feeling the cold sweat stain their uniforms, twitching at every sound. Until, at last, they heard their names being called.

"Gareth? Leo?"

This voice was familiar, though it wasn't the one Leo had been hoping for. "We're in here," Gareth shouted.

Leo pulled himself to his feet just as Captain Saito appeared in the doorway. She looked different from when he'd seen her earlier that day: her normally tightly buttoned uniform hung lose on her shoulders, one of which supported a makeshift sling for her arm, a spot of crimson soaking through.

"Are you hurt?" she asked.

Leo shook his head. "The Djarik? Are they . . ."

"Gone," she finished. "They took what they wanted and left."

What they wanted. No doubt in Leo's mind what that could be. Ventasium. More fuel for their fleets. The *Beagle* wasn't a military ship. It was a scientific research vessel. They didn't have any weaponry aside from what their small security force carried. Captain Saito was the most valuable officer on the ship. The only other passenger who was even a ranking member of the Coalition was . . .

Leo saw the look in the captain's eyes and felt a chasm instantly open inside him, a black hole forming at his center. He knew without even asking, knew by the twist in his gut, the tightness in his chest.

Captain Saito didn't look away.

"I'm sorry," she said, trying to steady her voice. "We tried to stop them. We did. But it was no use."

Leo reached out for something to hold on to and found his brother's hand as his whole world crumbled.

Again.